# UNHOLY

## *THE CHRONICLES OF BRIANNA BOWERS*

### Book 2

*Billy Stancil*

Unless otherwise indicated, all scripture references are from New International Version (NIV)



Published by TaylorMade Publishing

Jacksonville, FL

www.TaylorMadePublishingFL.com

(904) 323-1334

The holier a man becomes, the more he mourns over the unholiness which remains in him.

*-C.S. Lewis-*

Thank you to Brandy Cook for editing and business management.


This book is dedicated to the old gentleman in the fedora…


Night and day among the tombs and in the hills he would cry out and cut himself with stones.

~ Mark 5:5 NIV ~


…Many times it had seized him, and though he was chained hand and foot and kept under guard, he had broken his chains and had been driven by the demon into solitary places.

~ Luke 8:29b NIV ~


"What do you think? If a man owns a hundred sheep, and one of them wanders away, will he not leave the ninety-nine on the hills and go to look for the one that wandered off?

~ Matthew 18:12 NIV ~

# INTRODUCTION

*FAYETTEVILLE, ARKANSAS*

*39 years ago*

Melissa felt very pretty tonight. They usually didn't allow her such nice clothes to wear when she went out. Typically, a pair of shorts and a halter top was her costume for the night. Tonight though, she was going to a party. A black-tie event, they'd called it. She was given a shiny, black dress. The shiny things were sequins and they made her smile when she looked at them. She also wore tanned pantyhose and a pair of high-heeled shoes that were black and beautiful and Melissa had never worn anything so perfect in her life.

She imagined that she were Cinderella going to a ball. She checked her makeup the woman had put on her and it seemed like a bit much, but she imagined that this was probably how the pretty girls wore it. The man, Vernon was his name, came and collected her. He led Melissa out of the big house and into a waiting car. A limousine, she'd heard them call it. She felt very pretty as they prepared to take her to the ball.

Melissa sat back in the seat and looked down at her beautiful dress. It was uncomfortably short and came to about mid-thigh as she sat. She attempted to tug it lower. She thought of her mother...or the person she remembered to be her mother. She could barely remember her. She could barely remember anything from that world. She had been about four or five when the lady had taken her hand in the store and led her out to a van. Her mother had just stepped into the changing room to try on a blouse. "Stay right here, Missy. Mommy will be right out." That was the last time she'd seen her.

That had been a long time ago. By anyone's guess, Melissa was about fourteen now. Not a day had gone by that she hadn't thought of her mother. She thought about the beautiful song she would sing to her at bedtime. The way she would hold Melissa when she didn't feel good...her mom would stroke her hair and tell her a story about when she was a little girl. She missed her mother so much that it hurt her stomach to think about it.

"Are you ready!?" the woman sitting across from her asked. After all this time, she had never been allowed to say or even think about the woman's name. She knew it, though...Patricia. She was a beautiful woman. Tall and thin and elegant. Melissa heard someone call her elegant one time and decided she liked the word. She'd looked it up...pleasingly graceful and stylish in appearance or manner. That's how Melissa felt tonight.

"Yes ma'am," Melissa replied, sliding her hands down her sequins.

"Stop doing that!" the woman snapped. "You'll ruin the dress...and it's worth so much more than you are!"

"Well, I wouldn't say that," Vernon said as he drove. "Tonight she's worth a dang good penny." They both had a laugh.

"Tonight you are to be respectful, do you hear me?" the woman said. Melissa nodded. "You will do what you are told...no matter who is telling you or how bad you think it is. Another outburst like the last time and I will no longer be needing your services...do you understand!?"

"Yes ma'am," Melissa replied. She still couldn't believe the things that ugly old man had wanted her to do. She had screamed at the top of her lungs and scratched his face and arms in order to get away from him. He'd run out of the room holding a towel to his face and screaming for someone to call...her. That had been a very bad night for Melissa.

They rode in silence for over an hour before the car finally slowed down and turned onto the driveway of a large house beyond a tall iron gate. The words on the gate were in another language and Melissa thought they looked unusual. "What does that say, Vernon?" she dared ask.

"Something in Greek...Chi Alpha Pi or something like that. This is a fraternity house."

"I don't know what that means…"

"You don't need to know what it means!" the woman said. "You're too stupid to ever go to college anyway…so just sit back and shut up!"

"I'm NOT stupid!" Melissa shouted before she could stop herself. The woman had slapped her so fast and hard that she'd hit her head against the window.

"Speak to me like that AGAIN!" the woman leaned back and straightened her dress. "Compose yourself, girl…you've got quite a night ahead of you."

Vernon parked the car in front of the house, got out, and opened the door for them. Patricia told Melissa to exit first, then she followed. There were several young men mingling on the front steps, smoking something that Melissa thought smelled funny. Patricia checked Melissa's makeup and hair, took her by the hand and followed Vernon up the steps.

One of the young men smiled at Melissa and looked her over. "Is this the entertainment?"

"It could be," Patricia replied as they passed. "If you play your cards right."

"Oh, lady, I'm very good at cards…"

They entered through the large doors and Melissa gasped at the beautiful home. There was a grand staircase that went up from both sides of the room. The wood shined like it was made of glass. There were pictures lining the walls of young men from all the years the house had stood, or so it appeared. Some of the pictures were black and white.

A tall, older man, whose face looked like it was made of leather, entered the room through two large doors. He looked out of place in his swim trunks and tank top. Melissa noticed how his arms and legs were tanned to the point that he looked like he'd been left in the microwave for too long. The thought made her giggle inside. "Hello, hello, forgive my appearance!" He shook the woman's hand vigorously and she seemed uncomfortable at his touch. "I fell asleep out by the pool and appear to have lost track of time!" His laugh seemed to vibrate off the walls and made Melissa want to cover her ears. He turned his eyes toward Melissa and smiled. "Is this her?"

"It is indeed," Patricia replied, sliding a hair behind Melissa's ear. "This is Missy, and she is extremely excited to be of service for you this evening." Melissa cringed at the sound of the woman calling her Missy. It was what she remembered her mother calling her.

"Well, Missy," the man said, leaning down so that his face was level with hers. "My name is Thomas…" he looked her over and held out his hand. Melissa only glanced at it. She'd noticed that her entire body had tensed up at this point, and she seemed to be frozen in time.

"Take his hand, Missy," Patricia said, nudging her from behind.

Melissa smiled, placed her hand in his, and as sweetly as she could sound, replied. "Actually, I prefer Melissa."

"Well, Melissa," Thomas said, in an equally pleasant reply, "I couldn't care less what you prefer...for what I'm paying for you, you just need to do what you're told." Continuing to hold onto her hand, he quickly pulled her from the room, thanking Patricia and telling her that she would be paid at the end of the night.

As the doors closed behind her, Melissa started to panic and knew that despite her beautiful appearance...despite her gorgeous surroundings...despite the fact that she was still attempting to imagine that she was at a fancy ball having the best night of her life...this was, in fact, no fairy tale. It was, however, the beginning of an absolute nightmare.

# CHAPTER 1



*JACKSONVILLE INTERNATIONAL AIRPORT*

*Present Day*

Brianna took her window seat at the back of the plane. She was slightly surprised that the plane was full, with it being Sunday morning and all. She buckled in and took out her laptop. Her parents had driven her to the airport from Gateway and she'd said her goodbyes to them. Her mother had been sad that her visit was cut short by a phone call from an old friend...Pastor Jason Green. He had seemed in distress when he'd called her only two days ago. Jason had always been so energetic and crazy, that it had concerned Brianna to hear actual fear and sorrow in his voice.

She checked her emails and saw that she had only one of importance and it was from her new friend, Carmen Sanchez. Carmen had recently requested that Brianna help her find her missing daughter, Maria, who had been taken by child traffickers. That had been Brianna's ministry...locating missing or taken children. However, Maria had been burned alive in front of Brianna by the man in charge of the world's largest child trafficking ring, multi-billionaire, Joshua Coff. The memory still shattered her heart. Joshua had been discovered later that night, his body completely unrecognizable, in an automobile accident.

Carmen had told Brianna only days later that she felt like God was leading her into the ministry of rescuing children from trafficking. "Good morning, my friend," the email read. "I know you are heading out of town this weekend, and I wanted to wish you well. I also wanted to let you know that I will be meeting with a ministry team out of Wichita, Kansas. Please keep me in your prayers as I embark on this new part of my life, helping reunite families with their children and counseling those who, like myself, will never see their children again. I love you, Brianna Bowers...more than you will ever

1

✝

know. God used you to find ME. Forever your friend, Carmen Sanchez." Brianna found herself teared up. How beautiful a spirit, this woman who had just buried her daughter, had. Jumping right into a work for God. And to tell Brianna, the woman she'd sent to find that daughter, that she'd found HER instead. Just wow!

As a middle-aged woman took the seat next to Brianna, she replied to Carmen, telling her that she would be praying for her and that she was extremely proud of her. Then she typed an email to Jonah...Jonah Westbrook, her supposed boyfriend, which sounded very weird to say out loud. Brianna had not been searching for love when the ruggedly handsome stranger waltzed into her life, on the run from the same people that had been chasing her. They had found solace in each other's company, and then, thanks to the workings of the Holy Spirit, Jonah had given his life to Christ. They were literally a match made in heaven.

Their very different lifestyles, however, were not copacetic to having a relationship...so they'd both agreed to keep it casual for now. With him living across the country, in Colorado, that wouldn't be too difficult. "Heading to Knoxville. My flight should take about an hour. Pennington Springs from there. Miss you. Love, Bree!" She hoped he didn't read too much into the word love, they hadn't really gotten that far yet. In fact, their entire relationship up to this point had been an exciting, adrenaline pumping adventure right up to the gates of hell...which was why stepping back and reflecting slowly was a great idea.

Before she put her laptop away, she decided to look up Pennington Springs, Tennessee. She had never even heard of the place where one of her best friends lived and pastored. It was smack dab in the middle of the Smoky Mountains, not far from Pigeon Forge and Sevierville. The population was just under 9,000 people and it was famous for its small-town charm, cute shops, and a small bakery called Dalia's Delights, that people visited from all over the world.

2

✝

That's when it hit her...the dream she'd had last night. She leaned her head back against the seat and tried to remember. Rarely did she even remember her dreams and usually the ones she did were silly or unimportant. This one, however, had stirred something in her spirit. She had been lying down it seemed, yes, definitely lying down...but not in a bed...more like she was being pushed around...like maybe on a gurney. She couldn't remember where she'd been, but whoever was pushing or moving her had been in a hurry. There was someone beside her, but she couldn't remember the face...a boy perhaps...yes, a young boy was walking beside her. He'd kept glancing over at her, but his face was a blur. Why did that feel important? So strange.

"So, business or pleasure?" the woman beside her asked, breaking her concentration.

"Oh, um...business I guess," Brianna replied. "I'm not really sure." She smiled at the woman who raised her eyebrows.

"I'm intrigued," the woman replied. "Is a man involved?"

"A man?" Brianna asked. "Yes, but not a love interest...more of an old friend with a problem that apparently needs my expertise."

"And what exactly is your expertise, if I may ask?" she turned slightly in her seat to focus her attention on Brianna. "I'm Helene, by the way." She held out her hand to shake.

"Brianna," she replied, shaking the woman's hand and giving her a genuine smile. She loved getting opportunities to talk with strangers. "Well, my expertise, up until recently, has been rescuing children from traffickers...I led a ministry in Germany that investigated child trafficking...and adult trafficking occasionally...but have recently felt the need to move in a different direction."

"Oh my, were you involved in that whole Joshua Coff situation they've been talking about on the news?" Helene asked.



✝

"They're trying to say he was being wrongly accused, but I never know what to believe."

"I was…and he was as guilty as they come," Brianna replied.

"That is so interesting...so this old friend...does his problem have to do with child trafficking?"

"Honestly, I have no idea, Ms. Helene," Brianna said. "All he said was that he had a problem that he felt I needed to look into…"

"Now, you said you worked for a ministry," Helene replied. "Does that mean you're some kind of pastor or minister or something?"

"Not exactly, but I do have pretty much the same education as most pastors...and I share the same boss," she said with a big smile. Seeing Helene's blank stare, she added, "God...Jesus?."

"Oh, I see…" Helene turned back in her seat and faced the front. "I haven't been to church in a long time, Brianna." Brianna could see that her eyes had teared up. "Not since my Norman passed."

"I'm so sorry," Brianna said.

"Twelve years ago this weekend," Helene said, her eyes seeming to be reliving a memory. Brianna chanced placing her hand on top of hers and squeezed. "That's why I'm heading to Knoxville...he's buried there. That's where we lived...he was an insurance salesman...not a very good one," she said with a distant smile. Brianna squeezed her hand again. "We went to church every Sunday...every time the doors were open, actually. Norman was an usher...he always looked so handsome in his suits."

Brianna smiled. "How long were you married?"

"Thirty-three wonderful years…" Helene reached up and wiped a tear.

4

✝

"So, if I may be so bold as to ask, Ms. Helene," Brianna said. "Why did you stop going to church?"

"Well...at first, I guess it was because I was mad at God. Then, well...I moved closer to family in Jacksonville and none of them really ever went, .so It just became easier and easier to ignore that pulling at my heart."

"Well, I have good news for you, Ms. Helene...Jesus still loves you, and He desperately wants to fellowship with you. In fact, I'm pretty sure that's why He put us together this morning."

"I do miss spending time with Him," Helene replied. "And reading His Word."

"He misses that too," Brianna said. "May I pray with you?" Helene closed her eyes and nodded...tears streaming down her cheeks. "Father, I thank you for this chance meeting with Ms. Helene...thank you for bringing us together so that we could bless each other. Father, I pray that you would restore her to her place with You, God. Help her to get into Your Word, and to spend time fellowshipping with You. God, I pray Your blessings over her right now...that Your Spirit would shine through her...in Jesus' name...amen."

Helene, kept her eyes closed as she sobbed. She leaned over and gave Brianna a huge hug. "My Norman used to say those exact words...that your Spirit would shine through her! I feel like he's here, right now." She squeezed Brianna tight. "Thank you so much!"

The pilot came over the intercom saying they would be landing in twenty minutes and Brianna realized that she hadn't even noticed that they'd been flying. "Well, that was fast."

"Time flies when you're having fun, Sweetie!" Helene said, squeezing Brianna's hand.

"Apparently it does!" They exchanged numbers and email addresses before they disembarked. Helene gave Brianna another hug

5

✝

as they parted ways in the terminal. Brianna told her that she would be praying for her. As she headed to baggage claim, she thanked her old friend for allowing her to be a part of something as amazing as restoring someone to their place in God's kingdom.

As she stood waiting for her suitcase to make an appearance, she saw a tall, thin, older man with gray hair and glasses, wearing what appeared to be a tan police uniform, and holding a sign that read BRIANNA BOWERS. That was odd, she thought, since Jason had not mentioned having someone pick her up when she arrived. While watching him, she almost let her bag pass by. She quickly grabbed it, slid up the handle and wheeled it toward him. He saw her coming and produced a big smile that seemed to brighten the day. "Now you HAVE to be Brianna Bowers!" He held out his hand, "I'm Jerry Winkler! Police Chief of Pennington Springs! Most people just call me Chief!" He continued to smile and shake her hand.

"Pleased to meet you, Chief!" Brianna replied, unable to stop smiling herself. "How did you know it was me?"

"Solely based on the description the pastor gave me… 'she's short with thick brown hair and probably the most beautiful woman you've ever seen in your life!' His description, I promise." He let go of her hand and took her bag from her. "And while you are the most beautiful woman I've seen since kissing my lovely bride, Carolyn, on the cheek this morning, I have to admit, it was your countenance that gave you away. Pastor Jason also said you were so full of the Holy Spirit that it practically poured out of you."

"Well, I had no idea he was sending someone to pick me up," she said, while following him through the airport toward the front. "Especially the police chief! I had planned to rent a car; I have no idea why I'm here. Jason was not very clear…"

"You're here to assist federal, state, and local law enforcement in an investigation, Ms. Bowers," the chief said, smiling



✝

back at her. "As for a car, Pastor Jason said that you'll be using his...he has the church van to get around in."

"I'm sorry..." Brianna said, trying to catch up to the long-legged chief. "What kind of investigation? Does this have to do with child trafficking? Because I'm not involved with that anymore."

"While I am at liberty to tell you that it does not have anything to do with child trafficking, I am not at liberty to discuss any other details of the case, just yet. There will be a briefing tomorrow morning with the F.B.I." The chief held the door open for her to go through. "Just there to the right," he said, nodding her toward his squad car. He opened the trunk and set her bag in and walked over to open her door.

"Thank you...such a gentleman," Brianna said with a smile, while getting in the car.

"Nah, I even open the door for the people I put in the back," he said with a chuckle." He closed her door and walked around. As they pulled away from the airport, he told her to rest her eyes if she needed to, he understood how it was to get up so early. "Besides it's a little over a half hour before we get to church."

"Church?" she replied with a gasp. "Will we be there in time for church?"

"Of course we will," the chief replied. "We may miss a little bit of Sister Grace's organ playing, but we'll definitely be there in time for the word. Pastor made me promise."

"Don't get me wrong, I love church, but I'm not exactly dressed for it," Brianna replied, looking down at her blue jeans and black t-shirt that read, 'Daddy's Girl' across the front.

"You'll be fine...and probably one of the more appropriately dressed people there," he said with a laugh. "I swear, some of them women come to church looking like...bless their hearts." He looked over at her and smiled. "So, how was the flight?"

7

✝

"Fast actually," she replied. "And quite productive. The Holy Spirit sat me right beside a woman that needed what only He can offer."

Chief Jerry smiled at that. "I'll just bet He does that a lot with you."

"On occasion," she replied. "So, how is my friend, Pastor Jason Green, doing in Pennington Springs, Tennessee?"

"Well, at first he was like a fish out of water, I'm not going to lie," the chief said, with a smile. "Some of us wondered if he'd last...and thought it unusual that a man of his stature and flair...would even consider a town like Pennington Springs. But now, he's one of us. He loves it here and we love him."

"Flair..." Brianna smiled. "That about sums up Jason Green."

"It sounds funny hearing you say his name without saying Pastor," the chief said. "You've known him a lot longer than I have, though."

"Yes, I don't mean to be disrespectful, but I've known Jason since we were thirteen." Brianna remembered that time of her life. "The dragon incident..."

"I've seen the footage, you know..." Chief Jerry added. "I was a skeptic at first...in fact, I didn't believe it at all until Pastor Jason came here. There was no denying he'd been in the presence of God when I met him though. I see the same thing in you that I saw in him...it's how I knew you were Brianna Bowers."

"So, you can't tell me anything about what's going on in your small town, Chief?"

"I wish I could, Brianna, but I gave my word..."

"Say no more, Chief...your word is your currency...I can wait until tomorrow."

8

✝

Ten minutes later, they passed through the major metropolis of Pennington Springs, Tennessee. There were several gift shops, restaurants, coffee shops, bakeries, real estate businesses, a bank, a large courthouse, the police station, fire department, and a tall, white, beautiful classic looking small town church. 'Pennington Springs Community Church...All Are Welcome.'

"Here we are," the chief said, pulling into a half full parking lot on the right side of the building. "Usually more people, but...well, you'll find out more about that tomorrow."

Brianna saw the concerned look on the chief's face and said a silent prayer for whatever was going on in the town. She followed him across the parking lot and up the steps. The weather was nice today. A beautiful, crisp Fall morning in the mountains of Tennessee. Probably in the upper 60's lower 70's. She turned when they reached the top step and looked out across the street to the town park with its beautiful oak trees, park benches, paved walkway, and pavilion for events. Such a nice place. What could possibly be going on behind the scenes?

"Is everything okay?" the chief asked, turning back to see her just standing there.

"Just admiring your beautiful town," Brianna replied.

"I just love it when folks stop to smell the roses," the chief replied, opening the door for Brianna. "Not enough people do that anymore."

There was a small foyer where they walked in, with a table covered in pamphlets, a bulletin board with the weekly schedule, two velvet covered chairs that were a faded rose color, and on both sides of the table were double doors that led into the sanctuary where Brianna could hear the organ and a piano playing.



†

Before the chief opened the door, he turned to Brianna... "I'm going to go up front and sit with my bride, you're welcome to come with me or you can sit wherever you like."

"Thanks, Chief," Brianna said in a whisper. "I think I'll just sit in the back."

He smiled with a nod and opened the door. The organ music came blaring at them as they entered. The thirty or so people were standing, as the woman on the piano led them in an old hymn. Brianna slid into the back row as the chief moseyed to the front. He shuffled past a few people and slid his arm around a small older woman that Brianna assumed was his bride. As he joined them on the row, others began to look back as if they were expecting Brianna.

What had Jason Green gotten her into? That's when she noticed him smiling at her from the stage...and where had all his hair gone? All that pretty hair he'd had as a teen and young adult was now completely gone. Jason Green was a bald preacher in the mountains of Tennessee! Was that why he'd left the Dragon Slayers? He knew he would be bald? Brianna chuckled to herself and couldn't wait to tease him. His blonde goatee didn't look half bad, though.

The music ended and Pastor Jason walked up to the podium and thanked the ladies for that amazing time of worship. They stood, left the stage, and took a seat with their families. "Good morning!" Jason said with a big, contagious smile.

"Good morning!" a large portion of the congregation replied.

"Before we dive into the Word this morning, I would like to introduce you folks to a very dear friend of mine... Brianna would you like to stand up and say something?"

Brianna stood slowly, smiling at the crowd that was now turned around and watching her. "First of all, let me apologize for my appearance...I had no idea that Chief Jerry was going to be picking me up and bringing me to church this morning." A few people



†

laughed and smiled at her. "My name is Brianna Bowers and Jason and...I'm sorry, Pastor Jason and I go waaay back to the age of thirteen or so. We shared quite a few adventures together, as I'm sure he's told you about the big one."

"Oh, they know about the dragon!" Pastor Jason added. "That filthy sucker thought he could take on God's people!" Several people nodded.

"Anyway, I am presently between ministries right now, and when your pastor called me to come to Pennington Springs...I still have no idea why...but I feel in my spirit that this is exactly where God wants me right now." She smiled and sat back down. Several people clapped.

"Thank you, Brianna," Pastor Jason replied. "She was actually being quite modest...having just single-handedly brought down a multi-billion-dollar human trafficking ring...last week." Quite a few people stirred at that remark and began whispering to each other.

"Not exactly single-handedly!" Brianna said. "I had quite a bit of help!"

"Okay, everybody calm down!" Pastor Jason said, giving them just a moment to settle from telling each other what they'd seen on television concerning the human trafficking ring. "Turn in your Bibles to the book of Mark...chapter 5."



✝

# CHAPTER 2



39 years ago

Melissa immediately knew something wasn't right. She'd been sick before, but never like this. Unable to keep anything down, she once again was kneeling in front of the toilet with sweat dripping down her forehead and cheeks. She was miserable and nobody seemed to care. She tried to imagine what it would be like to have a mother and father that took care of her during times like this. A mother that would give her medicine, hold her hand, stroke her hair...smile at her and tell her that everything was going to be okay. A father that would hold her in his lap, rub her back, and whisper that he loved his little teacup. For some reason she'd always imagined being called a teacup by a father...who knows, maybe that's what her real father had called her. She couldn't remember him.

Just then, the door burst open, and Vernon stepped in, looking as agitated as always. He threw a small box at her and told her to read the instructions and do what it said.

"Is it medicine?" she asked between heaves.

"No!" he said in an irritated tone. "It's a pregnancy test, you idiot!" He slammed the door, and she could hear him walking away mumbling to himself.

"What!?" she gasped. "A pregnancy test!?" Why would he give her a pregnancy test? She knew what that meant but she didn't even know how a woman got pregnant. "I'm only fourteen," she muttered to herself and picked up the box. "I can't be pregnant." She sat up on the side of the bathtub and read the instructions. "Gross...I'm not doing that..."

Thirty minutes later, she picked the test up from the sink and couldn't believe her eyes. According to the box, it was positive. She



✝

was pregnant? What did that mean? How did it happen? She couldn't possibly be having a baby! What had she done to get this way? Was it something she ate? Or...that night...no...she'd tried to forget that night at the college three months ago. Those boys had...no! The room started spinning...she knelt in front of the toilet just in time.


*PENNINGTON SPRINGS, TENNESSEE*

*Present Day*


"They went across the lake to the region of the Gerasenes. When Jesus got out of the boat, a man with an impure spirit came from the tombs to meet him. This man lived in the tombs, and no one could bind him anymore, not even with a chain. For he had often been chained hand and foot, but he tore the chains apart and broke the irons on his feet. No one was strong enough to subdue him. Night and day among the tombs and in the hills he would cry out and cut himself with stones." Pastor Jason looked up from his Bible and stepped to the side. "Sound familiar to anybody?"

There was a light murmuring among the crowd and Brianna could see that he had somehow struck a nerve.

"Let's keep reading...starting at verse 6, it says...When he saw Jesus from a distance, he ran and fell on his knees in front of him. He shouted at the top of his voice, 'What do you want with me, Son of the Most High God? In God's name don't torture me!' For Jesus had said to him, 'Come out of this man, you impure spirit!' Then Jesus asked him, 'What is your name?' 'My name is Legion,' he replied, 'for we are many.' And he begged Jesus again and again not to send them out of the area." Pastor Jason looked up and smiled. "So, what did we just read?" He walked over and stepped down the three steps to the floor and stopped. "A man that had been possessed by thousands of demons...in Roman times, a legion of soldiers was

13

✝

somewhere between three and six thousand men. Now it says later that two thousand pigs rushed into the lake and were drowned. This man was eat up with demons, ya'll!" He walked back up onto the stage. "Talk about being in a hopeless situation! POSSESSED BY 2,000 DEMONS!!! And y'all think I'm crazy!" Several people laughed. "BUT!" He smiled and walked across the stage. "Ya'll say BUT!"

"BUT!!!" the people shouted.

"But...he went to the shore...to meet a man named Jesus!" Pastor Jason paused as several people shouted amen.

"Is anything impossible with our God?"

"NO!!!" someone in front of Brianna shouted.

"You're talking about a God that parted a sea and made it dry ground!"

"That's right Pastor!"

"You're talking about a God that shut the mouths of lions!"

"Come on!"

"You're talking about a God that not only rescued three Hebrew boys from a fiery furnace but got up in there with them!"

"Mmmhmmm!" an older gentleman stood up and lifted his hands in worship.

"The same God who turned water into wine! Healed the sick! Raised the dead! Cast out demons! Calmed a storm! Fed thousands of people with only five loaves of bread and two fish!" Pastor Jason yelled, "Get to your feet and give him some praise y'all!"

That's when Brianna saw Him...standing at the end of the first row. Her old friend...He held His hat in His hand and turned to watch the people praising Him. He saw Brianna looking at Him and started toward her...pausing for a second to lean down to a man sitting



✝

on the third row. He whispered something in the man's ear and Brianna noticed the man fidget in his seat. The Holy Spirit then raised back up and headed toward her. He slid into her aisle and stood beside her.

"Praise Him, Church!" Pastor Jason said. "He's worthy!"

It was an amazing service as Pastor Jason went on to talk about how no situation is impossible if God is on your side. "Even in death, we have victory in Jesus!"

After the closing prayer, the Holy Spirit leaned over to Brianna and whispered, "Praise is your weapon...and pray for Harley Thomas Linwood."

"Who is th…" and He was gone...of course. He would reveal the details as the drama played out, she thought to herself with a smile. "Father, please be with me on this next adventure...and bless this Harley Thomas Linwood." As she stood to leave her row, she saw the man that the Holy Spirit had spoken to glance at her and look away. "Hi, I'm Brianna!" she held out her hand to him as he was about to pass her by. He stopped and looked her over.

"You're the friend of the pastor...the one from Florida?" he replied. He seemed to be a few years older than her, with thinning hair and a thick waistline. His face was weathered and he seemed to have a permanent sour expression.

"Yes, Gateway," Brianna said. "Pastor Jason and I go way back."

"So, you were there for the...dragon thing…" he kept glancing toward the foyer.

"Oh yes…" Brianna chuckled. "The infamous dragon thing."

"Well, I'm Michael. Michael Nesmith… the town pathologist...hopefully you can help put an end to all this…"



✝

"Hello, Michael!" it was Chief Jerry that had walked up. "Good to see you in church this morning! I see you've met the lovely Brianna Bowers."

"Yes...hello, Chief," Michael said. "It was nice to have met you Ms. Bowers, have a lovely day." He nodded to the chief and walked away.

"Brianna, I would love for you to meet my beautiful bride of forty-two years, Carolyn," Jerry said, beaming with pride as the lovely woman standing beside him held out her hand to Brianna.

"It's a pleasure to meet you, Carolyn...you have the sweetest husband. The way he talks about you…" Brianna said, shaking her hand.

"Yes...he's quite the rascal…" she replied, smiling up at him. This was the relationship Brianna wanted when she got married. "So, Brianna, Pastor Jason is in a quick board meeting, but said he would meet us at Rodney's, so the plan was for you to ride with us and after lunch we'll take you to the inn."

"Rodney's?" Brianna asked, not really feeling up to a get together with a bunch of people right now.

"Rodney's Roadhouse BBQ," Carolyn replied.

"Oh, okay...perfect. Will it just be us?"

"Yes, I'm sure you're tired after getting up so early."

"Yes, ma'am...and I hardly got any sleep last night," Brianna replied, rubbing her eyes.

Fifteen minutes later, they were being seated in an old country restaurant, with tools, signs, and animal heads mounted on the walls. Brianna's dad had once told her that was how you knew the food was good. Of course, he also told her to only order sweet tea when at a barbecue restaurant, it wasn't good anywhere else except home. She had every intention of doing just that.

16

✝

"The food is excellent here," Carolyn said. "We always get the pulled pork, but it's all good."

Brianna smiled, "Yes ma'am, it smells delicious in here."

"Good afternoon, Chief!" a young teenage girl said, grabbing a stack of menus. "Your usual booth?"

"Yes please, Mandy," the chief replied. "We have one more coming."

Brianna felt her phone buzz as they headed to the back of the restaurant. She pulled it from her purse and saw that it was a text from Jonah. "Did u make to TN ok?" She quickly replied. "Yes, about to have lunch with some very nice people." Brianna sat across from Chief Jerry and Carolyn, and slid into the booth to make room for Jason.

"Can I take y'all's drink order?" Mandy asked. "Chief, I know you and Mrs. Carolyn want the sweet tea… and you, ma'am?"

"Same, thank you," Brianna replied.

"Sweet tea for me as well, Mandy!" Pastor Jason yelled across the restaurant as he headed their way. "And I want the rib plate! Greens and mashed taters!" He smiled a big, goofy smile as he took his seat next to Brianna. Noticing their expressions, he added. "Oh, you ain't takin' food orders yet?"

"No sir, but if you folks are ready?"

Jerry and Carolyn ordered the pulled pork and Brianna got a sampler with a little bit of everything.

"So!" Pastor Jason said, looking at Brianna. "How was the flight?"

Brianna nodded. "Short and sweet."

"You look tired."



✝

"Very… if it's okay with everyone, I will be taking an extended nap this afternoon."

"Fine with me," Pastor Jason replied. "We've canceled all of our evening services temporarily." He shared a grim look with the chief.

"Oh really?" Brianna said. "Any particular reason?"

"Yes, and that my dear Brianna… is why you are here." Pastor Jason leaned back in the booth and let out a big sigh.

"Okay… would you care to elaborate?" she asked.

"I would," he replied. "But I promised that I wouldn't."

"Can't you even give me a nugget?" Brianna asked. "Even the Holy Spirit is quiet on this."

"Well...keep praying… you're going to need it." Brianna had never seen Jason look more serious or concerned in her life.

"So, how are you liking the country life, Mr. Pittsburgh?" Brianna decided to change the subject since the one they were on was going nowhere. "And how have you not landed a wife yet?"

Jerry and Carolyn laughed at that last question and Jason turned red.

"The truth is Brianna…" Jason started.

"Oh Lord!" Jerry interrupted. "Here we go!" Carolyn laughed again.

"The truth is...no woman can handle all this man." They all laughed.

"Jason Green, I've missed your silliness!" Brianna patted his arm.

"So, what about you!?" he asked. "Has being an international woman of mystery kept you too busy to land a man?"



✝

"Actually, I just recently met someone," she replied. "His name is Jonah and he lives in Colorado."

"Oh really?" Jason replied. "Tell me about him."

"Well, he was with me on that last adventure. He was one of the construction workers that built the compound where they were holding the children. In fact, he was the only one to get out alive. We were both being hunted by them. That's actually when he got saved...he had an experience quite like Mark, you know...where he had the vision of the crucifixion."

"That's awesome, Brianna," Jason replied. "But be careful...relationships that start off under duress rarely last...but I'm just hoping." He smiled that big cheesy smile again.

Brianna shoved him lightly and looked awkwardly at Jerry and Carolyn. "Jason has been trying to get me to be his girlfriend for a long time now...I thought he was over it." She gave him a side glance. "I see him as a brother though." She placed her hand on his. "The best brother a girl could ask for," she added, squeezing his hand. "He saved me from some bullies one time in the ninth grade… just after he moved to Gateway. The three of them, much older, beat him up pretty good… but they never messed with me again."

"I would die for this woman," Jason replied. "Of course, I would probably do that for about anybody… if I had to."

"I know you would," Brianna replied.

After they ate, Chief Jerry and Carolyn drove Brianna to pick up Jason's car. She then followed them to a small bed and breakfast that Carolyn ran. They helped her get settled in and the chief told her that she needed to be at the police station at eight sharp the next morning. "It's just around the corner there...you can walk." After they left, she put her clothes away, showered, and practically fell into the bed. She barely remembered her head hitting the pillow.

**19**

✝

She was being pushed in the gurney again...or maybe it wasn't a gurney… it had sides. Wait, she could see her legs… they were small. Was she a child? Was this a stroller she was in? The boy walking beside her kept glancing at her, but she couldn't make out his face, no matter how hard she tried. She had a strange feeling that he was angry… that he didn't like her. They slowed down and came to a stop. The boy opened a door and she was pushed into a store. There were racks of clothes… they were at a mall. Whoever was pushing her stopped near some clothes racks and walked a few feet away. That's when he reached over and pinched her leg. He twisted her skin so hard that Brianna jumped up from the bed and yelled out in pain.

It was dark outside and according to the clock; she'd been asleep for about nine hours. She sat on the edge of the bed and rubbed her eyes. "Coffee… and my Bible." Feeling the stirring of the Holy Spirit, she knew it was going to be a long night.

Her phone buzzed on her nightstand with a text from her best friend, Gabi Morgan. "U good?"

"Yes, but I feel another storm coming." She sent the text, knowing that her friend would immediately be on her knees doing battle with her. The thought made Brianna smile. No matter what tomorrow held… she was battle ready.



✝

# CHAPTER 3



*FAYETTEVILLE, ARKANSAS*

*39 years ago*

Melissa had never been in more pain in her entire life. For a while after finding out she was pregnant and coming to terms with how it had happened, she had started feeling better and getting sick less. There had been a lot of discussions among Patricia and Vernon on whether it would be worth keeping the pregnancy. Although she knew this was no kind of life to raise a child in, Melissa had begged them to let her have the baby. In the end, Patricia had decided that she could keep it… it would be worth more to them alive than dead.

They didn't allow her to stop working though… apparently a young pregnant girl was worth a lot of money to some men. Now, here she was, fat bellied and seven months pregnant. Her stomach had started hurting about a week ago, and gotten worse with each day. She barely slept and pretty much lived on the bathroom floor. Patricia and Vernon both continually told her how worthless she was and reminded her of how much money she was costing them.

She pulled herself up from the floor and headed into her bedroom to get her vitamins, when she noticed that she was bleeding. She screamed for someone to come and after about five minutes Vernon poked his head in the door.

"What are you screaming about!?" he demanded. "SHUT UP!" Then he saw the blood on her legs and helped her lie down on the bed. "Stay here, I'll be right back."

About a half hour later, her doctor was standing over her, checking her vitals and trying to find out what was going on.

"Is the baby dead?" Vernon asked.

"What!?" Melissa yelled. "NO!!!"



✝

"Shut up, girl!" Vernon yelled. "You done killed your baby and cost us more money!" He raised his hand to slap her, but the doctor stopped him.

"Will you please leave the room?" the doctor said. "The baby is still alive, but I need to get him out now!"

"HIM!?" Melissa asked, tears streaming down her face. "I'm having a baby boy!?"

The doctor pushed Vernon from the room and went to work. She hung a bag of liquid from the bed post and ran that liquid right into Melissa's arm. "Okay, I'm going to need you to start pushing in just a moment."

Melissa nodded; she was starting to feel quite weak.

"Okay, let's get this little boy out here to meet his mama," the doctor said, kneeling down in front of Melissa.

For over two hours, Vernon could hear Melissa screaming upstairs. He couldn't even enjoy the football game he was trying to watch. It didn't matter, he figured, his team was losing anyway. He went to the kitchen to get himself another beer, when the screaming finally stopped. A few moments later it was replaced with the sounds of a different scream… a baby's cry. He rolled his eyes and went back to his recliner. About fifteen minutes later the doctor lady came down the stairs holding the baby that was wrapped in a blanket. "Is he healthy?"

"Yes… but the mother didn't make it."

"Whatta you mean!?" Vernon sat up quickly and swore, mostly because he'd spilled his beer.

"I mean, Melissa died giving birth… she was…"

He swore again and told her it was her fault and that she had to get rid of the body and to never mention it again. She handed him the baby and told him it was his responsibility to feed it. Swearing



✝

again, he tossed the child onto the sofa and went to call Patricia… she would not be happy about any of this.

*PENNINGTON SPRINGS, TENNESSEE*

*Present Day*

At exactly 7:55 a.m., Brianna stepped into the Pennington Springs Police Department with a large cup of coffee she'd acquired from Carolyn before leaving. She would need to ask Carolyn what roast this was because it was absolutely delicious. The building was tiny and stood alone between a small dry-cleaning business and an old Baptist church. It was only about five hundred square feet in total but from what Brianna could tell from the parking lot, there was only about six or seven police officers in all. She entered through a glass door and approached the small desk where a large older woman, who Brianna guessed was their version of a secretary slash dispatch, sat talking to someone on the phone.

"Yes, Wilber, it was most likely dogs or coyotes," she said into the telephone, rolling her eyes at Brianna as if whoever this Wilber was, he was on her last nerve. "No, I don't suspect it was Harley that killed your chickens and scared your horses."

"Harley?" Brianna thought. The Holy Spirit had told her to pray for a Harley...was it the same man?

"Okay, Wilber, I'll inform the chief...yes...thank you...bye now." Brianna could still hear the man yelling as the woman hung up the phone. "How can I help you, Dear?"

"Brianna Bowers to see the chief," she said with a smile.

"Oh...yes...CHIEF!" She yelled to the back, causing Brianna to jump. "BRIANNA BOWERS TO SEE YOU!!!"

A door directly behind the woman slung open. "For goodness sakes, Darlene!" Chief Winkler said. "Why don't you announce it to



✝

the next county...I'm right here!" He gave Brianna a big smile and shook her hand. "Come on back, Brianna, we're just finishing up. I trust you slept well? Having not seen you leave your room all afternoon and night."

"Yes, thank you...I was exhausted." She entered the chief's office, which was a little bit larger than the front room she'd just come from. There was a large wooden desk and chair backed up to a window, with four chairs facing it. Three men stood to their feet as she entered...all wearing suits except for the one closest to her.

"Good morning, Brianna," Jason said with a grim smile, and shook her hand.

"Ms. Bowers," the older, heavy set man next to Jason shook her hand. "I'm Detective Horne out of Nashville."

"Agent Eddie Young, Ma'am," the tall, thirty-something, fairly good-looking man said, shaking her hand with vigor. "It's good to finally meet you!"

"Agent?" Brianna asked as she took her seat near the door. The men each sat as well. "Are you F.B.I.?"

"Guilty," he replied.

"I recently had some dealings with Agent Donny Wright," she said. "Do you know him?"

"Only from what I read in in your file...I haven't had the pleasure."

"He's a good man."

"Well, from what I read about you, you're quite impressive yourself, Ms. Bowers," Agent Young replied. "Helping to bring down the largest human trafficking ring in the world!"



✝

"Impressive indeed," Chief Jerry replied. "And we are honored to have Brianna with us this morning." The three men nodded.

"Chief, if I may," Jason said, turning to Brianna. "First of all, Brianna...if there'd been any other way around it, I would not have allowed you to be pulled into this. Secondly, if at any point you don't feel safe or if you just want to get out of this, just let me know and I will personally escort you back to Gateway. And lastly, I'm sooo sorry for getting you involved in this. You have no idea..."

"Jason..." Brianna said, placing her hand on his arm. "I have absolutely no doubt that I am exactly where God wants me. You can relax...whatever is going on here...it's not my first rodeo...greater is HE!" She smiled at him, and he turned back around in his seat.

"Still," Jason replied. "I'm your shadow from this point on...as long as you're here. Anybody has a problem with that, deal with it."

"Great idea," Chief Jerry replied. "Now, let's get down to business. Brianna...I'm sure before you came here to Pennington Springs, you checked the local news for some sign as to what you were getting yourself into. We have, up to this point, been able to control the media. No news of what's been going on has been leaked so far...outside of town, that is. Pennington Springs is a small town that thrives on tourism...and without it, well, we wouldn't survive.

However, as the chief of police, I also can't allow innocent people to be placed into harm's way. We've issued a ban on the mountain for now...told them there'd been some black bear attacks. He paused and opened a file that was sitting on his desk. "Now, like Pastor Jason said, I too would rather have not involved you in this, but there was just no other way." With that, he pulled out a stack of pictures. "I'm sorry to make you look at these, but..."

"It's fine, Chief...I've seen some pretty horrible things in my..." She saw the first picture on the top of the stack and forgot to



✝

breathe. Taking the stack from the chief, she noticed that her hands were trembling. It took her brain a few seconds to realize that she was looking at the dismembered body parts of a human being. She quickly moved to the next picture hoping it would be less disturbing...it was not. Men, women, children. She allowed a sob to escape her mouth as she finally remembered to exhale. She could hear Jason praying beside her and felt comforted by that. "How many…" It was all she could say.

"Twelve so far," the chief replied. "Mostly men...plus," he paused. "There are missing women."

"Missing?" Brianna asked. "Is that why I'm here?" Then she saw the last photograph...On the wall of an old shack, written in blood, was...her mind began to spin. She dropped the stack of pictures and looked up at the chief. "Me? Why does he want me?" She looked at each of the men as they watched her. "Bring me Brianna Bowers? Oh wow….I did not see that coming."

"Are you okay?" Jason asked, placing his hand on her arm again.

She looked up at the chief. "Does Harley Thomas Linwood have anything to do with this?" You could've heard a pin drop in the office as the men just looked at each other.

"Ms. Bowers," Agent Young said, leaning forward in his seat. "How could you have possibly known that name?"

"Agent Young," Brianna replied. "You said you read my file. Well, does it say anything in there about my 'secret source'?"

"Actually...yes," Agent Young replied.

She just smiled at him. "So, tell me about this Harley character."



✝

Each of the men looked at one another and the job just kind of fell on the chief. "Well, for as long as I can remember, old Harley has been living on Pennington Mountain. Not sure that's his actual name, by the way. He goes by several names, depending on the day. He used to have a tent about two hundred yards up, behind Rodney's Barbecue...used to get food out of their trash. He was harmless enough. People always warned the tourists that he was there...just in case he startled them. The town had talked about voting to find him a place to live, but he just always seemed happy...so we left him alone. Then he moved up to the old shack." Chief Jerry took a sip of his coffee and leaned back in his seat, glancing at Agent Young. "Fast forward to about a year ago, and ole Harley began to change. Out of nowhere he would just start screaming in the middle of the night. I'm talking blood curdling, wake you up out of a dead sleep screaming. The complaints came in fast...people were terrified. We brought Harley to a doctor for a psychological evaluation, but as soon as we got him there, he broke the cuffs and went ballistic. He destroyed the doctor's office and pushed his way past the entire staff...left my deputy with a concussion. Ran out of there and apparently made his way back up the mountain. Nobody has seen him since; but my guess is, he's living in one of the hundreds of caves up there."

"And you're assuming that HE'S doing this?" Brianna asked, pointing to the pictures that were still lying on the floor at her feet.

"Who else could it be?" Detective Horne chimed in.

"Other than the doctor's office, has he ever shown any sign of being violent?" Brianna asked.

"We've found animal parts..." Chief Jerry said. "Ripped apart. Human teeth marks on the raw flesh."

"And were there any signs of human teeth marks on the flesh of these...people?" Brianna asked, reaching down to pick up the photographs.

"None," Chief Jerry replied, shaking his head.

**27**

✝

"You're not sure it's him," Brianna said to the chief.

He glanced at Detective Horne and smiled. "I'm not ruling it out, but no...I'm not sold on it."

"This man is dangerous, Ms. Bowers!" Detective Horne added. "The only possible conclusion to these heinous murders is this homeless, psychotic maniac that lives in the very forest where they are being done."

Brianna set the pictures on the desk and turned in her seat. "With all due respect, Detective Horne, it is not the only POSSIBLE conclusion. Pennington Springs has a population of what? About eight thousand people? Not to mention the surrounding towns...literally tens of thousands of conclusions. You're just looking at the simplest one."

"Well, then tell us, Ms. Bowers, what is your 'source' telling you?" Detective Horne asked, smiling at the chief. "Maybe we can wrap this up before lunch, now that you're on the case." All eyes were on Brianna.

"My source isn't telling me anything right now...except to pray for Harley Thomas Linwood...and I've been doing just that."

"Two different attacks..." Agent Young said, causing everyone to look his way. "Over the past seven days there have been two different attacks." He was looking at Brianna. "He's left no survivors...he's apparently very fast. He killed five in the first attack, a group of campers from Biloxi. Seven in the second attack...from Georgia somewhere. It's believed that he took one or two women or children from each attack." He checked his notes. "We're still confirming the total."

"Nothing about that proves that it was Harley, though, does it?" Brianna said.

"Footprints and..." he looked at Detective Horne, who nodded. "A knife...with Harley's prints."



✝

"Oh," Brianna said, sitting back down. "Well, you could've led with that."

"You're not law enforcement, Ms. Bowers, we don't have to share everything with you." Detective Horne said.

"So, tell me, gentlemen," Brianna said, sitting back in her seat. "What exactly is your plan? Do you intend to tie me to a tree and lure the killer out with some beating drums?" They all looked at her in complete confusion. "You know...like in King Kong?"

Pastor Jason smiled at her. "You're crazy."

"No, ma'am," Agent Young said. "We kinda hoped it would draw him out just having you here."

"That's why I said I would be your shadow, Brianna," Jason said. "Packin' my 9." He patted his jacket to let her know he had his gun under it.

"Well, I have another idea," Brianna replied. "Let's go find Mr. Harley...see what he has to say when he sees me."

"You want to go up there?" Chief Jerry said in disbelief, shaking his head.

"Fantastic idea!" Agent Young said. "You're braver than I thought, Ms. Bowers."

"Or dumber…" Chief Jerry added. "No, I can't allow this."

"It's not your call, Chief!" Agent Young said. "She's willing and I approve. Besides, we'll all be with her."

"Great!" Brianna said, standing up once again. "Let me go change clothes."

"Brianna!?" Pastor Jason yelled, giving her quite the look. "You aren't serious?"

"Dead," she replied matter-of-factly, opening the door and walking out of the office.



✝

# CHAPTER 4

*FAYETTEVILLE, ARKANSAS*

*36 years ago*

Vernon couldn't stand it any longer. The child just wouldn't shut up. He stormed up the stairs screaming expletives as if his life depended on it. "Three years of this is enough!!!" He snatched the little boy from the large wooden crate they kept him locked in and shook him violently. "SHUT UP!!!"

The boy's screams intensified and Vernon threw him onto a nearby bed. "PATRICIA! HE GOES OR I GO!!! MAKE A DECISION NOW!!!"

"Calm down, Vernon," Patricia said, walking into the room nonchalantly, while continuing to file her nails. "I would've gotten rid of the little piece of garbage long ago, but he's making us a mint! Who knew there was such a market for toddlers in our business!? Honestly, we should get some more."

"Then, can I at least put his crate in the basement so he can scream to his heart's content without disturbing my football games?"

"Put him wherever you want," Patricia replied. "Heaven forbids your precious quality time be disturbed." She gave him an evil grin. "Just don't forget to feed him," she added as she left the room.

"By the way," he called to her as she walked down the hall. "We still need to give him a name!"

"Doesn't matter," she replied, and stopped where she was. "Let's call him Micky...it was my first husband's name...I hate the name, Micky."

Vernon looked over at the sobbing child and shook his head. "Alright Micky, let's move your worthless butt to your new room."

*Present Day*

Matt Ramsey opened his eyes to complete confusion...for all of about two seconds. He was in his old bed, in his parent's house, in Gateway, and it was Monday morning. He had arrived home last night after an extremely long flight from Tokyo, Japan. His parents had picked him up from the Jacksonville International Airport, taken him to Chick-fil-A for his favorite spicy chicken sandwich and he'd told them all about the amazing things God had done during his time touring with the Dragon Slayers Conventions all over the world.

Matt was a thirty-year-old, 6'4" musician that had led the worship band with Gabi Morgan for several years as they toured around the world telling young people about the power of God in driving back the darkness. Of course, their tight little band of friends were quite experienced in that area and had actual news footage to prove it. Footage from an event that happened about sixteen years earlier. They actually battled the forces of darkness right here in Gateway when they were teenagers.

In fact, a massive dragon had appeared out of the ground right in the middle of the local football field. He and his friends, Mark McGee, Maria Lewis (now McGee), Scotty Morgan, Gabi Motes (now Morgan), Brianna Bowers, Yvette Turner, Jason Green, Andy Cruz, Eddie Schumer, and Jake Malkin (Mark's long lost cousin)...had single-handedly, with the help of a legion of angels, fought off thousands of demons and basically saved the entire town of Gateway from an evil plot to kill them all.

Now, Matt was back in Gateway, having accepted the job of worship leader at Lighthouse Christian Center. It was the biggest church in town and was led by his friend and mentor, Pastor Brian Jones.



✝

"Matthew!" his mother called to him. "Are you awake, sweetheart? Breakfast is almost ready!"

"Be right down, Mom!"

An hour later, Matt was on his way to the church for a meeting with Pastor Brian. He was using his mom's car, since he didn't have one yet...he smiled at the thought of being 30 and having never owned a car. Just way too busy living for God. That would have to change soon enough...getting a car, not the busy part. Luckily his dad, Lieutenant Ramsey of the Jacksonville Sheriff's Office, had made him get a license before he'd gone to college. He at least knew how to drive.

As he pulled into the parking lot, his phone buzzed with a text. He parked by the front door and checked his phone. It was a message from Pastor Brian telling him to meet him in the fellowship hall when he got there. He got out and walked across the parking lot to the large building on the other side. He hadn't been here in a while, but it appeared that not much had changed on the outside. His mother told him about a month ago they'd repainted some of the rooms in the church.

Just as he opened the door and stepped inside, about a dozen people screamed, "SURPRISE!!!" Matt jumped back and put his hand over his heart, but you couldn't have slapped the grin off his face as he looked into the faces of those present. Pastor Brian and his wife, who Matt had never actually met, stood the closest to him with huge smiles on their faces. Mrs. Gilmore, Mark's mom, was there alongside Mrs. Morgan, Scotty's mom. Larry Motes and his wife Gae were Gabi's parents. Larry was stepping down as the long-time worship leader and starting a new ministry in Jacksonville. Matt's eyes teared up when he spotted Mrs. Mumpower smiling at him...her son, Billy, had been Matt's childhood best friend...he'd died during one of their battles with the dragon.



✝

Mr. Bret was there, looking as intimidating as ever, though his smile showed his true heart. Matt nodded to him. That's when he saw Jake...Mark McGee's long-lost cousin that he hadn't even known about. They were united during that final battle with the dragon, where Mark and Jake successfully sent old Rusty to his eternal resting place in hell...Matt could only hope. Jake wheeled his chair over to Matt and the two embraced.

"Good to see you, my old friend," Jake said, through his tears. Matt had been the one to reach out to Jake when he was new to town and had no friends.

"You're looking good, Jake." Matt wiped his own tears away. "What are you up to these days?"

"I'm actually full time here at the church," Jake replied. "Sound, lighting, and media ministry. Not only am I heading it up, but I'm also teaching courses to some of the teens."

"So, we'll be working together?" Matt asked, quite excited at this idea. Jake nodded. "That's awesome, Jake, I'm so proud of you." Just then a woman with long brown hair and a pretty face, walked up behind Jake smiling from ear to ear at Matt. "Hi, I'm Matt Ramsey, the..."

She slapped his hand away as Jake burst out in uncontrollable laughter. "You know who I am, Matt Ramsey!" Seeing his confused look, she shook her head. "You're the reason I'm here...well, Jesus is the reason, but you were the vessel..."

"JO!?" Matt stepped back in shock that the beauty before him was Jake's older sister, Jo...who looked so much like a man the last time he'd seen her. "ARE YOU KIDDING ME!?" He swept her up into a massive hug. Matt had not returned home with the others after he'd left for college. He'd chosen to use his summer and winter breaks to serve in various ministries. This was literally the first time he'd seen these people since his send off after high school. "You're absolutely gorgeous," he whispered in her ear.

33

✝

"Well, thank you, Matt," she replied, breaking free from his embrace. "There's a couple of people I'd like you to meet." With that, she turned and introduced a tall, thin man with a beard that reached his chest...and he was holding a young, sleeping toddler. "This is my husband, Robert...and our son...Matthew Jacob Hall."

Matt was too stunned for words. He only nodded as he shook Robert's hand and leaned in close to look at his name sake. "Wow," was all he could manage as Jo patted his back. Again, he gave her a big hug and couldn't hold back the tears. "Oh, Jo...God is SOOO good."

"Yes He is...and I go by JoAnn now," she replied with a slight snicker.

"JoAnn," Matt stepped back and looked at her family...the one Satan had tried to rob her of. "So good to see you again." He wiped his eyes and realized that everyone was standing around them and watching the scene. They were also wiping their eyes.

They all swooped in and got their hugs and told their stories over the next half hour or so as Matt filled his face with cake...although he'd just had a substantial breakfast.

Just as he was about to excuse himself to go to the restroom, someone came up behind him and covered his eyes with their hands. "Guess who!?" a young female voice said.

"I honestly have no idea...but your hands smell nice," he said with a laugh, and they removed them from his eyes. He turned around and was greeted by what appeared to be an absolute angel from heaven. Matt's breath literally escaped his lungs as he stared at the most beautiful girl he'd ever seen.

Seeing his confusion, she playfully shoved his chest. "It's ME, silly...Bethany McGee!" Mark McGee's little sister, who was several years younger when the gang hung out, she had never been more than a little kid to Matt. Now...whoa!

34

✝

"No way!" he gave her a big hug. "Oh my gosh, Bethany...you're all grown up!"

She smiled. "And working at the church...I'm the Office Manager...hey, someone has to keep these slackers in line."

"That's impressive, Bethany!" Matt replied. "Why didn't Mark tell me about any of this?"

She shrugged. "He's just busy, I guess."

"Wow, Bethany McGee all grown up...and look at you, you're stunning." Matt watched as she turned about four shades of red.

"Well, thank you, Matthew," she replied. "You're too kind. Listen, I have some pressing issues I have to run by Pastor Brian...maybe we can get together sometime?"

"I'd like that," Matt replied as he watched her walk away. She'd called him Matthew...something he only allowed his and Andy's mom to call him...but hearing her say it…

"She's single, you know," Mrs. Gilmore, her mom, brought him back to reality.

"I'm, um, did you, what?" Matt stammered as she gave him an encouraging smile.

"She's single...and been somewhat excited about you returning."

"Me?" Matt was totally confused. "Why?"

"Why?" Mrs. Gilmore asked. "Why not? Matt Ramsey, the musical genius who can play practically any instrument, sing, write songs...and does it all for God...yeah, I got nothing." She gave him a light shove and rolled her eyes. "She loves Mexican food, and we never had this conversation." She gave him a wink and walked away.

35

✝

As Brianna made her way back to the bed and breakfast, she noticed that people were staring at her as she walked down the sidewalk. Cars were slowing down, people were stepping out of shops, heads were turning. At first, she just smiled and waved, thinking they were extra friendly here in small town America...then she realized that word must've gotten out somehow among the locals.

She turned her head to watch a slow car pass by with a young couple watching her and ran right into someone standing in her path. "Oh, my goodness...I'm so sorry...Mr. Nesmith, is it?" she said, seeing it was the man that had spoken to her in church yesterday morning. She reached up and straightened his tie, since she'd just slammed into him.

"Ms. Bowers," he replied with a nod. "I trust it's important business that has you in such a hurry?"

"Actually, yes, it is," she leaned in to whisper. "We're going up the mountain to see if we can find old Harley."

"Do you really think that's such a good idea, Ms. Bowers?" Mr. Nesmith asked. "I've seen what that man is capable of, and..."

"I'm not exactly sure that Harley is our man, Mr. Nesmith...but that's just my suspicion at this point."

"You've just arrived, and you haven't even met him, yet you've come to that conclusion, have you?" Mr. Nesmith seemed quite perturbed with her attitude.

"I'm not saying I'm right," Brianna said with a smile. "Something just doesn't feel right, you know? He just seems like a good scapegoat."

He looked her over as if plotting his next words carefully. "Well, alright...good luck with your theory. The entire town is pretty



✝

much sold on it being ol' Harley. But I suppose the only way to be sure is to investigate other avenues."

"That's the spirit!" Brianna replied. "Well, I need to get changed, so we can start our search. Sorry again for bumping into you!"

When she got to her room, Brianna rummaged through her clothes to find something to trek through the mountains in. That's when she realized that she didn't have any proper hiking shoes. She quickly shot a text to Jason to see if there was a nearby place to purchase some. She slid on some shorts and a t-shirt just as her phone rang. Without looking and assuming it was Jason, she picked it up.

"Hey, so anything nearby?"

"Unfortunately, I have no idea what you're talking about," she could hear Jonah's smile through the phone. "Also unfortunately, I'm not nearby."

"That IS unfortunate," she said, catching herself blushing. "Jonah! I didn't expect to hear from you for several days."

"I needed my Bree fix," he replied, and she smiled at the name he'd called her. Only her parents had ever called her Bree, and it felt special to hear him say it.

"Did you now?" she asked. "So, how's your Bible reading going?" She desperately needed to steer the conversation to God before she left this place, got on a plane, and found this man.

"That's actually why I'm calling you," he replied. "You know how you told me to start with the book of John and then Acts?"

"Yes," she replied. "How far have you gotten?"

"Well, actually...I've read both of them three times now."

"Oh, wow, Jonah," Brianna said, clearly impressed. "That's awesome!"



✝

"So, I have some questions about the Holy Spirit," he said. "Are there any books about Him that could help me to understand Him better? I know how important He is to you and how you said that He was the one who drew me to Christ through my visions and all."

"Yes, there's a few books about Him that I enjoy and if I were home I would send them to you."

"It's cool, I downloaded the Kindle app to my phone and have been itching to read something."

"Okay, ready?" Brianna asked. "There's two books that I highly recommend."

"Hit me…" Jonah replied, grabbing his pen and paper.

"Okay, John Bevere has an amazing book called The Holy Spirit, and Paul Yonggi Cho has one called The Holy Spirit, My Senior Partner."

"Sweet, thanks Bree!" Jonah said. "So, how's Tennessee?"

"It's beautiful here in the small town of Pennington Springs!" she replied, not sure how much to share. She didn't want him to worry.

"Uh huh, and have you found out yet why you're there?"

"Just some mysterious things going on that Pastor Jason thought I might be able to help with."

"Well, if you don't want to tell me, just say so," he said with a chuckle.

"Nothing for you to worry about, just be praying for me," she replied.

"Well, that I can do," Jonah said. "Okay, let me look into these books and let you get back to solving mysteries."

"Alright," Brianna said. "Thank you for calling...it was good to hear your voice."

38

✝

"You too...talk to you later, Bree!" He hung up leaving her with a big smile.

Just then her phone buzzed with a text from Jason. "Pennington Springs Country Store. How about I pick you up and take you there?"

"Sounds good."



†

# CHAPTER 5



*FAYETTEVILLE, ARKANSAS*

*34 years ago*

Officers Denise Gallagher and Eddie Halloway climbed the front steps of the massive home and rang the doorbell. Out of the corner of their eyes they saw several other officers circling around to the back of the house. The call box on the wall to their right buzzed and a woman's voice asked for them to identify themselves.

"Yes ma'am," Officer Gallagher replied. "This is the City of Fayetteville Police Department; we have a warrant to search these premises." There was silence for several seconds. "Ma'am, I'm going to need you to open the door immediately or we'll…"

"You're going to have to wait, I'm attempting to reach my lawyer!" the woman replied.

"Ma'am," Officer Halloway added. "This sure is a beautiful door…oak, is it? It would be a shame for me to have to break it into splinters…you have exactly five seconds to open up!"

The door immediately swung open and a tall, thin man that looked like he'd been in the process of several lines of coke and smelled as if he hadn't showered in days, stood there attempting to block their way.

Officer Halloway easily pushed past him, and Officer Gallagher informed him that he would need to step outside along with anyone else inside the home. An extremely thin woman whose skin was as white as paper came down the stairs speaking into a cordless phone. "Yes, Roger, they're actually in my home at this very moment and I would like to press charges against the Fayetteville Police Department…this is outrageous!"

"Out of the house, lady!" an officer commanded. "You can walk out, or I can carry you!"



✝

"Do you know who I am!?" she demanded as he shoved her toward the door.

"We have a warrant to search these premises on suspicion of drug distribution and prostitution!"

"My lawyer will have your jobs!"

"He can have it, lady!" the officer said, as he pushed her out the door. "Tell him it's tiresome work dealing with so many idiots, though." He closed the door and shook his head.

"Sarge!" an officer called from down the hall. "Jenkins says you have to see this!"

The Sergeant walked down the hall and looked in the direction the officer was pointing...which just so happened to be down a set of stairs. "Whatta ya got Jenkins!?" he asked as he descended the steps into the basement.

"Check this out," Jenkins said, pointing to several pallets of cocaine and bags upon bags of marijuana. "We've hit the mother lode!"

"Yeah, these morons are going away for a long time," the Sergeant said.

Just then, there was a rattling sound from behind them in a dark corner. The officers all turned and faced the darkness. "Somebody get a light back here," Officer Gallagher said, squinting at what looked like a box in the corner. Just then someone shined a light in that direction and revealed that it was a blanket draped over a box. It shook and made a rattling sound. "I think it's a cage, Sarge," Gallagher said as she warily approached it. She could hear ragged breathing and a light growl. "Some kind of animal..."

"Be careful, Officer Gallagher," the Sarge said, placing his hand on his sidearm.



✝

She reached out her hand cautiously and yanked the blanket off, jumping back at the scene before her. "OH MY GOD!!!"

The small child leaped at the side of the cage and screamed in a manner that made her skin crawl. It began to shake the cage violently, causing it to move across the floor. Drool and blood were coming from its mouth as it screamed and hissed at the officers.

"My God, what in the world!" The Sarge approached the cage and saw that it was an extremely young child, anywhere from three to five years old, practically a skeleton in size...with the eyes of a rabid animal.

"How do we handle this, Sarge!?" Gallagher asked, standing there with her hand over her mouth and nose...the smell was unbelievable.

"Get me Child Protective Services on the phone, somebody," he said, as he ran to another corner and threw up.


*PENNINGTON SPRINGS, TENNESSEE*

*Present Day*

Brianna and Pastor Jason met up with the others at the police station after purchasing her new hiking boots and a few other necessities for a day out on the mountain. She found Chief Jerry, Detective Horne, Agent Young, and two officers...Stevenson and Clark, being briefed on what was going to happen. Pastor Jason grabbed her arm as they entered. He gave her a frustrated look and said, "This is a bad idea, Brianna...I don't like it."

"And remember," Chief Jerry said, motioning for Brianna and Jason to join them in his office. "Unless I or Agent Young give you specific orders, we're all to stay together. No wandering off or going anywhere alone. I understand that you two..." he pointed to his officers..."feel like you know Harley...but I can't stress it

**42**

✝

enough...right now he is our only suspect in these gruesome murders...DO NOT UNDERESTIMATE HIM!!!"

"Brianna, good...you're back," Agent Young said. He reached into his ankle holster and produced a small pistol. "I don't need to ask if you know how to use this...I've seen the video footage." He handed it to her. "Keep it in your pocket, just in case."

"It's so small...is this a .380?" she asked.

Agent Young nodded. "Yes, it is...six shots. Hollow point so it still packs a punch."

"I'm sorry," Pastor Jason stepped forward. "Is it really necessary that we take Brianna up there?"

"Bring me Brianna Bowers," Agent Young replied. "Which word confuses you?"

"The word that says you're doing exactly what a killer tells you to do!" Jason replied. "It's like a lamb to the slaughter!" This made Brianna laugh.

"Sorry," Brianna said when she saw how furious Jason was. "That was a good reference. My King Kong reference was better, though."

"You're the one that called Ms. Bowers, Pastor," Detective Horne said. "Did you think we were just inviting her to tea? Getting her out in the open could bring this guy right to us! Not to mention, this is literally her idea!"

"And the faster we can catch this guy, the faster we can open the town back up to tourists!" Agent Young added, glancing at Chief Jerry.

"Well, let's go if we're going," Chief Jerry said. "We're burning daylight."

**43**

✝

Once outside, they piled into three different vehicles. Chief Jerry had Jason and Brianna in his Jeep, Agent Young rode with Officer Stevenson, and Detective Horne was with Officer Clark. They headed up the mountain toward where they'd found the last of the bodies. They would begin there, and make their way up the mountain on foot.

Brianna sat quietly in the backseat praying for their safety. Her old friend, the Holy Spirit, was beside her, staring out the window. Chief Jerry and Jason were in the front seat talking about how this was a crazy idea, but Chief Jerry did like the idea of getting this whole mess behind them. Brianna's phone buzzed in her pocket and she checked the screen to see a New York number she didn't recognize. Before she could decline the call, her old friend smiled at her and nodded to the phone. "Hello?" she answered.

"As I live and breathe! If it isn't the world famous Brianna Bowers!" a slightly familiar female voice said into the phone.

"World famous is a bit strong...but yes, this is Brianna Bowers."

"Hey girl!" the woman said. "You have no idea who this is, do you!?"

"You sound very familiar, but I'm sorry to say, no...wait a minute...Christina!?" Brianna almost screamed. She hadn't spoken with Christina Bulford in almost a decade...actually, it wasn't Bulford anymore, it was Gavins now. Her and Tyler had married about a year after the whole dragon incident. Later, they'd moved away to Atlanta.

Christina had been a news reporter in Gateway when Brianna moved there. She had been a huge help during the castle incident that started the spiritual battles of Gateway. She got involved when Matt Ramsey asked her to help investigate. Hotshot reporter Tyler had come from Tampa later on and swept her off her feet. They became overnight sensations after reporting on the dragon event live as it happened.



✝

"Yes!" Christina replied. "How are you doing, Brianna!?"

"I'm spectacular! Are you in New York now!?" she asked.

"I am!" Christina responded. "Tyler and I started a media outlet called, 'The Right News'. We attempt to present the news in a way that is not only truth, but also glorifies God."

"Christina, that's amazing!" Brianna was so proud of her friend. "I can't believe this is the first I'm hearing about it!"

"We cover a lot of what Dragon Slayers are doing, but I try and leave you guys alone for the most part. I know you're facing enough enemies, and well, we've made a few ourselves." Christina said with a laugh.

"I'm sure you have," Brianna responded. "So, to what do I owe the honor of this call?"

"Well, although we've never actually done a story on you, given your occupation and I'm sure, need for anonymity. We have, however, kept up with your every move over the last few months. Yes, Tyler and I have been stalking you!" This made Brianna laugh. "My sources have you in Pennington Springs, Tennessee right now, Brianna...and I've been sensing a secretive buzz out of that area. Anything you're able to share? Off the record, for now, of course."

"Christina, I can't right now," she glanced up and caught Chief Jerry watching her in the mirror. "But I can promise you a scoop when it's all said and done. And by the way...great investigation skills, girl!" They both laughed.

"Well, that's awesome, and thank you Brianna," Christina said. "I look forward to hearing from you. Until then, as always, you're in my prayers."

"Much needed...and thank you!" Brianna replied. "Give Tyler my love!"

"I will!" Christina said with a smile. "Bye, Brianna."



✝

"Goodbye, Christina." Brianna clicked off the call and looked over just as her old friend placed His hand on hers.

"Pray without ceasing, Brianna...there's a powerful storm coming...but I've prepared you for this. Trust me." He smiled at her.

"Yes sir," Brianna replied. "I always trust You."

"Do what?" Jason asked her.

She noticed that her old friend was gone for now, though not really. "Nothing," she replied to Jason. "Just talking to God." Little did she know...that would be the last time she would see her old friend for quite some time.


## CAIRO, EGYPT

Mark McGee and the rest of the Dragon Slayers planned to head back to the states after Tokyo. There were no other stops on the schedule for the next three months and they were looking forward to relaxing and settling back in at their homes. As it happened, however, a group of fans had petitioned the city of Cairo to allow them to come. They'd received over 250,000 signatures...so the city gave them a permit. The entire group agreed that if the people were that hungry for God, who were they to deny them the event. So, here they were, getting settled into their hotel rooms in the center of the booming metropolis of Cairo, Egypt.

"Did you know," Scotty Morgan said to his wife, Gabi, as they were unpacking their bags. "That Cairo has a bigger population than New York? According to that pamphlet I was reading, there are over ten million people here!"

"Yeah, that's crazy," Gabi replied. "Wouldn't it be amazing if we could reach that many while we're here?"

"Well, at eighty thousand a night, that would take over four months… or so."



✝

"With God, all things are possible...greater is HE!" Gabi replied, just as there was a knock at the door.

"I got it," Scotty said, walking over to open the door. He was greeted by Mark and Maria McGee. "Hey guys!" Scotty said, waving them in. "Come in and save me from this optimistic worship leader."

Maria laughed. "Gabi, an optimist...impossible!"

"Yeah, I find that hard to believe, myself," Mark added with a wink to Gabi.

"Hey, guys!" Gabi said with a smile. "Have a seat." Mark and Maria plopped down on the small loveseat in the middle of the room. "So?" Gabi walked over and sat in one of the chairs across from them and Scotty took the other one. "What's got you two so secretive lately?"

Maria smiled. "Well, we were supposed to be flying back to Gateway and were going to have a big party with everyone and give them the news...but then Cairo came up."

"You guys are pregnant!!!" Scotty and Gabi said together. Mark and Maria both blushed and smiled at them...nodding.

"Dude, that's awesome!" Scotty yelled and jumped up hugging his friend. "Marcus and Thomas are going to have a little...? Do we know yet?"

"Sister," Maria replied. "The whole reason I joined you guys on tour was so that I could give Mark the news in person," she said as Gabi pulled away from the bear hug she had her in. "We even have a name picked out."

"Do tell," Scotty said, glancing at Mark as Maria nodded for him to tell.

"Gabriella Angel McGee," Mark said as his eyes teared up. He looked over to see Gabi wiping a tear from her eyes as well.

47

✝

"Wow…" Gabi said. "I'm honored." She gave Maria another huge hug.

"Angel?" Scotty added. "As in…"

"She saved Mark's life…before I ever met you guys," Maria said. "I can't wait to meet her in heaven…to thank her."

Angel had been their friend in middle school for a brief time. She'd died saving Mark's life while in the mysterious castle. Scotty had led her to Jesus just before she died. A day had not passed where Mark McGee had not thought about Angel's sacrifice. She'd stepped right in front of an attacking demon. His sword, meant for Mark, had gone right through her.

Again, Mark wiped a tear and tried to smile. He placed his hand on Maria's stomach. "I hope you're as courageous as both of the women you're named after…" He smiled at Gabi as she approached him with a big hug.

"You guys should know by now that I really hate hugging," Gabi said. "So, consider this my baby gift…" they all burst into laughter.

There was another knock at the door. Scotty walked over and answered it. There was a young, extremely good-looking blonde man standing there, holding a backpack over his shoulder. "Can I help you?" Scotty asked.

"Yes, I was told this was Gabi Morgan's room," he held out his hand nervously to Scotty. "I'm Dustin…Dustin Knight."



✝

# CHAPTER 6



*LITTLE ROCK, ARKANSAS*

*33 years ago*

Dr. Alisha Morrow of New Hope Child Psychiatry Services, sat at her desk looking through Micky's chart one more time. She couldn't believe how far he'd come over the last few months. They'd pretty much written him off as a lost cause. He'd been distant, prone to extreme fits of rage, unable to communicate, terrified of being around people(mostly males), terrified of being alone, extreme changes in personalities within minutes and sometimes seconds. He'd been diagnosed with almost every psychiatric issue in the book. PTSD, anxiety, schizophrenia, paranoia, delirium, bipolar disorder, panic disorder, and dissociative disorder...to name a few. Then, just as they were about to have him committed permanently into a mental hospital, he seemed to just...snap out of it...almost perfectly normal, except for his complete lack of education at the age of six. He still spoke as an infant but was learning to communicate at an exceedingly high rate. Just yesterday, he smiled when she entered the room and said "Docker Mowo". She was excited about his sudden improvement, but had no idea what to attribute it to.

Today they were bringing in a tutor to expedite his learning skills. The goal was that Micky would be able to go to a normal school and be in class with children his own age within the next year. It would require several hours a day, seven days a week, but she felt confident that Micky was up to the task.

Micky...it was the only name he had. It made her sad to think about his past. Micky deserved a bright future, and she intended to prepare him for it. He deserved a last name...and she intended to help him get adopted once his age-appropriate education was complete. Micky...an anomaly.



✝

Dr. Morrow sat back in her seat and smiled. "I don't understand you, Mr. Micky...but it's kids like you that remind me why I do what I do." She closed the file and headed out to do her rounds.


## GATEWAY, FLORIDA

### Present Day

Matt was attempting to set up his new office. Pastor Brian had told him to just spend the day getting settled in and touching base with everyone on staff. His computer was finally hooked up properly and he'd found the perfect spot for his desk. He'd made a list of things he would need to buy tonight at the store, some important, some just to give the office his personal touch.

"Excuse me, Matthew," a woman's voice said from behind him at the door. He turned to see his friend, Andy Cruz's mom standing in the doorway. "I'm sorry to bother you…"

Matt jumped up and ran to greet her. "You could never bother me, Ms. Cruz!" He gave her a big hug that let her know how much he truly missed her. "It's so good to see you." Ms. Cruz had resisted coming to church for about a year after Andy had gotten saved. The gang had killed her with kindness as Gabi liked to call it. She'd eventually showed up for Mother's Day service and given her life to Christ. Matt had heard that she was heavily involved in various ministries.

"It's so good to see you as well, Matthew," she said with a bubbly smile, holding him at arm's length. "I was so excited when I heard that you were coming to lead the worship team. I only wish that Andrew had come with you!"

Matt chuckled. "Well, he wouldn't have been far behind me if Cairo hadn't fallen into their laps."



✝

"I know my son is doing God's work, but I miss him terribly," she said, taking a seat in one of the chairs Matt had slid up against the wall until he could figure out his feng shui. "Have a seat, Matthew...I need to talk to you."

"Yes ma'am," he replied, taking a seat at his desk. "What can I do for you?"

"Well, it's Daniel..." Daniel was her youngest son, Andy's little brother. "He's been getting into some trouble lately, nothing serious, but you know...he's on the wrong path."

Matt nodded. "How old is Daniel now, Ms. Cruz?"

"Sixteen," she replied. "Going on thirty, you'd think, given his attitude."

"Wow, I remember he was only five when you dropped Andy off at college," Matt said. "Where has the time gone?"

"Wait until you're my age, Matthew," she replied. "Anyway, he has shown a lot of interest in music ever since his big brother started playing. He's actually quite good on the guitar, Matthew. I was kind of hoping that maybe you could take him under your wing...you know...help him to find himself...and hopefully God."

Matt smiled at his friend's mother, who loved everyone unconditionally, and tried to imagine the pain of a child straying away. "I would be honored, Ms. Cruz. Give me his cell number and I'll touch base with him this week."

When she left his office, Matt closed the door and knelt next to his desk. He had a mission...and he would need all the wisdom God could offer.



✝

They slowed down and pulled off the road into a clearing in the trees. "We're on foot from here," Chief Jerry said. They all climbed out of their vehicles and gathered their gear. "Remember, no wandering off alone. And I want two people with Brianna at all times. No excuses." Each of his officers produced a shotgun and Officer Clark handed one to the chief.

Brianna stood to the side and watched as the men prepared for what felt like war. Jason walked over and stood beside her like a centurion soldier. He checked the rounds in his gun for like the fourth time since they'd arrived. "It's going to be okay, Jason."

He looked over at her. "I'm sorry for asking you to come."

"People have died, Jason," Brianna said. "This guy needs to be stopped. Besides, I'm still not convinced it's Harley that's doing it. Something about it just doesn't feel right."

"It's him...but either way, whoever is doing it, wants you dead." Jason looked around, scanning the tree line.

"Maybe not," Brianna said. "He said to bring me...maybe he just wants to talk...WHAT? I'm a good listener!" She laughed, but Jason just gave her a stern look. "Stop being so serious, Jason, it's not you, you were always the jokester!" She gave him a light shove. "Besides, I apparently just took down the largest child trafficking ring in the world...single-handedly!" She said, with a wink. "Old Harley is no match for me!"

Jason couldn't help but smile. "Just be alert when we get in there...and stay close to me."

"Yessir, Captain," she saluted him with a big grin on her face.

"Is everyone ready?" Chief Jerry called out. They all nodded and followed him onto a small trail that Brianna had not even noticed. "It's about an hour walk to the last murder scene."

"This doesn't look like a well-known trail," Brianna said.

"It's not!" Chief Jerry called back. He and Agent Young led the way, followed by Detective Horne, Jason and Brianna, and Officers Stevenson and Clark. "Only a few of the locals know it's here. Back in the eighties it was used by the park rangers. There used to be a fire tower near where we're headed. Now there's just an old shack. It's where the rangers would stay when they were on duty."

"Is that where Harley lived?" she asked.

"For a while," Jason replied. "He's believed to be further up the mountain now...in a cave most likely."

"So, what's our plan?" Brianna asked. "Are we hunting him or are you boys just giving me a tour?"

"Well, this was your idea Ms. Bowers," Agent Young said. "We're actually fishing...you're the bait."

"I get THAT much, Agent Young," Brianna said. "What I mean is...how far are we taking this today? Are we staying up here until we find him or heading back before dark?"

"Let's just see how things play out, Brianna," Chief Jerry replied. "We brought enough supplies to stay the night, but it isn't set in stone."

An hour later, they arrived in a clearing that was covered by tall trees allowing very little sunlight. There was police tape roping off a very large area. Brianna saw where there'd been a campfire and a smoothed out place where there'd been tents just a few nights ago. The shack was just up the hill, next to the base of what Brianna imagined had been the fire tower. Four concrete footings.

"So, this is where it happened..." Brianna said. She caught herself looking around for signs of a struggle or blood splatter.



✝

"We cleaned everything up as good as we could," Officer Stevenson said. "Except..." he glanced at the chief. "The inside of the shack."

"So...what he wrote?"

"It's still there, Brianna," Chief Jerry said. "Don't look if it's going to bother you."

She made her way up toward the shack with Jason right behind her. "I'm going to need you too, Holy Spirit." There was no door on the front entrance of the shack, but the police tape blocked her entrance. She bent down and maneuvered her way in. Jason followed her.

"Just like we found it except..." he started to say.

"Except for the body parts," she finished for him. She glanced up at the wall in the back. There it was...Bring me Brianna Bowers. A chill moved up her spine. "Okay, God...I need You here. What's going on? Please give me...give us Your wisdom in this situation."

"The man who did this is possessed, Brianna," Jason said. "Just like the man in the tombs from the Bible. Probably possessed by multiple demons...imagine those things we fought living inside you...controlling you."

"I'm sure you're right," Brianna said. "But why me?"

"Well, Harley wouldn't have seen you on television," Jason replied. "He wouldn't have any way of knowing who you are...but the demons would. They know...and tremble."

"That scripture refers to Jesus," Brianna replied, still looking at her name on the wall.

"And who lives inside you?" Jason responded. "You've stopped a lot of evil, Brianna. Satan wants you dead. That's why your name is on the wall...that's why you're here."



✝

She nodded. "Well, I'm here." She turned and faced Jason. "What now?"

Jason held both of his hands out to her. "Let's pray."

Outside the shack, the others were setting up a makeshift campsite. Officer Clark was gathering wood for a fire while Officer Stevenson tied up a tarp between some trees for cover. Chief Jerry produced a small table and set out some maps of the area. Agent Young and Detective Horne worked together to set up a large tent, just in case they decided to stay the night. Within fifteen minutes it almost looked like a respectable campsite.

Brianna came out and asked if there was anything she could do to help. Chief Jerry pointed to a small tent unrolled but not put up yet. There was a sleeping bag lying next to it.

"Since you're the only female, I figured you'd want your own tent. Just in case we decide to stay the night. You can wait until later to put it up if you want."

Brianna looked over and noticed Officer Clark watching her. He quickly glanced away and set down the limbs he'd been gathering. "Um, okay, I wasn't aware that we were definitely staying the night," she replied.

"Chief," Jason said. "I'm not sleeping in that tent with you guys while Brianna is out here all by herself."

"Well, it's not going to look right if you sleep with her, Pastor!" Chief Jerry said with a smile. "Relax, do you honestly think I'm not going to have someone standing guard all night?"

"Ms. Brianna, would you like to gather some limbs with me?" Officer Clark asked. "If you're looking for something to do."

"Yeah, um...I'll look over here." She headed in the opposite direction of where he was heading.



✝

"Ma'am," he said, holding out his hands. "It would probably be safer if you didn't go alone."

"Yeah, I'll go with you, Brianna," Jason said.

Twenty minutes later they were drinking fresh coffee that Detective Horne had made with the help of the fire. Chief Jerry was going over the map with them, showing them where he wanted to look. "We can cover more ground if we split into two groups. Agent Horne, and Officers Stevenson and Clark will take this section, and the rest of us will look over here. Now remember, Harley is not a sane man. He's extremely strong, and most definitely dangerous. He's killed before, so I can't imagine what he's going to do when cornered. Detective Horne and Officer Stevenson both have tranquilizer darts to shoot him with. I would prefer to take him alive, but if we have to kill him...well."

Officer Clark was standing extremely close to Brianna and making her quite uncomfortable. His hand was actually brushing up against hers. She moved away from him slightly and noticed him glancing at her. She thanked God that he was not in her group. This guy was definitely giving off a vibe she didn't like. She glanced over and Jason was giving her a confused look. She just smiled at him and continued listening to Jerry telling them to check any caves they found and to radio the other group if they find anything significant.

Five minutes later they split up and headed toward their destination, Brianna glanced back to see Officer Clark watching her as they headed in the other direction. He smiled when their eyes met and said something to Officer Stevenson.

"You okay?" Jason asked her as they walked up the mountain.

"Yeah, why do you ask?"

"Seemed like something was bothering you back there."



✝

"I'm fine." There was no way she was bringing Jason in on this. He would say something to Officer Clark and blow it all out of proportion. Nope, she was a big girl...she could handle a guy with a crush, even if he did give her the creeps.

The further up the mountain they went, the denser the forest became. With the trees overhead you could barely see the sunlight. Chief Jerry was having to knock the underbrush out of the way with a machete as they hiked.

"Hardly feels like a well-traveled path," Detective Horne commented. Something made a noise to their right and he drew his handgun. They all stopped and ducked down, scanning the area. A mother and baby deer fled into deeper forest. They all chuckled and composed themselves. "Better safe than sorry."

"Um…" Brianna said. "I have to use the restroom."

Jason laughed. "Restroom?"

"You know what I mean!"

Chief Jerry reached into his bag and tossed a roll of toilet paper to Brianna. "I like to be prepared," he said with a smile. "And leaves are just awkward."

"I agree," Brianna said with a laugh. "Thank you, Chief!"

"Head that direction," Jason said. "Looks a little more private."

Brianna looked that way and saw a huge boulder sticking out from the ground about twenty five feet away. "Yeah, I'll go over behind that big rock."

"Be aware of your surroundings, Brianna!" Chief Jerry called.



✝

"Probably a good idea to take care of some business myself," Detective Horne said, heading in the opposite direction. "No paper needed."

Brianna made her way around the boulder and found the underbrush to be a little thicker than she'd thought. She looked around for the best location and slipped in as close to the boulder as she could get.

"Yer Brianna Bowers...we're sure of it," a man's voice said from just above her on the side of the rock.

"Wha..." Brianna froze. "Who...Harley?"

"He told us yous comin to fine us, yes he did." He made his way into view as Brianna tried to dig the pistol out of her pocket. Her heart was pounding.

"Who told you, Harley?" She could see him now. He was a medium built man with cuts and scrapes all over his face and arms. She saw the broken handcuffs still clamped onto his wrists. He wore a pair of old jeans, a plaid shirt that was buttoned up wrong, and old boots with holes that exposed his dirty socks. That's when Brianna noticed the blood splatter on his jeans and shirt. He smiled at her and showed his almost black teeth.

"Yer purtyer than he said," Harley added. "Yor gone be our favrit."

"Who told you I was coming, Harley?"

"Brianna!?" Jason called. "Are you okay!?"

"Why Micky told us, o'course," Harley said. "He tells us evrythin." He twitched as he spoke. "Micky's the smart one. He takes care o us."



✝

# CHAPTER 7



*GATEWAY, FLORIDA*

Sixteen-year-old Daniel Cruz sat alone in the school courtyard just outside of the cafeteria of Gateway High School. His mother had prepared him a bag lunch consisting of a ham sandwich with mayo and mustard, an apple, and an oatmeal cream pie. She had also given him just enough change to get a soda from the machine...which at the moment, was out of order.

Right as he was about to take the first bite of his sandwich, someone snuck up behind him and knocked it out of his hand. Seeing it fall onto the dirty walkway; he heard a familiar laugh. Chris Norton, (the guy who had been bullying Daniel since sixth grade). Daniel jumped up and spun around. There stood Chris and his three sidekicks: Fred, Jarod, and Malcolm. They were all laughing as they waited to see what Daniel would say or do. "Dude, seriously!?"

"You're such a loser, Danny!" Fred said with a laugh, knocking the rest of his lunch off of the bench.

"Yeah, Dude," Malcolm replied. "Sit down and shut up, before you get hurt. LOOK, he's going to cry!" They all laughed as they walked away.

"WHAT A LOSER!" Chris yelled for everyone to hear. Several people were watching what was going on, but nobody dared to challenge Chris and his boys and risk becoming the new target.

Daniel picked up his bag and sat back down. He watched as they disappeared into the cafeteria, dreaming of several different scenarios to get revenge on those jerks. Just then, his cell phone buzzed in his back pocket. He pulled it out to find a text message from his brother, Andy, who was in Egypt, doing another of those Dragon Slayer shows. Daniel didn't care much for the church scene, he'd never been able to see the point, but he thought it was really impressive that his big brother was in a famous world touring band. He pulled up the text.

"Hey little bro! Praying for you this morning. Hope all is well. Should be heading home in a few days."

"Yeah, a lot of good those prayers are doing," Daniel mumbled to himself, putting his phone back in his pocket and taking a bite of his apple. He looked through the cafeteria window and saw Chris talking to Heather Greer. She seemed to be enjoying his attention. Of course she was...Daniel lost his appetite. He decided to go to the restroom and then head to his next class. Unfortunately, he had to cut through the cafeteria; but they seemed preoccupied, and probably wouldn't notice him.

He stuffed his oatmeal cream pie into his jacket pocket and headed for the door. He'd just keep his head down and walk fast. He opened the door and made his way around the tables, staying clear of Chris and the others. He was almost to the door.

"HEY LOSER!!!" Chris yelled. He kept his head down and pressed on. "HEY, I'M TALKING TO YOU, DANNY BOY!!! DON'T YOU WALK AWAY!!" Daniel stopped and looked over at them. They were all laughing.

"Chris, be nice," Heather said. "Leave him alone."

"But look at him," Jarod said, with a smirk. "He's literally a loser. Look at those pants."

Daniel just couldn't help himself with the finger gesture he gave them. "At least I'm not Chris' side chick, Jarod!" He turned and walked out of the cafeteria as fast as he could, hearing their chairs scraping on the floor as they took chase.

**60**

✝

Gabi Morgan had started the evening, once again, with a heavy heart for her friend, Brianna. Before doing anything else, she dropped to her knees in her dressing room and prayed. No matter how much she tried to concentrate on all the things she needed to take care of before the show, the Holy Spirit had drawn her back to pray. She texted Scotty, her loving workaholic husband, to get his help with some of the things that needed to be done. She knew he was running late with a problem he'd had to run take care of with the city. Something to do with a last minute permit they required him to sign off on. She hadn't heard from him since, which led to her taking things in a direction she had not originally planned. Just as she was kneeling down again to pray for Brianna, there was a light rap at her dressing room door. "Come in!"

"Hey, Gabi," Dustin said. "I was told to find you?"

"Yes," Gabi replied. "Come in, leave the door open." She stood and took a seat at her makeup table. "Pull up a chair."

"Okay," Dustin replied. "Is everything alright?"

"Yeah, you remember Brianna? She's apparently gotten herself in another jam or something and God has me praying for her," she said with a smile.

"What's going on?" Dustin asked with serious concern.

"She's fine, I'm sure...but I have no idea."

"So, what...God just tells you to pray for her? How do you know." Dustin, a new believer, was clearly confused.

"You just know in your spirit," she said. "It takes time to get to know His voice, Dustin, but with a lot of time in prayer and the Word," she held up her Bible. "You eventually recognize when He's talking...just like you would recognize any familiar voice."



†

"Anyway, listen. I know I told you to just observe tonight's event, but Scotty is MIA, and with God having me pray for Brianna, I really need your help." Dustin was a rising pop star, and had been given an opportunity of a lifetime. All he'd had to do was take one eight year old girl, given to him by some very powerful people, and do some very bad things to her. His career would have taken off beyond his wildest dreams. However, Dustin had refused...and it almost cost him his life. That's when he'd met Brianna Bowers...and witnessed the power of God as a mighty billion-dollar empire had crumbled in a single moment. He gave his heart and life to Christ that very day and Brianna helped him to get in touch with the Dragon Slayers Ministry...who just so happened to be losing one of their main members, Matt Ramsey.

"I'll do anything you need, Gabi," Dustin replied.

"Perfect," she replied, handing him a hand-written list of things that needed to be checked on or taken care of. "Get with Yvette if you have any questions."

"Okay...no problem," he replied as he perused the list. "This seems simple enough." He stood to leave. "I'll be praying for Brianna as well...if that's okay."

Gabi smiled. "Of course it's okay...and thank you." Dustin Knight was going to be a perfect addition to the team. He just needed to get a bit closer to God, grow in his faith, and be more comfortable with his new lifestyle. Christianity was not for the faint of heart.

As Dustin closed the door, Gabi knelt back down on the floor. "Dear Heavenly Father, I lift up my friend, Brianna Bowers to you again. Father, I thank You for my friend...for her heart to serve You as a mighty warrior. Father, I pray that You would surround her with Your angels." Her mind went back to her days as a preteen, the first time she met an angel...Topher. He was a messenger angel, so excited to serve his King. Then later, she met, and fought alongside, the warrior angels: Daniel, Adam, Brandon...and so many more. They

62

✝

were so powerful. So intent on vanquishing the evil forces that hinder us...fueled on by our prayer life. Gabi smiled. "Yes, Father, surround her with Your mighty angels and guide her with Your Holy Spirit. Protect her from the flaming arrows the enemy is constantly firing at her, I pray. Cover her with Your peace, Your joy, Your love. Let her be a light in the darkness. I pray that You would be with the people she is working with as well...Pastor Jason Green...and the local police department...and" There was another knock at her door. "Yes?"

Mark McGee opened the door and stood there with a grim look on his face. He had taken his wife, Maria, to the airport earlier. She'd needed to get back to their sons, since the stop at Cairo had not been planned. She assumed Mark was just feeling sad over that. Then...he closed the door.

"Is everything okay..."

"Gabi, I just received a call from the Cairo Police...Scotty's been in an accident."

With one swift motion, she was on her feet. "And?" Tears were already forming in her eyes.

"Gabi, he's in surgery...they had to revive him at the scene. Scotty was dead for over five minutes."


*PENNINGTON SPRINGS, TENNESSEE*

"BRIANNA!!!" Jason called, running toward the direction she'd gone. "I'm coming back, so you'd better answer me if you're okay!" The others followed behind him.

"Brianna!" Chief Jerry called. "Brianna!? Can you hear us!?"

"JASON!!!" she screamed from some distance away. "Jason! Over here! HURRY!"



✝

They made their way through the thick brush about fifty feet beyond the rock. Brianna was sitting on the ground with her hair disheveled and her shirt torn.

"Brianna!" Jason called. "What happened!?"

"He was here!" she cried out. "Harley was here! He took my gun! He was so fast...I pulled it out and within a split second, he cleared five feet, and grabbed the gun...then he pulled me through the brush like a rag doll!"

"Which way did he go!?" Detective Horne asked. Brianna pointed up the mountain and he pulled out his radio. "Team 1 to Team 2, this is Detective Horne. The suspect made an appearance and is heading up the mountain near..." Chief Jerry was holding the map. "Section 11...maybe 12. Be aware...he now has a gun!"

"Copy that," came the reply from Agent Young. "We're heading that direction. Are you guys okay?"

"Yes, Ms. Bowers is a little shaken, but we're good."

Jason helped Brianna up and made sure she was alright. Her arms and face were cut up from being pulled through the thick brush, but she was fine.

"Jason...I think he really is possessed," she said. "He kept referring to himself as we...and he mentioned the name Micky...as the smart one who takes care of them."

"I tried to tell you he was," Jason replied. "Are you still convinced he's innocent?"

"He said I was going to be their favorite," she let out a slight sob at the thought of the others who hadn't managed to get away. "He was so fast."

Jason wrapped his arms around her. "Thank God you're okay. How did you manage to get free of him?"

64

✝

"I said the name of Jesus over and over and he kept telling me to stop. Then when you called my name the second time, he panicked. I think he might've thought you were Jesus coming to save me."

"Well, I would've sent him to see Jesus!"

"We should let them search for Harley," Chief Jerry said. "We'll head back to camp...I'm not putting Brianna through anything else."

"NO!" Brianna said. "This was my idea and I'm seeing it through! Harley needs to be stopped and the sooner we can do that the better!"

"Are you sure you're up to it?" Detective Horne asked. When Brianna nodded, he lifted his radio to his mouth. "Team 2, we're coming up from the area of Section 9...be aware and please don't shoot us."

"Roger that Team 1," Agent Young replied. "We should be at Section 11 in about ten minutes. All quiet at the moment."

"So, where was he at, Brianna?" Chief Jerry asked.

"Over by that rock where I'd gone to use the bathroom...he just appeared and started talking to me like he'd been expecting me."

"Well, he did request you," Detective Horne added.

"Okay," Chief Jerry said. "Let's spread out a bit, so we don't miss him. I'm going to go about twenty feet to the right, Pastor and Brianna can stay in the middle, and Detective Horne you go twenty feet in that direction. That way we can still see each other. Guns ready...and remember, I prefer him alive but do what you have to do." They all nodded and headed up the mountain.

It was dead quiet...no bug sounds, no rustling trees, no birds chirping, just the quiet calm before the proverbial storm. They were unaware that they were being watched as each of them climbed the



✝

mountain. Hundreds of demons were waiting patiently as these men delivered their prey to them. Brianna Bowers was the trophy they so desperately wanted. The thought of it made them salivate. Harley was hidden away in a cave where they would never find him. Micky would be so proud of the events that were playing out. Brianna Bowers' days were numbered and they would be spent in much, much suffering.

## *GATEWAY, FLORIDA*

Matt was almost ready to head home from his first day at work. All he'd really done was set up his office and send out emails to some of the band volunteers giving them a schedule of when they would be needed and letting them know when practice was. He couldn't lie though, his mind had wandered to Bethany McGee several times...and each time, the butterflies got more violent. Was she truly excited about him coming to work at the church? And to make things worse...or better...she worked in the church office too. Of course, he hadn't seen much of her today, but just knowing that...focus Matt...don't get distracted. "Eyes on the prize, Dude!" He often had to encourage himself out loud...especially when Eddie wasn't around...that was usually what he did.

Andy and Eddie...those guys were awesome. It had been so difficult leaving them behind...though he knew they'd be coming home soon enough for their break from the tour. He missed them already. They were like the three musketeers, well most of the time they were more like the three stooges. They had come so far since that horrible bus accident that had changed all their lives. So much had been lost during that time.

Matt lost his best friend, Billy Mumpower to what the doctors called a massive heart attack. Matt knew the truth though...the dragon...Rusty Staggerbush...Anansi...whatever you wanted to call the evil jerk. He was responsible for killing Billy. Matt witnessed the knife being plunged into his heart.

Matt gathered his things and left his office. He headed down the long hallway past several other offices and happened to look into one of them. He saw Bethany sitting behind a desk, on the phone, with a very serious look on her face. He waved at her and passed by, wondering if she was okay. Maybe he would text her later...he'd looked up her number in the church directory.

He headed out to the parking lot and got in his mother's car. Starting it up, he made sure his Bluetooth was on. Just as he was about to pull away, somebody slapped his passenger side window so hard it scared him. He jumped and looked over to see Bethany standing there with tears in her eyes. He quickly unlocked the door and she climbed in. "Bethany, are you alright?"

She shook her head as she wiped her eyes. "No...that was Mark on the phone, Matthew." She looked over at him as she sobbed. "Scotty was in a car accident."

"No!" Matt said. "Is he okay!?"

She shook her head and put it on his shoulder. "He's in surgery...Mark said the doctors aren't very optimistic."

Matt put his arm around her and began praying for Scotty. "Father, we lift Scotty Morgan to You right now! God, he has been Your faithful servant for years now and his life has been dedicated to spreading Your word and leading others to Christ! I come against this attack of the enemy, right NOW in the name of Your son, Jesus Christ! I pray that You would guide the surgeons' hands and completely heal Scotty's body! I also lift his wife, Gabi Morgan, before You now, Father! Give her a peace that passes all understanding. I pray all this in the name of Jesus! Thank You, God! Amen!" He was taking this one to the battlefield.

Bethany looked up at him and smiled. "Amen."



✝

# CHAPTER 8



*LITTLE ROCK, ARKANSAS*

*30 Years ago*

Micky was now 9 years old and the smartest kid in his class. In fact, it could be argued that he was the smartest kid in his school. And that was saying a lot, since he was presently attending the Catherine J. Wallace School for Gifted Children. He excelled at every subject he studied. Not only had it taken him less than a year to master the English language, but by the age of 8, he was speaking fluent Spanish and French. The strange thing was, he hadn't taken any classes in those languages.

Dr. Alisha Morrow still followed his case, doing a thorough study into his mind. She'd found Micky to be a scientific mystery, and had written several articles on his path to academic success. "You're a marvel, Micky Doe," she whispered to herself as she watched him, through a two-way mirror, answer question after question in his classroom.

"Quite the marvel, indeed," Professor Johansson replied from behind her.

She turned to smile at the professor who'd spent so much time working with Micky. Training his mind. Molding him. "I didn't hear you come in, Professor."

"You know, he really is the smartest child I've ever had the privilege of working with...perhaps even the smartest person."

"Even smarter than me!?" Dr. Morrow teased her old professor.

"Perhaps even smarter than the two of us combined," Professor Johansson replied, not taking his eyes off the boy in the adjoining room. "He is most likely the anomaly of our careers."



✝

"The cure for cancer could be in that brain," Dr. Morrow pondered.

"Perhaps," Professor Johansson said. "However, I feel as if this boy has the potential for even more than that…"

"Still," Dr, Morrow said. "What he needs is the love of a mother and father. For as smart as he is, he has frighteningly little social skills and seems to be skeptical of everyone he meets. His past is something out of a horror movie. It's a wonder he can even function."

"I agree he needs a family, Doctor," the professor replied. "But not only someone who can show him love and trust, but can also push his potential to its limits. I believe we may very well have found the perfect place for him…that's right, Micky has already been placed with a family…he leaves at the end of the month."

"Who?" Dr. Morrow asked. "Where will he be going?"

"Some very special people are taking him in. They actually live in a castle in a small town in Florida," Professor Johansson replied. "I believe they called it Gateway."


*CAIRO, EGYPT*

*Present Day*

Gabi stood in the waiting room of the large hospital in downtown Cairo. She'd never seen so many people waiting to be helped. If her husband wasn't in surgery fighting for his life, she would be walking around asking people what she could pray for them about. As it was, she was terrified and anxious. Mark had made his way to the front of the line after telling her to hang back and pray. Try as she might though, she just couldn't find the words to take to God.



✝

Before they'd left the arena, Yvette had taken to the stage as people were coming in and explained what was going on. She was leading them in prayer as Mark and Gabi had left for the hospital. Hopefully their prayers were enough to get heaven's attention. Andy was left with instructions to lead the worship team. He'd never done it before but Gabi had no doubt that he was capable. Dustin had said he would help in any way he could, though he didn't know any of their songs.

"GABI!!" Mark called from the reception desk.

She looked up to see him waving her up. She had to make her way through a literal sea of people...all of whom did not want anyone cutting in front of them.

"Gabi! This way!" Mark said as she drew closer. "They're taking us back to where he is!"

She numbly followed Mark as they were led down a long, narrow hall. Her mind was racing at a million miles an hour. How had she not seen this coming? Why did God have her praying for Brianna while her husband was fighting for his life? Why was God allowing this to happen? Had they canceled their plans to come here just so this could happen? Were they out of God's will for coming here?

"You okay?" Mark asked, bringing her out of her fog.

She nodded. "Have they told you anything?"

"Just that he's still in surgery," Mark replied, putting his arm around her and allowing her to lean on him. "Are you sure you're okay? You know God's got this, right?"

"Do I?" she asked before she could stop herself. Gabi had never questioned God in her life. She'd given her life to Jesus at a young age and had never regretted it...she'd been as faithful a follower as she could be...why was He doing this to her? "Sorry, I just don't know WHAT I know."



✝

Mark squeezed her shoulder. "It's okay, I know He does. You just breathe."

The orderly led them into a small waiting room and told them that a nurse would let them know as soon as Mr. Morgan was out of surgery.

"Thank you," she heard Mark reply as the room began to spin. Mark helped her to a seat, and she could hear him whispering a prayer over her. She lowered her head and closed her eyes...not wanting to talk to God right now. She just wanted her husband to be okay and to find out why God was punishing her. She felt a tear hit her arm. Gabi was not a crier...why was God breaking her heart?

## *VALLEY OF THE SHADOW OF DEATH*

Scotty began coughing as he awoke. His throat was so dry, he could hardly breathe. He slowly opened his eyes, blinking in the scene around him. He was lying in the dirt...or was this clay? He slid his fingers through it to make sure it was real. The sky was...orange...with black smoke moving slowly by like clouds on a windless day. He felt as though he'd been here before, as he eased himself up from the ground. There was something familiar about this place. He had to remember...he'd gone into town...Cairo...yeah, that was it. He had to sign some permits and...he'd been on his way back to the venue...he couldn't remember anything else. He stood up and brushed himself off, turning in place to take in his surroundings. A distant thunderous sound caused him to notice the mountains that surrounded him on every side. "You have got to be kidding me..."

"That's right, Scotty Morgan!" A familiar voice said from behind him.

Scotty spun around and faced off with someone he never thought he'd see again. The red headed teenage boy smiled as he watched Scotty's brain compute what was going on. "Rusty!? Rusty

Staggerbush!? I watched you die!" It was Rusty, the demonic dragon that Mark and Jake had defeated.

"You're the one that's dead!" Rusty said with a laugh. "You're dead and everything you ever knew was a lie!" He snapped his finger and instantly they were surrounded by what appeared to be millions of demons and foul creatures. "Imagine that, Scotty Morgan!" Rusty said as he watched Scotty begin to panic at his predicament. "Everything you've done...a waste of time! Your faith in a God that doesn't even exist! That entire DRAGON INCIDENT that you losers have continued to hold to...was just a ruse to lead you down a path of lies!" Rusty's laughter became the very thunder that boomed around them. "Now!" Rusty took a step toward Scotty and instantly became the dragon. "Now, you will have a front row seat as I personally peel the skin from each of your friend's bones!"

"You're a liar!" Scotty replied. "Your boss is the Father of Lies!!!"

Lightning flashed and thunder roared around them. The black smoke began to form into a cyclone that was heading straight for them.

"You shall see, Scotty Morgan!" The Dragon called. "One by one your friends are about to join you!" He laughed again. "And then I will personally escort each one of you through the gates of hell!" At that, Scotty fell to the ground...covering his eyes and hoping this was just a dream. "Judgment is upon you, Scotty Morgan!"

Scotty looked up at the fierce dragon and began to panic. This was real! This was the Valley of the Shadow of Death that they'd come to after the bus accident when they were teens! This was where the dragon had killed Billy Mumpower!



✝

The search for Harley had come up empty. They'd found several caves, but none appeared to be housing a psychopath murderer, or any sign that one had ever been there. After several hours of looking, Chief Jerry had called off the hunt. They'd made their way back to camp in the dark.

Presently, Brianna was sitting at the entrance of her tent, reading her Bible, and praying silently. She thanked God for keeping them safe today; for protecting her from harm at the hands of Harley. She prayed for each of the men that were with her...especially Officer Clark, whom she'd caught staring at her several times and totally giving her the creeps. She asked God to help her to be a witness to him.

The others were sitting around the fire and discussing how they would do the night watch. Two hours per man starting with Chief Jerry, then Officer Stevenson, Officer Clark, and Detective Horne. Pastor Jason insisted on putting his sleeping bag just outside Brianna's tent door so nothing would happen to her. She interjected that she would probably step on him if she got up to pee and that it would not be necessary for him to do that. He laughed and replied that she wasn't allowed to go to the bathroom anymore until she got back to her room at the inn.

About a half hour later, Chief Jerry told them all to get some sleep. They had a long day planned tomorrow and needed their beauty sleep. Everyone except him, turned in, after saying their good nights. Brianna zipped up her tent, tucked herself into her sleeping bag and fell fast asleep.

She was in her family's living room...from her childhood. She walked slowly into the kitchen and caught a glimpse of herself in the mirror. She appeared to be about one year old...which explained why she was moving so slow. Looking around, she saw a young boy sitting at the dining room table working on something. He glanced at her as she rounded the corner and his face seemed to show irritation. She said something unintelligible to him and he rolled his eyes.

Then, he slid his chair back quickly and walked over to one of the drawers. He opened it and pulled out a long knife. Running his finger along the sharp blade, he smiled when he saw that it had drawn blood. He turned and faced Brianna… "I really do hate you…" He lifted the knife above his head and smiled down at her. Just then, Brianna's mother appeared behind him and screamed. "WHAT IS GOING ON IN HERE!!!???" She grabbed the knife from his hand and snatched him away from Brianna. "No!" He cried out. "She had the knife and I took it from her!" He showed her his bleeding finger. Brianna couldn't believe her ears. "BRIANNA!!! NO MA'AM!!!" Her mother screamed and whisked him away to put a band-aid on his finger, tossing the knife into the sink. "We can't leave the camp in the dark!!!" she heard a man yell.

Brianna jumped awake because of a heated argument between what sounded like Officer Clark and Agent Young. Brianna checked her cell phone to see that it was 4:35 in the morning. She heard Chief Jerry shush them and say something about not waking Brianna up.

"We need to start a search right now!" Officer Clark said through what Brianna imagined was gritted teeth.

"I've contacted a search and rescue team that will be here by sun up!" Agent Young replied. "Nobody is leaving this camp until then!" He didn't even pretend to be quiet.

"What's going on out there!?" Brianna asked into the darkness.

"Everything is okay, Brianna…you just go back to sleep," Chief Jerry replied. "Sorry we woke you!"

"Why don't I believe you, Chief?" Brianna asked, as she unzipped her tent. Pastor Jason was sitting in front of it like a posted



✝

guard. Brianna could hear him praying quietly. She placed a hand on his shoulder as she stood up and around him. "Why is everybody up?" She asked, scanning the group to see everyone except..."And where is Officer Stevenson?"

She looked directly at Chief Jerry and he nodded to a nearby log where there seemed to have been a scuffle. The leaves were bunched up and there were boot marks in the dirt as if someone had kicked out...and then Brianna saw a handgun lying amid the leaves. "He appears to have been taken," the chief said.

Brianna stood frozen in place as she realized the severity of the situation. Officer Stevenson, a full grown, armed man, had been taken right out from under their noses in the middle of the night...and nobody had heard a sound.

"The rest of you can stand around with your hands in your pockets if you want to!" Officer Clark said, appearing from the tent with a shotgun in hand. "I'm going to find my friend!"

"Officer Clark!" Agent Young yelled. "I'm ordering you to stand down! Chief, you need to control your officer!"

"Toss me my shotgun as well, Clark!" Chief Jerry said, giving the federal agent a glance. "My officer is missing, and his family isn't going to accuse me of sitting idly by waiting for the sun to come up just because you're afraid of the dark, Agent Young!" He took the weapon from Officer Clark and checked it over. "The rest of you, stay here! And for the good Lord's sake, keep Brianna safe!"

Just then, a man's scream in the distance caused them all to jump. It sounded as if it were far up the mountain. Officer Clark grabbed his flashlight from near the tent and sprinted in the direction of the scream.

"Stay here!" Jerry said to Agent Young, as he began running after Clark.



✝

"CHIEF!" Jason called after him. The chief glanced back and Jason tossed him a radio. "Keep us posted...and shoot to kill!" No sooner had the chief turned back around, than there was an even louder scream.

Brianna dropped to the ground in prayer. "Father, I pray that you would protect Officer Stevenson, right now. Keep him and Officer Clark and Chief Jerry in your hands. I come against this evil in the name of your Son, Jesus Christ!"

"This is Agent Young; I need an ASAP on that search and rescue!" He was speaking into a satellite phone. "We have an officer down and I'm calling a 911 on the situation. Get a team to my location as soon as possible! Armed and dangerous suspect on the scene!"

There was another scream in the distance, but it didn't sound like the same person.

"Talk to me, Chief..." Jason said softly into the radio, just in case the chief needed silence. There was a long pause where it seemed like none of them were even breathing.

The radio crackled and they could hear a man weeping. "It's not good," Chief Jerry said quietly. It was apparently someone else weeping.

"Did you find Officer Stevenson?" Jason asked.

"Affirmative," the chief responded. "But it's not good." They could hear someone retching in the background.

Brianna closed her eyes and began to cry. She could only imagine what they had found.

"So…" Pastor Jason began.

"He's dead...Officer Stevenson is dead…" Chief Jerry began to weep just before he went to radio silence.



✝

# CHAPTER 9



*GATEWAY, FLORIDA*

Daniel woke up a little earlier than he usually did on a school morning. After yesterday's confrontation with Chris and his gang of misfit ruffians, he was a little worried about what might go down today. He was so sick of those guys...they'd been messing with him for years and he was ready to put an end to it.

A friend of Daniel's, that had also been hassled by Chris and his boys, had told him how to access a site on the dark web. At first, he'd thought, no way, but after not being able to sleep for most of the night, he was quite ready to entertain the idea of being able to defend himself. He quietly got onto his computer and quickly accessed the site. It was a prepper's dream website. They offered everything from two-way radios to hand grenades...and pretty much everything in between. He paused when he got to the handguns...scrolling through them slowly.

They were a bit pricey, but everything was under the table...which allowed a teenage boy to purchase things he would normally not be allowed to. He had a little money stored away for a car, but right now he had priorities. After looking for several minutes, he saw a 9mm that was not only affordable, but exactly what he was looking for. He punched in his friend Jeremy's code and made the transaction, adding in a box of ammo, of course. He would have to pay Jeremy as soon as he saw him today.

Daniel shut down his computer and climbed back into bed with a smile on his face. "Chris Norton...you've tormented me for the last time," he thought to himself. He grabbed his cell phone to text Jeremy and saw where he had a message from his brother, Andy.

"Hey little Bro, I know you don't pray much but send one up for my boy Scotty if you will. He's been in a bad accident and is in a coma. Love you, Daniel."



✝

Daniel hated that Scotty was in an accident, he was a good guy. But pray? God would never listen to a guy like him...not with what he had planned. No, he'd leave the praying to his mom and brother. He typed back, "You got it Bro! Keep me posted."

†

Maria McGee had been up most of the night praying for Scotty and conversing with Mark, who was keeping watch over Gabi in a Cairo hospital. Mark had told her that Gabi was losing it. She was so distraught that she'd refused to even pray. "She's just sitting in the waiting room rocking back and forth and staring at her shoes," Mark said. Maria desperately wished that she could be there for her friend.

As it was, she needed to be here in Gateway for her kids. Marcus had school this morning, and she was presently attempting to get him out the door, as her youngest, William, was clinging to her and whining about not getting to go to school with Marcus.

What she didn't realize was, that just outside the door there were several demonic forces waiting for young Marcus McGee to step outside, so they could send him to the Valley of the Shadow of Death, and hopefully into eternity.

"He's coming!" One of the demons shouted from behind the bushes. "Prepare the attack!"

"I'll shove him into the path of a passing car!" another demon said, licking his vile lips.

The front door opened, and his mother led him out toward the street to wait for the school bus. She was holding Marcus' little brother in her arms and not really paying attention to Marcus running ahead.

"Get ready!" one of the demons said, flying overhead and preparing to attack.

78

†

A minivan turned onto their street and the woman driving was changing the playlist on her phone and not paying attention to where she was going. Marcus saw something shiny in the middle of the road and darted ahead to investigate. Just as he reached the curb, the demon flew toward him to give him the shove. Just as the demon's hand reached out, suddenly, a bright flash of light swept across the sky and the demon disintegrated into thin air. The mighty hand of the warrior angel, Adam, reached down and knocked Marcus backwards and onto the grass, just as the minivan whizzed past.

"Marcus!" his mother yelled. "You need to watch what you're doing, son!" She helped him up and wiped off his pants. "And how in the world did you manage to fall backwards?"

Adam stood next to the child, watching his surroundings. He saw several demons gathering around him, though none dared to come any closer. "You're wasting your time with this one!" Adam said, his flaming sword drawn and ready for battle. "You won't touch him on my watch!"

"Soon enough, Adam!" a demon perched on the roof of the house called out. "Soon enough!"


*SAN DIEGO, CALIFORNIA*

Jonah Westbrook sat at his parent's dining room table desperately studying his Bible. It was still early, and his parents had not gotten up yet. His notes were laid out around the table as he poured over God's word. He couldn't believe how hungry he was for it...more so than for food. Ever since his vision and encounter with God just a few short days ago, he had been consumed with learning as much as he could. Brianna had given him several tips in studying the Bible and had even put him in contact with a pastor back in Gateway… A Pastor Brian Jones. Pastor Brian had been extremely helpful with study tips and devotions that helped him to see God from a new perspective.



✝

His sister, Jaclyn, had taken things quite differently. She'd withdrawn. Afraid to leave her house for any reason, she just sat there on her sofa in a daze. Her husband was at his wit's end with what to do. Jonah understood her response. She had gone through an extremely traumatic situation and almost lost her life. She'd witnessed a horrific murder...of a child no less. Jonah had prayed with her and was constantly in contact, but she seemed to have slipped into a bad place.

Lacey, his ex-girlfriend, had been there as well. Both women had been kidnapped in an attempt to get to Jonah. It had worked, but in the end, God had miraculously intervened and rescued them all...except for poor little Maria Sanchez. At first, Lacey had blamed Jonah. She'd released a fury on him like he'd never heard, saying that the whole thing had been his fault and he should've died.

Later, however, she'd called him to apologize, telling him she'd just needed to vent. He'd understood and easily forgiven her. And just like that...she wanted to rekindle the old flame. He'd had to explain to her that he was interested in someone else and that he felt that their time together, though wonderful, was over...for good. They could either be friends or…she'd hung up on him at that point and he'd not heard anything else from her.

Jonah wasn't sure where his life was heading right now, what with being unemployed and all. His entire work crew had recently been killed by an organization of child traffickers, which now left him jobless. He lived in Colorado, and the area he was in was not going to offer him a lot of options in his area of construction. He seriously needed some guidance, which was why Brianna had told him to seek out the help of the Holy Spirit.

Now, as he read through his John Bevere book, The Holy Spirit, on Kindle, a quote caught his attention. "So if you really want to know more about Jesus, you must spend time with the Holy Spirit. The Spirit will clearly reveal Jesus to you. But the Holy Spirit will



✝

only manifest where He is honored. As we honor the Spirit, He will reveal himself to us, and we will enjoy both His amazing presence and a greater awareness of the One He reveals."

"Holy Spirit...I know it was you who gave me those visions...thank you for that. Thank you for revealing Jesus to me. I want to spend time with You...I just don't know how."

"Well, this is a great start," someone said from behind Jonah, startling him. He quickly turned to look as an older gentleman wearing a gray suit and a fedora, walked up and stood beside him. "Hello, Jonah," The Holy Spirit said, smiling down at him.

Jonah's chair involuntarily slid back and Jonah dropped to his knees. "My God..." He covered his face and began weeping.

The old man knelt next to him and placed his hand on Jonah's shoulder. "You truly are off to a good start, Jonah." He gave Jonah a moment to compose himself and then helped him back up into his chair. "Just continue to seek Me and obey My words and you'll do just fine." He squeezed Jonah's shoulder. "As for your employment...I have something else for you to do right now...so pay close attention..."


*GATEWAY, FLORIDA*

Matt had been awake for at least two hours and was still lying in bed...not that he'd gotten much sleep at all last night. Between praying for Scotty and freaking out about Bethany, his brain had been in overdrive.

So far there'd been no update on Scotty. As of twenty minutes ago, according to Andy, he was still in a coma. Matt couldn't help but wonder if Scotty was in the Valley of the Shadow of Death or if that was just a one-time thing. Andy also said that Gabi was in a bad place. She wasn't speaking to anyone...even God. That was just



✝

weird...she'd been the one to keep the entire gang in line all these years. Matt made sure to say a special prayer for her.

Then there was Bethany...Bethany McGee...all grown up. She was so beautiful now...easy Matthew. It was, after all, Mark's little sister. What was it Mrs. Gilmore, her mom, had said? "She's been quite excited that you were returning…" The way she curled into his side and let him comfort her...well, he needed to pray again.

"Text Daniel," a familiar voice whispered in his ear.

"Oh, that's right!" Matt said out loud and sat up in bed. He found Daniel's number and punched it in. "Hey Danny Boy! It's Matt! Not sure if you heard or not but I'm back in town...for good. We should get together one evening. Let me know when is good for you!" He hit send and sent up a prayer for Andy's little brother. Just as he was swinging his legs out of bed, his phone chimed that he'd just received a text. "Well, that was a quick response, Daniel," he said, lifting his phone up.

"Hey there, it's Bethany! Just wanted to thank you for being there yesterday. You have great shoulders to cry on." Matt's heart literally skipped a beat.

"Hey Bethany! I was glad that we had each other! I've been praying for you this morning."

"Thanks, I need it. Haven't gotten an update on Scotty yet, but they're saying that Gabi isn't doing well."

"Yeah...but she's Gabi! She'll come around."

"By the way...I wanted to thank you properly. Care to join me for lunch today? I remember that you loved Gateway Barbecue!"

"Sounds awesome!" He replied and jumped out of bed with a little pep in his step.



✝

"What's gotten into you?" Matt's mother asked as he stepped out of his room with a huge grin on his face. "You look like you just got your first kiss."

"Mom!" He kissed her on the cheek. "I don't want to jinx it, but I think I'm in love."

"Well, Matthew Ramsey, if it's God's will, you can't jinx it...and if it's not...then it needs to be jinxed." She grabbed his arm. "Banana pancakes if you tell me who!"

He just couldn't stop himself. "Bethany McGee!"

"Oh, Matthew! She's stunning!" She gave him a light shove. "And way out of your league!"

He gave her a shocked look as she headed for the kitchen. "What did you say!?"

"Would you like bacon with those pancakes, sweetheart!?"

Bethany had been awake for several hours, praying for the gang in Cairo...especially Scotty...and texting back and forth with her brother, Mark. They were six hours ahead, so it was quite weird to think they were already past lunch. Mark had sounded more concerned about Gabi than he did Scotty. He said he's never seen Gabi just shut down...she'd even refused to pray.

Then, of course, there was the whole Matt Ramsey being in Gateway thing. She'd been so excited about it when she'd heard that he was going to be the new worship leader. Bethany had been crushing on Matt Ramsey since she was eleven...of course he was about eighteen or so back then, so she'd had to keep it to herself. Now, here he was, back in Gateway, and still single. She fanned herself and poured another glass of orange juice. "You have to pace yourself, girl!" she said aloud. "Don't scare him off."

"Bethany?" her mother said, walking up behind her in the kitchen. "Are you talking to yourself?"



✝

Bethany jumped and spun around, almost spilling her juice. "Oh, hey Mom! You caught me!" She smiled a big cheesy smile and headed for her room. "Sorry, I have to get ready for work!" Just then her cell phone rang, and she thanked Jesus and answered it. "Hello?"

"Bethany!?" a familiar, extremely chipper voice said into the phone. "It's your very favorite cousin!"

"Good morning, Jake!" she smiled, picturing her handicapped cousin sitting in his electric chair with a big smile on his face...you rarely saw Jake without a smile. The happiest person she'd ever known. "What can I do for you?"

"Funny you should ask," Jake replied. "My van won't start and I hate to bother JoAnn, with the kid and all."

"So, you need a ride?" Bethany asked, knowing she couldn't get his chair into her car.

"Actually, I think it just needs a jump...can you swing by?"

"Absolutely, I'll leave here in about ten minutes."

"Thanks, Bethany!"

*PENNINGTON SPRINGS, TENNESSEE*

It had seemed like an eternity before the search and rescue team of federal agents had arrived, but in truth, it had probably only taken them about an hour. Agent Young had already informed them that they'd found the missing officer deceased. There would be no keeping this whole thing quiet now...the feds were clearly taking over the search for Harley. There were presently a team of at least fifty men and women standing under a makeshift canopy, receiving instructions on the search that lied ahead. Chief Jerry had been informed to go with Agent Young back into town and prepare for the news briefing that was sure to hit like a storm. They had already loaded Officer Stevenson's remains into one of the vehicles as Jason



✝

led Brianna back to the car. They all seemed to be moving like zombies...not sure what to do or if any of this was real.

"What are we supposed to do now, Jason?" Brianna whispered to him as he opened her car door.

He shook his head. "With the Feds completely taking this thing over...probably nothing. We shouldn't have come up here in the first place." He closed her door and walked around the car. "You okay?" Jason asked the chief, who had a deer in the headlights look on his face.

"He was a good man, Pastor..." he choked out, covering his face. "Now, I have to go tell his wife."

Pastor Jason put his hand on the chief's shoulder. "I'll go with you." They both got in the car and just sat there while Chief Jerry composed himself.

"This is all my fault," Brianna said. "I was so gung-ho about coming up here and ending this thing. I didn't spend enough time in prayer...I should've let the Holy Spirit guide me and kept my big mouth shut." She began crying. "I'm sooo sorry."

"Brianna!" Jason said, turning around in his seat. "I was stupid to even call you in the first place! This was a police matter and Detective Horne insisted on getting you involved and I knew better! If this is anybody's fault..."

"Pastor," Chief Jerry said, placing his hand on Jason's arm. "Brianna...I don't think any of us has put the amount of prayer into this situation that we need to. We can't change what's happened...but we can still put God in the center of what's going to happen. Let's pray now." He took Jason's hand and Brianna put a hand on each man's shoulder and pray they did. For thirty-five minutes, in that squad car, on that mountain, they called on the God of heaven to comfort the families of the victims, to bless the search efforts, and to give them wisdom for the coming storm.



✝

# CHAPTER 10



*GATEWAY, FLORIDA*

Matt had eaten breakfast and showered. Presently, he was standing in his room, trying to decide what to wear today. Having a girl to impress changed how he felt and thought, so he assumed it should change how he appeared. "Might want to up your game today, Dude," he said to his reflection in the mirror on the back of his door. Of course, his own mother telling him that Bethany was out of his league had not helped either. "Should I wear a tie?" He opened his closet and immediately a thought hit him right in the chest.

"I didn't call you to be a worship leader so that you could impress Bethany...keep your focus, Matthew." Sometimes the Holy Spirit didn't pull any punches.

"I'm sorry, God," Matt said aloud. "Let my life be about you and nobody else. YOU are my Lord, and my life is yours."

"Besides, she's already impressed with you," the Holy Spirit whispered in his ear. "Regardless of the way you dress."

Matt grabbed a pair of jeans, a shirt, sprayed on a hint of cologne, checked his hair, and headed for the door. "Bye, Mom!"

"Matthew!" she yelled to him from the kitchen, stopping him in his tracks. "I would have thought you'd dress to impress today...what with having a beautiful young lady on your mind and all." She straightened his collar and ran her fingers through his hair.

"Yeah, I thought about it, but I need to keep my main focus on God," Matt replied. "That IS kind of the reason I came back to Gateway, you know."

His mother nodded as if in deep thought. "That's very mature of you, Matthew." She rose up and planted a kiss on his cheek. "But I want grandchildren...have a nice day, sweetie." She turned and walked back into the kitchen.



✝

Matt just stood there, dumbfounded. Grandchildren? "We haven't even been on a date, Mom! You're going to need to pace yourself!" With that, he headed to the car.

As he drove down the road on his way to the church he realized he needed to stop for gas. He pulled out onto the main road and noticed that the traffic was backed up and he could see there was an accident up ahead. There were police and rescue vehicles with lights flashing. "Father, bless whoever has been in an accident." Just then, his phone began to chime with a call. He saw Pastor Brian's name on the screen of the car display. He pressed the button to answer. "Good morning, Pastor…"

"Matt!" Pastor Brian interrupted him, sounding quite upset. "Bethany McGee has been in an accident!"

Matt's heart seemed to stop beating for a moment. "Is…is she…"

"It's not good…they've revived her…but it's bad. Meet me at the hospital chapel, we're all gathering to pray!"

"Y…yeah…okay…okay," Matt clicked off the call and stared straight ahead. He could see Bethany's small car upside down in the ditch. The entire driver's side was crushed. "No, God!" First Scotty…now Bethany… "Not again!"


## *VALLEY OF THE SHADOW OF DEATH*

Rusty had vanished in a mixture of laughter, dust, and black smoke...leaving Scotty standing there in the dark, dry valley feeling angry and confused. Why was this happening again? They had vanquished Rusty! Jake had severed his head. Of course, none of them had been exactly sure how that worked in the spirit realm...and apparently it meant nothing. Perhaps until Jesus cast them all into hell, they were "unkillable".



✝

He looked around at the familiar scene of dry, orange sand that went on for miles with an occasional boulder. There were mountains in the distance in every direction. The sky was a dark orange with pitch black clouds. Such a depressing place to be. He heard a loud roar in the distance and turned to look in that direction. That's when he noticed that the sky was beginning to come to life. The clouds were swirling and moving faster toward a central location in the valley. Scotty heard a scream coming from that direction and saw dust clouds forming around what appeared to be a large gathering of...something...alive.

"Father, I pray for your protection in this horrible place," he said and began to head in that direction. "Even though I walk through the darkest valley, I will fear no evil, for you are with me; your rod and your staff, they comfort me." Scotty paused as he attempted to remember the rest of Psalm 23.

"Something, something…Surely your goodness and love will follow me all the days of my life, and I will dwell in the house of the LORD forever." Gabi would give him a disappointed look...Another scream caused him to break into a run. It was a female scream and it seemed that the cloud of dust in that direction had settled. That's when he saw all the foul creatures he remembered from the last time he was here. Disgusting cross breeds of various animals and insects, larger than life. Some as small as a house cat and others as large as a whale. Then there were the black, leathery demons...who seemed to be quite aware of Scotty's approach. They drew their swords and took their battle positions.

The clouds began to swirl faster and faster, forming a slight funnel in the midst of these creatures...who seemed to be taunting someone.

As Scotty drew closer, he slowed and screamed out, "I come against you in the name of JESUS CHRIST!!!" The swirling stopped and the valley grew silent. Each of the creatures turned their attention



✝

to Scotty as the demons took a step backwards at the mention of that name. "That's right!" Scotty yelled, making a path through the center of the hordes of hell. They moved out of his way and formed an opening that led directly to the center...where a young woman stood looking up at the sky with sheer terror in her eyes.

"WHERE AM I!? WHAT IS THIS PLACE!!!???" She spun and looked around until her eyes met a very surprised Scotty Morgan…

"Bethany!!!???"

A bolt of lightning struck Bethany right in the chest, and she dropped back to the ground like a rag doll.

"NOOOO!!!!" Scotty screamed as the demons began to move toward her.


## PENNINGTON SPRINGS, TENNESSEE

After filing a report at the police station and dealing with several reporters that she was informed to "say nothing to," Brianna headed back to her room at the Inn. As she walked into the lobby, Carolyn greeted her with a big smile, and nodded toward the dining area. Brianna turned and looked that way and gasped as her friend stood to hug her. "CHRISTINA!!!" She wrapped her arms around the woman and squeezed her tight. "You have no idea how good it is to see you."

"I heard that something bad happened while you were on the mountain," Christina whispered. "I've been praying you were okay."

Brianna nodded. "I'm fine," she pulled away from her old friend and smiled a grim smile. "Extremely shaken up, but fine."

"Good!" Christina pulled her into another hug.



✝

"So, what are you doing here!?" Brianna asked. "Not that I'm complaining…"

"Business AND pleasure," Christina replied. "Come on, let's go up. The lovely Mrs. Carolyn, here, put me up in the room next to you."

"Are you doing okay, Brianna?" Mrs. Carolyn asked. "Jerry told me what happened."

"Chief Jerry is the one we should be praying for," Brianna replied. "All this mess in his sweet little town." She didn't want to be too specific with her reporter friend right there. She was under strict orders to be silent...although she knew this story wouldn't take long to leak...especially with a local officer dead.

They went upstairs to Christina's room where they decided to step out on the balcony with a glass of Mrs. Carolyn's sweet tea.

Taking a seat on a patio chair, Christina looked out over the beautiful town with the mountains in the distance. "This is picture perfect, Brianna."

"Yes, it is," Brianna eyed her friend. "Just so you know, I'm under strict instructions to NOT speak to the press."

Christina smiled from behind her glass. "I'm sure you are...but what CAN you tell me? And I promise that any information you divulge will not be printed or repeated without your express approval. You have MY word."

Brianna took a drink of her tea and set her glass down. "I received a call from Jason...Green?"

"I remember Jason...crazy kid from Pittsburgh…"

"Well, he's the pastor of a small church here in Pennington Springs now."



✝

"Okay, that's cool," Christina replied. "Not what I would've pegged him to be doing, but cool."

"Jason is an awesome man of God who hasn't even begun to hone in on the amazing things God has for him," Brianna said, smiling at the thought of how protective he'd been of her. "Anyway, he called me the other night right after I'd gotten back from that whole child trafficking thing. The Holy Spirit had already revealed to me that He had something else for me...so I was ready when the call came. Jason said he needed my help with something here in Pennington Springs..." Brianna proceeded to tell Christina everything that had happened up to the point of them going up into the mountains. That was the thing she couldn't talk about.

"Wow, Girl!!!" Christina exclaimed. "Your name was on the wall!? That would've freaked any normal person out! Not Brianna Bowers! No sir! She wants to go up and have a look!" Christina stood up. "Are you crazy or what!?"

"That about sums it up, I guess," Brianna said with another grim smile.

"I'll get us some more of this amazing sweet tea," Christina said, taking their glasses inside.

Brianna stood up and leaned against the balcony. She watched all the activities going on in town as she thought about everything that had led to this moment. A young family was walking along the sidewalk, browsing the shop fronts. A group of teenagers were hanging out near the fountain over at the park, laughing and carrying on without a care in the world. A businessman was walking by just below her, wearing a suit and looking all serious... "Mr. Nesmith!?" Brianna called down from the second floor balcony.

Mr. Nesmith stopped and looked up at her. "Brianna? Hello..." He looked around as if he'd been caught doing something he shouldn't. "I trust you're alright."



✝

"Yes, thank you. I'm fine."

"Well, I'm off...Officer Stevenson has been delivered to my...well, you know." He seemed extremely distraught...what with being the town's medical examiner and having to deal with all this death.

"I'll be praying for you, Mr. Nesmith," Brianna said with a slight smile. He shuffled away after a quick glance back.


## CAIRO, EGYPT

Gabi sat there in the waiting room with nothing in her heart but anger towards God. She couldn't feel anything else...nor did she want to. She had literally given her entire life to serving Him...practically every second of every day since she was a small girl. She couldn't remember a time when He wasn't her all. She had personally led countless people to Christ...not to mention the tens of thousands they'd reached through the Dragon Slayers Ministry.

She had even been a big part of the reason that Mark McGee and most of their staff were Christians. After all they'd been through as kids with the castle, the Valley, the dragon...did she complain? No...she only asked God for one thing. Protection over her husband. Something happening to Scotty was her greatest fear...especially now...with the…

"Can I get you anything, Gabi?" Mark asked.

"No…" she replied. "Thanks." To be honest, Mark was getting on her nerves. He'd stayed by her side every second of every minute, regardless of how rude she'd been to him. He'd read her scriptures, prayed over her and Scotty, said encouraging things, heck, he'd even had the nursing staff set up a room for her so she could sleep right there in the hospital...while he sat outside the room. He'd practically become her shadow and she was honestly about to scream



✝

with an overwhelming feeling of suffocation. "Actually...yes," she added. "A coffee sounds good."

"Absolutely!" Mark said, standing up and setting his Bible in the chair. "I'll be right back." He left the room.

As soon as he was gone, she stood up and walked over to the door. She watched him round the corner to the left and she went right, where she headed to the staircase and walked down them quickly. Luckily Mark had sent the others back to the hotel so they could rest...otherwise she'd never have been able to escape all the 'support'. She made her way through the main lobby and out the front door of the hospital. She spotted a park across the street and made her way over. There were enough people there to be able to blend in, in case Mark went searching for her. She wouldn't be long, just enough time to breathe and let out her frustration with God. How was He allowing her to go through another major trauma? She shook her head. "If anything happens to him…" she sucked in a sob and made her way over to a nearby bridge that crossed over a small pond.

It was a beautiful day. The sun was shining, the birds were chirping, and Gabi couldn't have cared less. She reached the center of the bridge where only a few people were walking across and draped her arms over the rail. "Okay, God, I'm barely hanging on, here…" Tears were flowing down her face...and Gabi had never been a crier. "Please don't do this to me right now...I can't…"

Her cell phone buzzed in her pocket and she pulled it out. It was a text from Mark..." where did you run off to???" She slid it back into her pocket and walked across the bridge.

She watched as a couple of families were sitting together enjoying lunch at the various picnic tables. Laughing and carrying on as if her husband wasn't presently fighting for his life...apparently being punished for doing God's work. She made her way past them and followed a small trail into a forest...completely unaware of the



✝

large, black, scaly demon walking beside her...his hand pressed to the back of her head.

"That's right, Gabriella...no good deed goes unpunished...why do you even bother with God...you could be leading a happy, healthy life like everyone else. Don't you have enough to worry about without God allowing so many bad things to happen in your life?"

The sun went behind a cloud and it seemed to get much darker in the midst of all the trees. Her phone buzzed again and she just ignored it. Couldn't Mark see that she wanted to be alone?

"If Scotty survives this, you should resign from the ministry and buy a house back home and live a comfortable life...like you deserve. You have sooo many things to worry about...and your future shouldn't be one of them." The demon smiled as she allowed him to keep speaking into her life.

"Scotty would never want to leave Mark to do this on his own," Gabi said out loud. "Maybe I could stay home like Maria..." Someone rounded the corner ahead of her and she hoped he hadn't heard her blabbering to herself. She reached into her pocket to check the last text. Mark again… "No change with Scotty...you deal with this however you need. I love you, Gabi. I'm praying for you and I hope you're praying now. Scotty needs that."

"Excuse me!" the boy walking toward her said, a little too loud. Gabi looked up and gasped at the red headed boy standing before her.

"If you think what I've done to Scotty is bad!" he said with a big smile. "Just wait until you see what I have in store for your unborn baby!!!" He touched her stomach, laughing hysterically as he vanished into thin air.

Gabi cried out and fell to the ground screaming in fear. "NOOOO!!!! GOD!!!! NOOOOO!!!!"



✝

# CHAPTER 11



*ST. AUGUSTINE, FLORIDA*

The Uber driver pulled into the parking lot of Flagler Hospital. "Where would you like for me to let you out, sir?"

"The front entrance is fine," Jonah replied. He truly had no idea why he was here...just that he was supposed to be. The Holy Spirit had told him to catch the first plane from San Diego to Jacksonville, then to go straight to Flagler Hospital in St. Augustine. Other than that, his faith would guide him. Jonah thanked the man and exited the vehicle with his bag. He'd only brought a couple of changes of clothes and his necessities.

He stared up at the large building and took a deep breath. "Okay, Holy Spirit...what now?" He stood there for a few seconds, not sure exactly how this whole praying thing worked. He then glanced around, and half expected to see the old gentleman sitting near the fountain, smiling at him. But...nothing. "Alright, I'm going in."

Stepping into the front lobby, Jonah looked around for some kind of sign. Nothing in particular caught his eye. People were milling about heading in different directions for various reasons and not one of them was paying him any attention. Realizing that he hadn't eaten anything all day other than the small bag of Cheez-its he had on the plane, he decided to follow the signs for the cafeteria. Once inside, he grabbed a tray and walked down the line grabbing a few items to eat. He paid and headed for a table near the window. With it being late morning, there were only a few people left. He chose a table near a man who seemed to be texting someone furiously on his phone.

"Oh, for God's sake!!!" the man slammed his phone on the table and leaned back in his chair with a loud sigh. He saw Jonah glance at him as he was sitting down. "Sorry, there's just no cell service in this blasted place."

Jonah checked his phone. "I have a few bars if you'd like to use my phone."

"No, it's fine," the man replied. "I'll just go outside in a moment…it's been a long night."

"Everything okay?" Jonah asked, turning in his seat and for the first time noticing the man's haggard appearance. He appeared to have been crying at some point in the last hour.

"My wife," he said, looking down at a picture on his phone. He held it up for Jonah to see an attractive brunette in what appeared to be her mid to late thirties, smiling back at him.

"She's beautiful," Jonah replied.

"It's an old picture…" he seemed to be fighting several emotions. "She makes fun of me for keeping it…as if she's still not presently the most beautiful woman in the world." He teared up and glanced out the window. "Sorry, she's in surgery right now…fighting for her life. Stage 4 brain cancer."

"I'm so sorry," was all Jonah knew to say. He felt a tinge of guilt for not having something wise to say. What kind of Christian was he?

"She's been fighting it for years. She was 36 in this picture…she's 43 now." He choked a sob out and put his head down. "We'd wanted to wait to have kids…but it looks like that won't happen now."

Jonah closed his eyes and asked God for wisdom. He stood up and slid into the seat across from the man at his table. Without a word, he placed a hand on the man's arm and began to pray for him. "Father God," Jonah began and he felt the man shaking as he cried. "I pray Your blessings over my new friend here, God…I don't know



✝

his name yet, or the name of his wife, but You do. Take this situation, Father, and show them what You are...WHO You are...be glorified in this, God." Jonah paused, in awe of his prayer. Had it been God praying through him? He would never have thought to pray that God be glorified. He would've begged for this woman's healing...but this...WOW!

"Thank you..." the man spoke up, bringing Jonah back to reality. "And my name is Wayne...my wife is Catherine...I call her Cat." He smiled. "She hates cats..."

"Jonah," he replied, smiling back. "I hope that was okay."

Wayne nodded. "I'm no believer, but hey, I'll take what I can get. Her side of the family are Christians and they've been praying for her as well."

"Yeah, I'm brand new to this, myself." Jonah replied. "Do you need anything?"

"My wife back...my life back...just...peace."

Jonah nodded. "I get that. And it just so happens that God offers that."

The man looked uncomfortably at Jonah and then checked the time on his phone. "So, what brings you here to this wonderful place, Jonah?"

Well, that was a loaded question and Jonah had no answer. Who would believe that he'd just flown all the way across the country because the Holy Spirit had given him a direct order and no reason whatsoever except "Trust Me?" Jonah had no idea why he was here or what the God of the universe wanted him...wait...no.

"This is going to sound a bit crazy, but I think YOU did."

"I'm sorry?" Wayne asked, taken aback.



✝

"All I know is, twelve hours ago, I was in San Diego, California when God told me to go to Flagler Hospital in St. Augustine, Florida. I had no idea why...until now."

*PENNINGTON SPRINGS, TENNESSEE*

After chatting with Christina a bit, Brianna decided it was time to get back to her room and take a much-needed shower. She pulled her cell phone out of her bag, having not checked in a while because there was no service in the mountains. "Oh wow!" Among other people, Mark McGee had left her twenty-three text messages and had tried to call her eight times, leaving three voice messages. She decided to start with the texts.

"PRAYERS NEEDED!!! SCOTTY IN BAD ACCIDENT!!!"

"Oh, Jesus!" Brianna cried out. "Father, please be with him!"

"He's been rushed to emergency surgery." the texts went on giving her updates and telling her how Gabi was not handling it very well. She was basically a basket case and wouldn't let anyone near her...apparently not even God.

Then when she got to the last text...Brianna's heart almost exploded.

"BRIANNA WHERE ARE YOU!!!??? SOMETHING BIG IS GOING DOWN!!! BETHANY HAS BEEN IN AN ACCIDENT IN GATEWAY!!! THEY'RE SAYING IT DOESN'T LOOK GOOD!!! WHAT IS GOD DOING!!!???"

Brianna dropped to her knees in prayer for her friends. After several minutes of calling out to God on their behalf, she decided she needed to respond to Mark. She dialed his number.

"Thank God, Brianna!" Mark said. "Not sure what's going on, but we're under attack!"



✝

"That's what I'm gathering!" Brianna replied. "What's the latest?"

"No updates on Scotty, which as I'm trying to see it, is good news."

"And Gabi?"

"She's vanished," Mark replied. "I knew she was feeling overwhelmed and tried to keep everyone away from her, but I think my staying with her was getting on her nerves. I left the room for a second and when I came back, she was gone. Now, she's not replying to my texts or answering my calls. She's in a dark place, Brianna...I've never seen Gabi like this."

"Yeah, she's usually the one rallying the troops." Brianna was seriously concerned about her friend. "Let me try calling her, Mark."

"Good idea," Mark replied. She could hear how tired he was in his voice. "Keep me posted."

Brianna clicked off the call and said a quick prayer before dialing Gabi's number.

"HE WAS HERE!!!" Gabi screamed into the phone, sounding like she was having a mental breakdown. "BRIANNA! HE WAS JUST HERE!!!"

"Gabi!" Brianna yelled, trying to get her friend's attention. "Gabi? Who? What's happening?" She tried her best to sound calm, but the fact that Gabi was frantic was really freaking her out.

"RUSTY!!!" Gabi screamed, and Brianna felt an icy cold chill run down her spine. "RUSTY STAGGERBUSH WAS HERE!!!"

"Gabi, are you sure!?" Brianna asked. "We killed Rusty!!!"



✝

"He's a demon, Brianna!" Gabi replied, sounding like she was turning in place, making sure he didn't return. "All we did, was send him away to regroup! Now he's back and he said he was the one that got Scotty and he's coming for my baby!!! Brianna! I don't know what to do!!!" She seemed to have collapsed and was sobbing.

"Gabi?" Brianna said, taken aback. "Did you say baby?"

"Y..yes...Brianna, he said to wait and see what he was going to do to my unborn baby!!!" Gabi was hysterical.

"First of all," Brianna replied. "I don't give a rat's patootie what that demon from hell said...he has NO authority in your life!" She closed her eyes and tried to calm herself. "Secondly...unborn baby?"

"Yes!" Gabi replied with a snap and then seemed to realize that up until that point that she was the only human in the world that had known that information. "Yes...I haven't even told Scotty yet."

"I'm going to be an aunt???" Brianna asked in as calm of a voice as she could.

"You are," Gabi replied and Brianna could hear the smile in her voice. "Brianna, I'm having a baby!" They both laughed at the thought.

"That is amazing, Gabi!" Brianna replied. "I'm so happy for you!"

"But what is going on!?" Gabi asked, seeming to come down from her high a little too fast. "What is happening, Brianna!? Why is Rusty back in my life!?"

"Well, maybe it's because you're still alive and you're still God's child and Satan hates you and wants to destroy you!" Brianna replied. "And to be honest, you must have some seriously powerful hormones working against you right now, because the Gabi Morgan that I know would've sent 'ole Rusty with his bags packed back to



✝

hell for threatening her family…or are you actually operating in fear!?"

Gabi sat down on a park bench and hung her head. "You're right…I've never felt like this before. When I found out about Scotty's accident, all I wanted to do was blame God and scream at Him for abandoning me. I wonder if it IS hormones? Either way, I feel like an idiot now."

"Yeah, you might want to call Mark and throw some love his way," Brianna said. "He's worried sick about you."


## VALLEY OF THE SHADOW OF DEATH

Scotty had watched Bethany drop to the ground when the lightning bolt had struck her right in the chest. He screamed out the name of Jesus and charged in as the demons had attempted to pounce on her. He made his way through the hordes of hell, screaming and pushing his way in under the protection of Jesus' name. He'd found her lying there, limp as a child's doll. The demons around him were laughing and screaming curses from all directions. He lifted her head. "No, in Jesus' name!" Bethany's eyes had shot open and a bright light shined all around them. The demons and foul creatures had scattered. Scotty had looked up and into the face of the One whose name he'd called on. Jesus himself was smiling down on them.

"Get up my children," He'd said. "The battle is mine."

That seemed to be about an hour or so ago. Scotty wasn't sure how time worked in the Valley. All he knew was…as soon as he helped Bethany up, everything and everyone had vanished. No demons, no creatures, no Jesus. Just the two of them. Bethany looked around in total confusion.

"Scotty???"



✝

"Hello, Bethany!" Scotty replied with a big, cheesy smile. "Welcome to the Valley of the Shadow of Death! Do you remember what happened that brought you here?"

"This is the Valley!?" Bethany exclaimed, looking around. "Wow! I don't know...wait a minute. I was on my way to get Jake...and somebody..."

"Car crash!?" Scotty exclaimed. "Me too!"

"So, what do we do now!?" Bethany asked, continuing to look around at the vast nothingness.

Scotty shrugged. "Not much we CAN do. Our bodies are lying in a hospital somewhere. Mine in Egypt and yours in Gateway."

"Isn't that wild?" Bethany asked, just as they heard a noise in the distance. They both turned to look. It appeared to be a woman coming toward them waving her hands.

"Excuse me!!!???" she yelled. "Can you help me!?"

"Be cautious," Scotty said to Bethany. "Things aren't always as they seem in here."

Bethany laughed out loud. "With our gang, things aren't as they seem ANYWHERE!"


## GATEWAY, FLORIDA

Matt was pacing back and forth in the waiting room as Bethany's mom and stepdad sought answers from the medical staff. All he knew at this point was that her heart had stopped twice already...once at the scene and once when they'd gotten her in the ambulance. They said she had internal bleeding and had to have emergency surgery.

Pastor Brian was on the phone getting the prayer chain rolling. Everybody at the church loved Bethany and wanted to help



✝

in some way. He was attempting to coordinate all that and keep too many people from flooding to the hospital.

Jake came wheeling into the waiting room with a look of sheer terror on his face. "Matt!" he exclaimed. "How is she???"

"She's in surgery," Matt replied. "Internal bleeding is all we know."

"Is it true that she died?" Jake asked, worry in his eyes.

"Yes, but she's alive now, Jake! Be praying!"

Jake's sister, apparently the one to bring him, walked in...also looking sick with worry. She made a beeline for Matt and wrapped her arms around him. "Is she okay?"

"Hey JoAnn, no word since she went in."

She glanced over at Jake, who had his eyes squeezed shut in prayer. "He blames himself…"

"What on Earth for?" Matt asked.

"He had called her for help. She was on her way to give him a jump."

Matt walked over and put a hand on Jake's shoulder. "Hey, man," Matt said, causing Jake to look up with tears in his eyes. "This is spiritual warfare. Don't you dare blame yourself for something that was designed by the enemies of God. All any of us can do is trust that Jesus is going to take care of the situation. This is HIS story."

"Thanks, Matt," Jake replied.

Matt nodded to his friend. "This isn't my first rodeo. Satan wants a fight...he came to the right neighborhood."



✝

# CHAPTER 12



*PENNINGTON SPRINGS, TENNESSEE*

Brianna finally made it to bed after dealing with all the spiritual warfare and drama that came with it. She lay there wondering how Scotty was doing. Mark had called to tell her that Scotty had come out of surgery and was stable, but they would have to wait it out with him being in a coma. There could possibly be brain damage. She'd prayed over that thought alone for over an hour. There was still no word on Bethany, Now, physically, mentally, and spiritually drained, she attempted to close her eyes and drift off. Christina had told her she was turning in hours ago. They'd planned to grab breakfast in the morning and head to the police station.

Just as she was beginning to drift off, she heard a scraping sound coming from the direction of the window. She raised her head and peered over, realizing that there were bars next to her head. "What in the world?" she thought. "Why am I in jail?" She began to sit up and realized that it wasn't as easy as she thought. She was a small child and wrapped up tightly in a blanket. Then she realized she was in a crib. Another noise took her attention back to the window near her bed. She could see a shadow moving and then heard the window sliding up.

Moments later, a head appeared to be coming through the open window...followed by a small person...a child...him...the boy who'd tried to hurt her before. He made it in, and stood up. He quietly walked over and picked up a small pillow. He looked down at Brianna...or whoever the small child was...and smiled. At first, she thought he was smiling at how cute she was or something.

Suddenly, he raised the pillow and brought it down toward her face. On instinct, she jumped, her leg struck the side bar hard, and it pinched the boy. It caused the child to instantly scream out in pain. The noise caused the boy to panic. He quickly set the pillow back



✝

down just as she heard her mother scream. The boy scampered out the open window as Brianna's mother attempted to grab him. She quickly picked up Brianna and held her tight, as she ran to her own room, she grabbed her phone. She began to feel tired. As she began to drift off to sleep again, she heard someone shouting from outside the window. "Brianna Bowers is dead! Brianna Bowers is dead! I cracked her on the head! I cracked her on the head!" They just kept shouting it over and over again.

Brianna shot up out of bed and looked around the dark room. Glancing at the clock, she saw that several hours had passed since she'd laid down. "What a crazy dream!"

"Brianna Bowers is dead! I cracked her on the head!" She heard someone gleefully yelling from outside her back window and a chill ran down her spine. She jumped up and ran to the window, sliding the curtain back from her second story window. There in the middle of the street in front of the inn, jumping up and down and shouting, was Harley. He was waving his hands around and spinning in place. "Brianna Bowers is dead! I cracked her on the head!"

"HARLEY!!!" Someone that sounded like the chief yelled from somewhere Brianna couldn't see. "STOP RIGHT THERE!!!" Chief Jerry came into view wearing a pair of sweat pants and a t-shirt, pointing his pistol right at Ol' Harley.

"I killed her!" Harley yelled. "She is no more!" He laughed a wicked laugh with his face to the sky. That's when Brianna saw the hammer in his hand.

"Drop the hammer, Harley!" Jerry yelled.

Just then someone started banging on Brianna's door. She looked away for just a second and that's when the gun went off...three shots from Chief Jerry's gun and Harley Thomas Linwood dropped to the ground.



✝

Brianna jumped at the sound of the gun going off, and stood stunned at the scene before her. She saw Chief Jerry run over and kick the hammer away, then he bent down to check Harley for a pulse. She saw someone else run over and heard him and the chief discussing what had just happened.

Just then, Brianna's door swung open and Mrs. Carolyn turned the light on to find Brianna at the window. "Oh, thank God you're okay, Brianna! We thought Harley had hurt you...or worse!" There were several others from the inn standing behind her with concerned looks on their faces.

"I'm fine!" Brianna said, walking over to assure them that she was unharmed. "To my knowledge he was never in my room!" She gave Mrs. Carolyn a hug and had the woman sit down.

"All that screaming," Carolyn said. "I wasn't sure what I would find when I opened that door." She was breathing heavy and holding her hand over her heart.

"Why did he say he'd killed you if he hadn't even been in here?" one of the women at the door asked.

"Harley wasn't exactly right in the head," Brianna replied. "He was very disturbed."

Just then, Pastor Jason came running down the hall and into the room. "OHHHH, Thank God!!!" He pulled Brianna into a hug. "He's dead now…"

Brianna nodded. "I saw…" Tears sprung to her eyes at the thought of what just happened.

"Thank God, you're okay," Jason said as he pulled away from her. He looked back toward the hall. "Where's Christina?"

A chill immediately shot down Brianna's spine. "Is she not in the hall!?" One of the women looked around as Brianna shot past her. "No way a world class reporter just slept through all that!" She



✝

knocked on Christina's door, which was right beside hers. Nothing..."CHRISTINA!!!"

Mrs. Carolyn came up beside her and unlocked the door. Brianna quickly opened it, flipped on the light and gasped at the sight before her. Christina's lifeless body lay under the blood splattered covers...her head and face were crushed in. The balcony door was wide open.

"He thought it was you," Jason said somberly.


## VALLEY OF THE SHADOW OF DEATH

"Hello!" Scotty said to the approaching woman, placing himself in front of Bethany. "I'm Scotty and this is my friend Bethany. What's your name?"

"I'm...I...I'm not sure...WHY CAN'T I REMEMBER MY NAME!!!???" She put her hands over her head and screamed. "Where am I!? What is this awful place!?"

"It's okay," Scotty replied. "Don't panic. Memory loss is apparently a common thing here."

Bethany put an arm around the woman and attempted to comfort her. "It's okay. I'm just figuring this out myself. Do you remember being in an accident or being sick?"

"I do remember something about being in a hospital...was I in an accident!? Why can't I remember anything!?"

"It's alright," Bethany said. "We call this place the Valley of the Shadow of Death."

The woman stiffened and looked at Bethany quizzically. "Like in the Bible?"



✝

"Exactly...yea, though I walk through the valley of the shadow of death, I will fear no evil. I think that's in Psalm chapter 23."

Scotty nodded, "Yes, verse 4."

"I don't really believe in that stuff...what does it even mean?" the woman continued to rub her temples and began pacing. "Am I dead!?" She looked over at Scotty. "WAIT!? Why can I remember that was from the Bible and that I don't believe in the Bible, but I can't even remember my own name!?" Bethany put a hand on her arm to calm her.

"The memory is a funny thing," Scotty replied. "And to answer your first question, no...you're not dead. You ARE, however, in the place where that is literally the next step. Your body is most likely in a hospital somewhere. Mine is in Cairo, Egypt and Bethany's is in Gateway, Florida. We were both in car crashes."

"But you knew each other before?" she asked.

"Yes," Bethany replied. "Scotty is best friends with my big brother."

She seemed to be trying to process everything. "So, if this is all in my head, so to speak...how are we here together? And what happens next?"

"I'm not sure how this works, but I think God decides who comes here...and you either wake up in the hospital, or you...die," Scotty replied. "The death thing is pretty intense down here, by the way."

"WHAT DO YOU MEAN!!!???" she backed away, clearly distraught.

"I mean, if you're not a believer in Jesus Christ, it's an extremely horrible experience...that most likely gets worse after you're dead...you know...hell."



✝

She shook her head. "You're just trying to scare me! I know the scare tactics of you Christians! Scare me out of hell!"

"And what exactly do you think I have to gain by doing that in this place!?" Scotty asked. "Do you think I'm making some kind of commission!? I'm just telling you what I've seen, Lady! There's a lot of screaming and pleading when death comes!"

"Death!?" She began to turn in place. "There's an actual Death!!!??? What, like the Grim Reaper!?"

Just then the ground began to shake. The woman grabbed onto Bethany and screamed. Bethany looked over at Scotty, who gave her a puzzled look and...vanished. Scotty Morgan was gone.

## *CAIRO, EGYPT*

Mark and Gabi had called everyone to let them know that Scotty was out of surgery, everything had gone well, and it was just a waiting game at this point. He was in a deep coma and they didn't expect him to come out of it anytime soon. They had then gathered with the few that had made their way to the hospital, in the chapel. Mark had led the prayer for a while, then Gabi had taken over, then Yvette, Andy, Eddie, and so on.

Dustin had come up and was enjoying watching how the believers had come together to fight for one of their own. This is how life was supposed to be. It was what the world promised but fell short of delivering. Here it was though...directly in the presence of God. He smiled and let out a huge sigh.

"You good?" Yvette asked, walking over and taking a seat next to the former pop star.

"I'm great!" he responded. "Just enjoying being right where God wants me."

"Well, you did amazing at the show...especially considering you'd never even heard any of our songs!"



✝

"Thanks," Dustin replied. "Music was always my first language." He smiled as if remembering something from his childhood. "My mom always said I would dance inside her stomach when she would listen to music."

Yvette smiled. "That's crazy. By the way, I just wanted to say how proud I am of you for the stand you took for that little girl. I can't even imagine the pressure you were under to give into that world of darkness."

"Thank you for saying that, Yvette," Dustin said, lowering his head. "I just wish I could've saved her."

Yvette placed her hand on top of his and squeezed it. "You did," she replied and they both just sat in that moment, crying together. It was exactly what Dustin needed...once again.

Mark's knees were killing him. He'd been kneeling in prayer for hours and he felt like if he tried to stand, he would fall right here on the hardwood floor of this chapel. He looked up at his friends gathered around...doing battle...and it melted his heart. Scotty would be okay...he had to be, and so would his sister. He met Gabi's eye and gave her that, what do we do now, look. She stood up and headed over to him.

"You look like you're in pain," she said with a smirk.

"Slightly," he replied and attempted to adjust to a sitting position on the floor. "Do you want to tell everyone it's okay to go back to their hotel rooms?"

"They all know they could've done that hours ago," she replied. "Everybody looks so content."

Suddenly, Dustin stood up with a gasp and pointed toward the altar at the front. "I remember you! You were at the compound with all those children!!!" He began to sob.

Everyone turned to look...but nobody was there.



✝

"Who, Dustin!?" Yvette asked. "Who are you talking about?"

"The old man! Don't you see him!?"

"There's nobody there," Yvette replied, placing a hand on his shoulder. "But I know who He is."

Mark was about to say something to Dustin when a large, gentle hand pressed on his shoulder.     "Go home." Mark looked over just in time to see the old gentleman vanish.

"But Scotty!?" Mark blurted out as if to bring the old man back. Everyone looked confused as to what was going on. "We can't leave Scotty here, Lord! And I need my sister to be okay!"

Just then, the door to the chapel opened, and a nurse stuck her head in. "I'm sorry...Mrs. Morgan!?"

"Yes!?" Gabi replied, standing to her feet. "I'm Mrs. Morgan!"

"Your husband is awake!"


## GATEWAY, FLORIDA

Matt had been pacing back and forth down the hospital corridor. He'd prayed with practically everyone who'd visited Bethany. He frequented the hospital chapel several times, praying fervently for his friend each time. This couldn't turn out like the other times. Not like Billy or his cousin Megan or her fiancé Caleb...God had to heal Bethany. Matt couldn't take another death. Not this close to home.

"Father, I plead with you...heal Bethany in Jesus' name." He leaned back against the wall and did everything in his power to muster the faith he so desperately lacked. "Please…"

"Well, well, well!!!" Someone was laughing from the other end of the hall. There was nobody else around. Matt looked in that

**111**

✝

direction and his heart nearly stopped. "If it isn't the worst Christian in the history of the world!!!" Rusty's laughter shook the walls.

Matt pushed off from the wall and rushed toward him. "I come against you…" Rusty vanished in a puff of smoke.

"She's mine, you know!" Rusty said from behind him, causing Matt to spin around. "I have her in the valley!"

"YOU HAVE NOOO AUTHORITY…."

Rusty held up his hand. "Listen, Matthew…I know MY place in all this. Do you know yours?"

"I'm a child of the living God, you foul stench!" Matt replied.

"Such hatred in your soul…" Rusty began laughing. "All those butterflies you had in your heart for the lovely Bethany McGee…do you love her???"

"YOU KEEP HER NAME OUT OF YOUR MOUTH, DEMON!!!" Matt screamed.

At that moment, Rusty waved his hands in the air and was immediately transformed into a giant dragon, causing the very walls to crack around him. "SHE'S MINE!!!" He roared. "BETHANY MCGEE HAS ALWAYS BEEN MINE!!!"

Matt could smell sulfur and blood on his breath as he took a slight step backwards. He cocked his head to the side and took in the terrifying sight before him. A giant, black, scaly dragon taking up most of the room in the hallway was towering over him. For some reason it excited him. Here he was, little old Matthew Ramsey, worship leader of a small church in Gateway, Florida…being used by God…to slay a dragon from hell.

"You really do believe your own lies, don't you?" Matt asked calmly. "Bethany McGee is a blood bought Christian, you idiot! Even if you kill her…she's God's property. She goes straight to heaven!" He said it with a laugh. "A place you'll NEVER see!"



✝

And with that, the dragon shook his head in a puff of thick, black smoke...and vanished.

Matt's phone chirped and he pulled it out of his pocket without looking away from the spot where the dragon had stood. After several seconds, he looked down...it was a text from Mark. "Scotty is awake. We're coming home."



✝

# CHAPTER 13



*PENNINGTON SPRINGS, TENNESSEE*

Brianna was sitting in the front room of the police station and had just gotten off the phone with Gabi. She'd called to tell her about Christina, but Gabi told her that Scotty had woken up and the gang was about to board a flight to Atlanta. Scotty was under strict orders to seek medical advice as soon as he landed. Everyone there had seemed in high spirits until Brianna had delivered the horrible news about Christina. Mark told Gabi to let Brianna know that he would contact her when they landed.

She looked up as Chief Jerry opened his office door and motioned for her to come in. She put her phone away and walked into his office where Jason was already seated. "Oh, hi Jason!" She said. "I didn't realize you were in here."

"Hey, Brianna," Jason stood. "How are you doing?"

"Well, I spoke with Tyler...Christina's husband." She looked away as a tear fell. "That wasn't an easy conversation."

"It never is..." Chief Jerry said. "How is he?"

"Confused...if it were anyone else but me, he would've called them a liar." She pulled a tissue out and dabbed at her eyes. "We prayed...we asked God for protection...Jason, why did it have to happen!?" Brianna stood up and walked across the small office. "Why COULDN'T it have been me!? I'm ready to meet Jesus! I'm not married! I don't have a spouse who will suffer over this for the rest of his life!"

"Brianna, we HAVE to trust that God knows what He is doing," Jason replied. "And a lot of people would suffer if anything happened to you."

"For I know the plans I have for you, declares the LORD," Chief Jerry chimed in. "Plans to prosper you and not harm you, plans



✝

to give you hope and a future." He looked up at Brianna and smiled. "Jeremiah 29:11, one of my favorites. God has a plan, Brianna...if you believe that...then you know that Christina is right where He wants her to be. By His side, worshiping Him. She's probably feeling sorry for US right now."

Just then, there was a knock at the Chief's door. Pastor Jason reached over and opened it and Mr. Nesmith, the Medical Examiner, walked in. He looked around at each of them. "Sorry for interrupting…"

"It's fine, what is it Michael?" Chief Jerry replied.

"Just wondering where exactly you wanted me to have...the body sent?" He asked, glancing over at Brianna, then back to the Chief.

"Tyler sent me an address, write down your email address and I'll send it to you," Brianna said.

He quickly scribbled down the information and handed it to Brianna. "Thank you...and I'm sorry for your loss."

"Thank you, Mr. Nesmith."

He smiled and turned to leave. "I suppose you'll be heading back home, Ms. Bowers?" He turned back around after opening the door. "What with the killer being taken care of and all."

"Yes, my flight leaves out early tomorrow morning," she replied. "Which reminds me…" she looked at Jason. "Can I possibly get a ride?"

"Absolutely, just text me a reminder and what time," Jason replied.

"Well," Mr. Nesmith said with a grim smile. "It was a pleasure meeting you, though I wish the circumstances had been different."



✝

"You as well, Mr. Nesmith," Brianna replied as he closed the door.

"Why don't the two of you come to the Inn this evening for dinner," Chief Jerry said to Jason and Brianna.

"Chief Jerry, you can't go offering Mrs. Carolyn to cook for us," Brianna replied. "She's a busy woman!"

"Trust me," Chief Jerry said. "She'll be mad if I don't offer. We may never get to see you again, Brianna! Besides, I'll help her cook...I make a mean can of biscuits!"

"Okay, if you're sure," Brianna replied. "Oh, wait!" she added. "Why did you want me to come down here, Chief?"

"I just wanted to make sure you were okay, Brianna," Chief Jerry replied. "You've been through a lot over the past few weeks."

"That's putting it mildly," she replied. "I'll be okay though. Greater is He that is in me…"

"AMEN!!!" Jason replied.

"Well, if that's all," Briana said. "I have a few more people that I need to notify about Christina, including her old news station in Gateway." She stood to go. "Oh, and I need to call my mom about a dream I had."

"You're not having nightmares like Mark used to have, are you?" Jason asked.

"No, nothing like that," Brianna replied. "Just let me know what time tonight, Chief...I'll see you guys later."


*VALLEY OF THE SHADOW OF DEATH*

Bethany had managed to calm the woman down after Scotty vanished. She'd told her that though she knew very little about this place, she could only imagine that he'd woken up in the hospital.



✝

Though, in the back of her mind, she knew it was possible that he'd died. Presently, they were both sitting on a large boulder discussing the plan of salvation; something that the woman clearly wanted no part of.

"Listen," Bethany said, interrupting a rant about how horrible Christians had treated her family in the past. "I'm terribly sorry for all of that, and if it truly happened the way you say it did, then there's no excuse for it. However, I'm not attempting to get you to follow a specific church, organization, or group of people. People are human and quite frankly, most of us are idiots. I'm trying to get you to follow Jesus..." Bethany let out a frustrated sigh. "We need to give you a name...how about Brandy? Until you can remember your actual name, at least."

"Brandy?"

"Yeah, I had a friend in college named Brandy McKie, that was SO amazing. She was a total Godsend that helped me out of more than one jam. She even convinced me to stay in college when I wanted to quit. If I ever have a daughter, that's what I intend to name her."

The woman nodded. "Then Brandy it is." She smiled and squeezed Bethany's arm. "I think you're a Godsend to me in this place...you know, if there actually was a God." She gave Bethany a light shove.

"Let me explain it this way," Bethany retorted. "Okay, Brandy, I know your memory is crazy right now but answer these questions to the best of your ability. Have you ever told a lie?"

"Yes, in the past...but I try to always be honest now."

"In the eyes of God, time doesn't erase sin, even a small lie years ago is remembered by Him. Have you ever stolen anything?"

"Hmmm, I went through a rebellious phase as a teenager, did a lot of bad things, so yeah, shoplifting was my jam."



✝

"Okay, have you ever cheated, like on a test or homework, or anything?"

"Oh yeah," Brandy laughed. "I used to pay Ashley Benton to do my homework. I won't even begin to tell you some of the other things I used to do to get by."

"That leads me to my last question...have you ever committed adultery...and by adultery, I mean sex outside of the bonds of marriage."

"Wow, isn't it funny how I could remember Ashley's name but I'm still a huge blank as to any part of my present life. Bethany, I don't even know if I'm married or have ever been. But to answer your question, yes, I do remember that. Adultery is a big fat yes. I mean, hasn't everybody done all these things?"

"We're just talking about you right now," Bethany replied. "When the time comes for you to stand before God, nobody else is going to be there but you and Him...the perfect Judge."

"Wait!" Brandy held up her hand. "I told you..."

"Let's just say, for argument's sake, that I'm right, Brandy!" Bethany interrupted her. "Let's just say that in twenty minutes from now, Death shows up and drags you away for all eternity. Let's just say that you are taken to stand before a Holy God who will not allow any kind of sin to enter heaven...EVER!" Bethany gave her a minute to process the picture she'd just painted. "Now, you just admitted to me that you're a lying, thieving, cheating, adulterer, who doesn't even believe in the very God you're standing in front of...what exactly do you think He's going to say to you?"

"First of all," Brandy replied slowly. "If that's the case...that no sin is allowed into heaven. There isn't a single person in the history of the world that hasn't sinned...so by your standards, everybody goes to hell."

"They're not my standards, Brandy, they're God's."



✝

"Well, regardless of who's standards they are...we're ALL going to hell."

Bethany smiled. "You're exactly correct."

"Wait, what?" Brandy gave her an extremely confused look. "Are you saying that you believe we're all doomed to hell? That's worse than not believing in God!"

"We ARE all doomed to hell, by God's standards ...however...that's the very reason that He sent His Son to die on the cross for our sins. He was the sacrifice that God required. You said earlier that everybody in the history of the world had sinned...but that wasn't totally true. Jesus NEVER sinned, and that's what made Him that perfect sacrifice. He took our sins upon Himself when He was nailed to that cross...and according to the Bible, when we BELIEVE in Him and call on His name...we too are saved from hell forever. He washes our sins away and ONLY then can we stand before God completely spotless."

Brandy looked away and Bethany could swear she'd seen a tear. "I've never heard it put that way, Bethany." She reached up and wiped her eyes. "It makes it so personal. It shows God in the most loving way possible." She looked back at Bethany as tears rolled down her cheeks. "It really isn't about the church...at least not how I always thought. It's ALL about His love for us."

"He IS love!" Bethany replied. "And don't misunderstand me...we need the church. We need to surround ourselves with fellow believers who are also attempting to work out their salvation. We just need to remember that they also aren't perfect. They're probably going to do or say something stupid...just like you and I are just as likely to do."

"But it's God that we keep our focus on?" Brandy replied and Bethany nodded. "I want to believe in Him, Bethany!" She let out an uncontrollable sob. "God, please forgive me for my unbelief!" She buried her face in Bethany's shoulder.



✝

"Let's pray," Bethany whispered into her ear.

## *ST. AUGUSTINE, FLORIDA*

Jonah stood across the bed from his new friend, Wayne. Catherine lay unconscious between them. Wayne had asked Jonah to join him in the room. "If I go in there alone, I'll probably lose it." He told the administrator that Jonah was his pastor. A lie...but not really. A pastor was a shepherd and right now Jonah was Wayne's shepherd. She lay perfectly still with tubes and wires running all over and around her. The bedside monitors were humming and beeping, making Jonah remember being in the hospital with his dad not so long ago.

"You okay?" Jonah asked Wayne, who nodded, though he never took his eyes off his wife.

"I have a personal question to ask you, Jonah," Wayne replied after several seconds of silence.

"Shoot," Jonah said, hoping he could answer whatever question about God this man was about to ask him.

"What in the world happened to your face?"

Jonah had completely forgotten about his bruised face and how it must look to those who didn't know what he'd been through not so long ago. He smiled at Wayne, even though the man still stared at his wife. "If you think this is bad, you should see my back, abs, and chest."

Wayne broke his eyes away from Catherine and looked at him. "Were you in an accident?"

"Did you hear about what went down a few days ago in Wyoming? The child trafficking ring?"

Wayne nodded. "Were you involved with that?"



✝

"I kind of had a small part in helping to bring that down."

"You're the construction worker! The one they were hunting!" Wayne seemed beyond impressed. "WOW! I'm in the presence of a hero!"

"Just a guy that was in the wrong place at the right time," Jonah replied.

Wayne extended his hand to shake Jonah's. "It's a pleasure, sir!" He wrapped his arms around Jonah and hugged him as he came in for the handshake. "Please, I'd be honored to have you pray for my wife!"

"Actually, Wayne," Jonah replied, pointing to the two chairs in the room. "I think I'm supposed to pray with you first."

"Well, you already did!" Wayne replied, thinking back to the prayer in the cafeteria.

"I mean for you!" Jonah said. "You're clearly willing to believe in a miracle for your wife. Well, how would you like to accept the miracle of having your soul saved from hell? The same God can do both!"

Wayne was caught off guard with what Jonah had said. His eyes teared up as he turned to stare at his wife. His beautiful Catherine...so helpless...so hopeless. Could God really heal her? Would God really heal her? Neither of them deserved anything that a loving God could offer. "I don't know, Jonah...I may be beyond that."

"Are you saying you found a way to sin that was more powerful than the God of heaven? That the Creator of the entire universe is weakened in the presence of the great Wayne's terrible past? Please tell me what you've done so I can steer clear of..."

"Okay, okay," Wayne held up his hands. "I surrender!"



✝

"That's all He asks us to do, Wayne," Jonah replied. "Just surrender YOUR life for His." Wayne nodded. "Close your eyes and pray with me."


## VALLEY OF THE SHADOW OF DEATH

Brandy finished her prayer of salvation and opened her eyes. She looked right at Bethany and gave her the biggest smile. "Thank you, Bethany!" The two women hugged. "Thank you for sharing eternity with me!" She started crying again. "I really feel as if I'm ready to face ANYTHING right now...even death."

"Ummm," Bethany replied, pulling away from the hug and looking over Brandy's shoulder. "Speaking of ANYTHING!"

Brandy turned around and looked behind her, where the sky was beginning to churn. Lightning bolts were striking in the distance and the rumble of thunder began to shake the ground. "Does this place HAVE storms?"

"Yes," Bethany said, sliding off the boulder and taking Brandy by the hand. "And from what I'm told, they're not very fun! Let's go this way!" The two women began to walk quickly in the opposite direction of the coming storm, when the ground began to shake even harder. Bethany let out a scream when just ahead of them a huge monster-creature topped the hill and began to charge toward them. It looked like a giant yak with sharp teeth and legs like a cat.

"What in the world!?" Brandy yelled. They turned and ran in a different direction just as hundreds of demons and foul looking creatures began to approach them from every direction.

Bethany stopped and attempted to block Brandy from their view. "Pray," she said over her shoulder to her new friend.

"I'm a step ahead of you there, girl!" Brandy replied. "Is this the end of the line?"



✝

The sky above them grew dark and the clouds seemed to swirl as if they were angry. Lightning struck the ground not far from where they stood and a loud boom followed. The women could make out the shape of a face beginning to form in the clouds.

"I think that's Death!" Bethany said over all the noise. The creatures continued to move closer. "Father God, I call on you to protect us in the mighty name of your Son, Jesus Christ!" Another lightning strike even closer than the last. Then...laughter.

The giant black leather-skinned dragon stood towering over all the other creatures as he roared with a sinister laugh that shook the ground. "YOU'RE FRIENDS ARE PRAYING FOR YOU LIKE THE FOOLS THEY ARE, BETHANY MCGEE!" More laughter.

"You know him!?" Brandy asked over the sounds of thunder and the demonic sneering from the creatures.

"We've met!" Bethany replied.

"BUT I'M HERE TO SEND YOU INTO ETERNITY!" The dragon roared.

"Eternity with Jesus, you freak of nature!" Bethany replied.

"PERHAPS," the dragon conceded. "BUT MY END GAME WILL BEGIN!"

"And what's that!? Spending eternity in HELL!?" Bethany said the last word with emphasis and took a step toward him.

"NO..." He lowered his head, and a smile slid across his twisted face. "The destruction of the man who would give you his heart...my target all along...Matthew Ramsey. I will destroy him with your death...I will see his soul in hell when he loses all hope in a God who has continually abandoned him!" His laughter shook the very foundation of the valley.



✝

# CHAPTER 14



*GATEWAY, FLORIDA*

Matt had drawn quite the crowd with his screaming at the dragon episode. Doctors, nurses, and security came running out into the hall to find him standing there alone just staring at his phone. He looked up and realized how crazy he must seem to them. "Sorry!" he said, raising his hands. "Heated argument with an old...enemy." He noticed one of Bethany's nurses among the group and headed toward her. "Is there any word on Bethany?"

"No, sir," the nurse replied. "Her condition hasn't changed since the last time you asked ten minutes ago." She gave him a slight grin. "You should go home and get some sleep. I have your number and will call you the moment anything changes."

"I appreciate it, but there's no way I could sleep knowing that she's in here." Matt followed her down the hall and replied to Mark's message. "Let me know when you're here. No change in Bethany's status." He joined Bethany's mom in the waiting room, plopping down on the seat beside her.

"Everything okay?" she asked.

"Mark and the gang are heading home. Scotty's awake."

"I got that text too," Mrs. Gilmore replied. "I mean with you, Matthew..."

He glanced over at her. "Nothing that you need to worry about."

"I'm not deaf, Matthew...you were screaming at the dragon, weren't you?"

Matt looked down at his shoes and nodded slowly. "He said Bethany was his now."



✝

"You know he's lying, right?" she replied, putting her arm around him. "It's what he does. You need to stand on the truth."

"I'm trying, Mrs. Gilmore...I'm trying…"

Just then, several nurses, including the one Matt had just spoken to, ran past the waiting room. Matt jumped up and ran to the door. They went down the ICU hall to where Bethany's room was, but the door closed and locked behind them...then he noticed an orderly heading toward it.

"Excuse me!" Matt called to him. "Could you hold the…"

That's when the orderly turned to face him and he saw that it was Rusty...smiling at him as he went through the doorway.

"NOOO!!!" Matt screamed and banged on the door.

"Matthew!" Mrs. Gilmore called out to him and he turned to face her. "Let's pray!"


## *ST. AUGUSTINE, FLORIDA*

As Jonah and Wayne sat at the foot of Catherine's bed praying, her body began to twitch and convulse. One of the machines that was hooked up to her began to beep and an alarm went off. Both men looked up and saw that she was shaking violently. Wayne immediately ran to her side.

"HELLOOOO!!!???" He screamed toward the hall as Jonah swung the door open to run out.

A doctor and three nurses ran into the room almost immediately and one of the nurses pushed both men out into the hall. "Give us a few minutes to see what's happening!"

"But...what's she!!!???" Wayne was a mess. "I can't lose her, Jonah!"



✝

Jonah placed his hand on Wayne's shoulder and squeezed. "Trust God, my friend…" was all he could think to say. He began to pray out loud for Catherine. As he prayed, he heard the shuffling of feet at the other end of the hall. He glanced in that direction and saw Him...the old gentleman was sitting down with His back to the wall, reading what appeared to be a newspaper. Jonah smiled and continued to pray. When he looked back, the Holy Spirit was gone.

"Thank you, Jonah," Wayne said. "I felt a peace when you were praying." He stepped away, "Excuse me, I never did get in touch with her family, I need to call them."


## *VALLEY OF THE SHADOW OF DEATH*

The dragon moved closer with one swift motion. Bethany and Brandy held their ground, looking up at him while praying under their breath. "That's right, Bethany McGee!" He roared. "Matt Ramsey was my target ALL ALONG!!! I intend to remove everyone he loves from his life...until he stands alone, begging ME for mercy!!!!" His laughter shakes the entire valley, even startling the demons and creatures that surround him. "I, of course, will show him NONE!!! But I will gladly have his soul dragged to hell after he denies the God who has abandoned him!!!"

"That's where you're wrong, you LYING STENCH!!!" Bethany yelled over the brewing storm. "As long as MY God is in heaven, Matthew will NEVER be alone!!!" She took a step toward him and pointed a finger directly at his face. "And you're the only one getting dragged to hell you deceived serpent!!!"

"ENOUGH!!!" He raised his long neck upward and roared. "DEATH!!! SHOW THEM YOUR STING!!!"



✝

*GATEWAY, FLORIDA*

Several other people ran in and out of the doorway to the ICU while Matt and Mrs. Gilmore stood there praying. Matt could hear shouting coming from down the hall every time the door opened. He was so happy that Mrs. Gilmore was there to lead the prayer, because he would probably be down there getting yelled at and kicked out.

"And, Father God!" Mrs. Gilmore continued. "I pray that you would protect and guide Matthew, here!" She squeezed his shoulder. "Give him the wisdom of your Holy Spirit, I pray! I know, God, that you have BIG plans for Matthew; I've known this for a long time. Prepare him, Father, for what lies ahead in his life. Your will be done, of course, but I think he'd make an AMAZING son in law."

Matt couldn't help but grin at that last part. He opened his eyes and shook his head. "Yeah, in my dreams…"

"Trust me, Matthew...in her dreams too."

As the door swung open one more time, Matt heard a male voice shout, "Come ON!!! We're losing her!!!" His legs buckled and he swayed toward the floor.

"Jesus!" Mrs. Gilmore called out. "Save my daughter!!!"

*VALLEY OF THE SHADOW OF DEATH*

Two massive hands formed in the clouds and began to move toward them. Brandy screamed and grabbed on to Bethany. The demons moved in closer and pushed them both to the ground. The demons were laughing and sneering. The sky grew darker and the clouds above them swirled as if a tornado were forming.

"Bethany!" Brandy screamed. "Are we about to die!?"



✝

"Trust Jesus, Brandy!" Bethany yelled back through the sounds of the storm and the creatures. "Trust Him, regardless! This weapon WILL NOT PROSPER!!!"

The giant hands wrapped around each of the women and lifted them off the ground. The demons and the creatures all began to cheer. The dragon let out an earth shaking roar of victory. They were lifted higher and higher into the air. The sky itself was alive and the thunder and lightning was nonstop. Boom after ground shaking boom as the women were lifted higher toward the sky.

"IT'S OVER FOR YOU, BETHANY MCGEE!!!" The dragon roared. "AND YOUR NEW FRIEND IS ABOUT TO BE CAST INTO THE PITS OF HELL!!!" He laughed again.

"Liar!!!" Bethany screamed. "Don't listen to his lies, Brandy!!!"

"She knows her prayers were made in fear!" the dragon replied. "They didn't count...did they, Brandy!?" He laughed. "You don't even know your own name! Your mind isn't right! Your prayers weren't even heard! YOU'RE ABOUT TO GO TO HELL FOREVER! CATHERINE LUTRINGER!!!"


*JACKSONVILLE, FLORIDA*

Officer Ramsey was just getting off work after pulling a double shift. Several city-wide human trafficking sting operations had needed all hands-on deck, and he had been going nonstop for the past eighteen hours. Now, he was exhausted. Having grabbed a cup of coffee before heading to his car, he checked his phone and saw where his brother-in-law, Wayne, had tried to call him several times over the past few hours. He hoped everything was okay with his sister, who was battling brain cancer. Quickly he hit Wayne's number and called him. Wayne picked up on the first ring.



✝

"There you are, Lieutenant!" Wayne said, seeming exasperated. "I haven't been able to find either one of you!"

"Well, I've been working a double shift undercover and my lovely bride is volunteering at a homeless shelter for the day. I'm heading over to pick her up now...is everything okay? How's Cat?"

"She had an episode yesterday," Wayne began. "And when I brought her in, they rushed her in for surgery."

"Oh my...so what are they saying?"

"Well, I'm not sure what's going on right now," Wayne said, clearly choked up. "She was sleeping in her room when all of a sudden she began to convulse...everybody seems shaken...it doesn't look promising…"

"Listen, Wayne," Officer Ramsey said. "We'll be there as soon as we can...you're at Flagler Hospital, right?"

"Yes," he responded and then someone spoke to him and he clicked off the call.


## *VALLEY OF THE SHADOW OF DEATH*

"NO!!!" Brandy, or Catherine screamed. "LET ME GO!!! I KNOW I'M SAVED, YOU EVIL LIZARD!!! YOU'RE THE ONE GOING TO HELL!!"

Bethany couldn't help but smile, although she needed to wrap her brain around Catherine being her name.

The storm grew louder and the black clouds began to envelope the women.

"Hold strong, Catherine!" Bethany yelled. "No matter what happens, God is in control!"

The dragon laughed, whipped his tail in anger and let out a final roar. "DEATH! I COMMAND YOU TO TAKE THEM…."



✝

It was at that very moment that a bright light pierced through the black clouds and seemed to drive them away. The thunder ceased and the face in the clouds seemed to let out a dull groan.

"Bethany!" Catherine yelled. "What is happening!?"

"I'm not sure, Catherine, but I think we're being rescued!" Bethany replied, trying to see through the piercing light to its source.

"NOOOO!!!" the dragon roared. "THIS IS MY DOMAIN!!!"

"OH DEATH!!!" a powerful voice commanded from directly within the light. "WHERE IS YOUR STING!!!??? OH GRAVE!!! WHERE IS YOUR VICTORY!!! KNEEL BEFORE YOUR KING!!!"

"NEVER!!!" came a voice from the clouds. "YOU ARE NO KING OF MINE!!!"

"YOU WILL HEED MY WORDS NONE THE LESS!!!" the smooth as glass voice spoke with confidence. "EVERY KNEE WILL BOW; EVERY TONGUE CONFESS THAT I AM LORD!!!"

"It's Jesus!" Bethany cried out and began to sob. "Thank you, Jesus!" She had no idea what was about to happen, but all her worry and concern seemed to melt away at the sound of His voice. She could hear Catherine thanking Him as well.

Then….the storm went silent. Both women were standing on the ground, looking around in every direction. The dragon, every demon, and every creature were gone. They stood there alone...and began to laugh. They reached out to embrace one another when…


## ST. AUGUSTINE, FLORIDA

A nurse had moved Wayne and Jonah down to the closest waiting room. She told Wayne that Dr. Andrews would be by to see



✝

him in a few moments. That was two hours ago. He was beside himself with worry, pacing back and forth. "What is taking so long, Jonah!?"

"It's a hospital, Wayne...you just have to be patient." He was also getting a little concerned about the long delay. Not to mention, the nurses were keeping their lips sealed. All they would say was that the doctor would come by when he could. When he could? What did that mean? "Just keep praying, my friend."

Just then, there was a rap on the door and Dr. Andrews, a tall, thin older man who looked as tired as Jonah felt, walked in. "Mr. Lutringer?"

"Yes?" Wayne replied, turning toward the man. "How is she, Doctor? Is she still…" He choked up, unable to finish his sentence.

"Could you step out into the hall, Mr…"

"It's okay," Wayne said. "Jonah is sort of my Pastor...he can hear this."

The doctor nodded. "Well, Mr. Lutringer, I have to say...Catherine gave us quite the scare. In fact, we lost her for about ninety-three seconds." He pulled out a handkerchief and wiped his brow. "In fact, to be honest with you, I don't know how we got her back...or anything really." He looked from Wayne to Jonah. "You fellows must've been praying hard is all I can say, because not only did we bring her back...but after running a few emergency tests on her...the reason you had to wait so long. It appears that every single bit of cancer is completely gone. Not a trace."

At that...Wayne just crumbled into Jonah's arms and cried. "Thank you, Jesus!"



✝

After what seemed like an eternity, a young doctor walked out into the hall and found Matt and Mrs. Gilmore leaning against the wall with their eyes closed in prayer. He removed the mask from his mouth and asked, "Mrs. Gilmore?"

Her eyes shot open and within a second, her and Matt filled the gap between them and the doctor. "What's going on, Doctor!? Is my baby alright?" A sob escaped before she could stop it, and she placed her hand over her mouth.

"Yes, Ma'am," the doctor replied in what seemed like a surprised tone. "Somehow, miraculously...she IS alright." He wiped a tear away that seemed to escape the corner of his eye and stepped back. "I've never seen anything like it. We literally lost her three times!" He grinned and looked at them both. "Whoever you were praying to was working overtime."

"IT WAS JESUS!!!" Matt shouted and spun around. "THANK YOU, JESUS!!!"

"Thank you, Doctor!" Mrs. Gilmore replied with a huge sigh. "When can we see her?"

"She'll need to remain in recovery for another hour, but I'll have a nurse notify you when she's back in her room."

Mrs. Gilmore and Matt hugged each other. "Oh, Matthew! God is SO good!"

"Yes, He is!" Matt replied. "I need to let everybody know!"

"OH!!!" she replied. "SO DO I!!!! I'll text the family, you take everyone else!" She turned toward the waiting room just as one of the Gateway police officers made his way down the hall.

"Officer Butler!" Matt called out. His dad had worked with Officer or Captain Butler for many years. He was a dear friend of the family. "Bethany is okay! The doctor said it was a miracle!"



✝

"That's great, Matt," Captain Butler replied, and stopped Mrs. Gilmore as she walked by. "Pastor Brian said I could find you here." He looked solemnly at Matt and lowered his head.

"What's wrong, Wally?" Mrs. Gilmore asked "Is everything..."

"Matthew, your parents were killed in a car accident in St. Augustine about an hour ago... I'm so sorry..."



✝

# CHAPTER 15

*PENNINGTON SPRINGS, TENNESSEE*

Brianna couldn't believe the things that had transpired since she'd arrived here just a couple of days ago. Three people had died...one that should've been her. Poor Christina...so full of life. So happy with the life her and Tyler had built for themselves. Doing so much good in the world. How could God...she couldn't think like that.

It was God's plan...his story...not hers. She hadn't read her Bible today...and other than with a few people on the phone...she hadn't prayed either. She needed that time with her best friend. Her spirit stirred, and come to think about it, she hadn't seen or heard from the Holy Spirit either...not since before going into the woods to look for Harley. She closed her eyes and took a deep breath. "I need you, old friend..."

Her phone chirped on the nightstand beside where she sat on the bed. She looked over to see a message from Jason. "You on your way?" Dinner at the Chief's.

She stood and headed for the bathroom where she checked her hair and let out a long sigh. She didn't feel like being social, but with flying out tomorrow morning, this would probably be the last time she'd see Jerry and Carolyn. She also knew that it would probably be a long time before she'd see Jason again. She put on her best smile and headed for the door. "Heading out now," she replied to Jason.

*ATLANTA, GEORGIA*

*Hartsfield-Jackson Atlanta International Airport*

The gang had landed safely in Atlanta after the nine plus hour flight from Morocco. There hadn't even been any issues with booking the flight together....and for their extremely large group, that had



†

been a miracle. When they tried to book a flight to Jacksonville from Atlanta, however, they were told they would have to split up and fly separately. Several of the crew that had children waiting for them were allowed on the first flight, along with Andy and Eddie...who just needed to get home to be there for Matt. They had all been devastated when the news came through about his parents.

That left Mark, Scotty, Gabi, Yvette, Dustin, and a few other crew members in Atlanta until the next flight departed for Jacksonville in three hours. Mark sat in a chair in the terminal watching everyone's luggage and talking on a video call with Maria and the boys. His call to Brianna had gone to voicemail. The others roamed the airport stores aimlessly.

Dustin was browsing some ridiculously priced golf shirts in one of the shops when someone brushed against him. He turned to look into the eyes of the most beautiful woman he'd ever seen.

"Excuse me," the beautiful blonde said with a sly smile and continued on. She briefly glanced back to see if he was still watching her...he was.

"Whatcha doin'?" Yvette asked, bringing him back to reality.

Dustin shook his head and felt instantly guilty for checking out the extremely hot blonde. "Just killing time...how about you?"

"Same," Yvette replied. "Hey, I slept through most of that flight and didn't get to talk to you again, but let me say it once again, you were amazing...how you just stepped in like you've been leading worship your whole life."

Dustin smiled. "Yeah, thanks...I was actually terrified."

"Well, it didn't show," she replied. "You have amazing stage presence...and your voice...I could listen to you sing forever."

135

✝

"That's very kind of you, Yvette," Dustin said. "You're pretty amazing yourself...not just your story, but how you sort of orchestrate the entire event. It's your calling."

Yvette blushed about three shades of red and turned her head away. "I really love what I do."

"It shows," Dustin replied. "I look forward to working with you in future events...if, you know, that's what God wants me to keep doing...I'm still trying to figure all this out."

"That would be nice," she smiled. "Us working together...well I'll leave you to your browsing, I need to find the little girl's room and go see if Mark is okay."

He smiled and nodded as she walked away. He liked Yvette...she was different from all the girls he'd previously hung out with. She was professional, smart, and super saved...was that a thing? Still, he needed to take everything slow until he got his Christian 'sea legs' under him so to speak. He turned around and found himself slightly disappointed that the blonde was gone. "What's wrong with you, Dustin? Old habits die hard, I guess. Please help me, Holy Spirit."


*PENNINGTON SPRINGS, TENNESSEE*

Brianna sat listening to Chief Jerry tell story after story about various silly and crazy cases they'd had in the small town of Pennington Springs over his many years on the force. Until recently, speeding was the worst crime to be committed, except for the time Wallace Cunningham was caught with Jasper Murphy's chickens in his living room. Jerry had to make his first arrest over that incident.

"Remember that time, Pastor Jason, when I had to come get your assistance over Thelma Thompson's daughter pretending she was possessed by the devil?"



✝

Jason almost spit out his tea laughing at that one. "Yeah, picture this, Brianna...we walk into the living room of this small trailer and this little girl of about five or six is laying on the floor reading a book, but as soon as she realizes we're there...she starts growling and writhing around. Her mama just sat there on the couch shaking her head and rolling her eyes."

"She said," Jerry continued. "I have NO idea where she got this from but she's relentless! What can you do, Preacher!?"

Brianna laughed. "So, what DID you do?"

"I said," Jason replied. "Well, we have two options here Mrs. Thompson...one...we can pray over her...and then, if that doesn't work...we'll have to stick her in the fireplace and burn that devil out! Devils don't like fire, you know!"

"And she said, do what you have to, Preacher!" Jerry said, with a laugh. "But little Shelby's eyes got big and she calmed down.

"She grunted in a deep voice, pray for me!" Jason said, with tears rolling down his cheeks he was laughing so hard. "And we did...and she never had that devil bother her again!"

"Well, praise the Lord!" Brianna said with a snort. Just then, Carolyn came out of the kitchen with a large platter of food.

"Speaking of praising the Lord!" Chief Jerry said. "Look at this beautiful woman coming over here!!! With food no less!"

They all laughed and Brianna got up and helped Carolyn bring everything out of the kitchen. They took their seats and it was at that moment that the atmosphere seemed to change. They all took each other's hands and bowed their heads.

"Holy God," Chief Jerry began. "We thank you! We praise you! We glorify you! Though sometimes our circumstances appear to be grim and hopeless, You are ALWAYS true to Your word. It's that word we stand on. It's that word that we place our hope...our



✝

faith...our lives. Thank You for this food, Father. Bless it in Jesus' name...and everybody said..."

"AMEN!"

*ATLANTA, GEORGIA*

*Hartsfield-Jackson Atlanta International Airport*

They'd finally been allowed to board the plane, and it was then that they realized exactly how far apart they'd been placed. Scotty and Gabi were the only ones that had managed to get seats together, while the others were scattered all over.

Yvette was sitting in the very front of the plane next to an older, overweight man who was breathing heavy after finally getting his bag into an overhead compartment. She had the window seat and attempted to hug the wall for all she was worth...giving him as much room as she could. She couldn't help but wonder how far back Dustin was. Dustin Knight...so handsome...so talented...so...dangerous.

She knew better than to let her mind wander, but he was so intoxicating. "Calm yourself, Yvette," she thought. "He's a new believer and needs to grow before you go putting your claws in him." She closed her eyes and said a prayer for herself and even threw one towards Dustin. If God wanted them to be together, then this was His problem. She would do her best to cast it His way as often as she needed to.

Mark was sitting about five rows behind Yvette. His heart was heavy for so many reasons. There was definitely an assault from the enemy happening and it felt strangely familiar. He wasn't sure why he'd thought these things were behind them. The Bible promised that we would have peace in the storm, almost guaranteeing that there would be storms. Even Jesus faced storms for crying out loud.

138

✝

Matt and Gabi had both mentioned seeing Rusty and even in the brief conversation he'd had with Bethany, she'd mentioned him being back and seeing him in the Valley. "What's happening, God?" he asked aloud and the man beside him glanced over. Mark covered his face and began to pray. There was a storm coming...he just had to trust that Jesus was on the boat with them.

"WHAT!!!???" Scotty Morgan yelled from several rows back, causing people to glance back uncomfortably. A flight attendant looked in his direction. "ARE YOU SERIOUS!!!??? HEY, EVERYBODY!!! MARK!!! I'M HAVING A BABY!!! I MEAN WE'RE...GABI IS PREGNANT!!!"

Everyone on the plane laughed and applauded Scotty and he reached down and squeezed his blushing wife. "So much for keeping it quiet," she whispered in his ear when he sat back down.

"Sorry not sorry!" he smiled at her with more excitement than he'd experienced in his entire life. "I'm going to be a daddy!"

"Congratulations, Scotty and Gabi!" Dustin called from the back of the plane. "That's so exciting!" That's when he saw her...the blonde from the gift shop...walking toward him. "Oh no," he thought. "The only empty seat on the plane is next to me and she's heading this...." "Hi," he said out loud as she slid into the seat and set her small bag between her feet.

"Hello," she held out her hand. "You're Dustin Knight, aren't you?"

He was taken aback, remembering that he'd actually released a few songs and had been a hot ticket for a brief moment. "I am..." He shook her hand.

"Sorry, but what are the chances I'd be sitting next to the biggest crush I've ever had?" She touched his leg as she spoke and he pulled away. "Can I take a picture of us?" Before he could answer, her phone was in the air and he was staring at the two of them in the



✝

screen. He attempted his best smile and tried to relax. It's only a short flight. He could do this. She wasn't that hot...yeah, right. "By the way, I'm Jessie."

"Nice to meet you, Jessie," Dustin replied. "So, do you live in Jacksonville?"

"No, going on business...just outside of Jacksonville. What about you?"

"I'm actually heading just outside of Jacksonville myself." Dustin said. "Gateway...I'll be staying with some friends...they just announced they're having a baby." He pointed toward Scotty and Gabi.

"Oh yeah, he seemed just a little excited," she replied with a smile and looked away. "How do you know them?"

"Something you may not know about me yet," Dustin answered. "Is that I decided to become a Christian."

She whipped her head around and seemed to study his eyes. "You're kidding, right?"

"Nope," he replied. "I've recently given my life to…"

"DUSTIN!" she yelled, catching him off guard. To his relief, nobody seemed to pay her outburst any attention. "You can't...NO...listen to me."

Just then, the flight attendant began to prepare them for departure and asked for everyone's attention.

"Dustin," Jessie leaned close and whispered. "There are so many things better than Christianity that you can get involved with. I can help you." She placed her hand on his arm and a shiver shot down his spine.

He instinctively pulled his arm away and gave her a sideways glance. "Don't be silly...what could be better than the one true God?"



✝

That statement caused her to snort. "Don't be stupid, Dustin," Jessie replied. "You're smarter than this."

"What do you actually know about Jesus?" he asked outright. "Sounds like you may have had a bad experience."

The flight attendant finished her speech and told them they would be departing in a few moments and to remain in their seats.

"Oh, I've had a bad experience alright!" Jessie replied, with fire in her eyes. "Your Jesus can…" she paused her rant and gave him an innocent smile. "Sorry…it's not your fault. Just trust me, Dustin…no good will come from following that…Jewish fraud." With that she unbuckled her seat belt, grabbed her bag, and stood up.

"Um, I think we're supposed to remain in our seats," Dustin said.

"I need to go to the ladies' room," Jessie replied and turned toward the back room.

Moments later they began to taxi down the runway and within seconds they were airborne. Jessie had still not returned. At the first sign of a flight attendant, Dustin waved her over. "Excuse me, but the woman that was sitting here...she went to the bathroom just before takeoff and she hasn't returned."

"Who?" the flight attendant asked, taking a small pad from her pocket and checking it.

"The blonde woman that was sitting here," Dustin replied. "She said her name was Jessie."

"I'm showing this seat to be open, sir," the woman replied. "Besides, the door shows the bathroom to be vacant. She must've gone to her actual seat and you just didn't see her."

A creepy feeling washed over Dustin and he just nodded. "That must be what happened."

141

✝

When Brianna got back to her room, she started getting ready for bed. She had an early flight home to Florida, then she would have to get ready to fly to New York to be with Tyler, Christina's grieving husband. As she brushed her teeth, she thought about her dreams, how they felt so real. So weird, a little boy trying to hurt or even kill her. Were they memories? She was apparently a small child in the dreams. Maybe she could ask her mom. She knew that her mom had occasionally babysat other kids when she was young, but Brianna could barely remember any of them. "Are these dreams significant, Holy Spirit?" He was still silent. She would need to pray for a peaceful night's sleep before she got in bed.

She finished getting ready and walked out of the bathroom. The television was on and the news started talking about Harley. They were saying that the state police were now taking over the case. They were trying to find out why Chief Jerry had kept all the murders quiet. Brianna knew that was not the case. He had worked not only with the state, but the FBI as well. The media was just upset that they had been kept out of the loop.

Sitting on the edge of the bed, Brianna grabbed her phone and sent her mom a text. Knowing her mom would want to chat about everything that had been going on, she didn't have the energy to call her. "Hey Mom, silly question. When I was an infant, did you babysit a little boy that was maybe troubled or creepy or I don't know...suspicious? Anyway, heading to bed. Love you! See you guys in the morning, don't forget to pick me up at the airport. I'll text you when I board."

She turned out the light and climbed into bed. As soon as she closed her eyes, sleep overtook her. Not a thought from the day haunted her. Not a care in the world.

The demons outside her window smiled as they watched her fall into a deep, exhausted sleep, having forgotten to pray. "Sleep well, Brianna Bowers...it's your last night alive."



✝

# CHAPTER 16

*ST. AUGUSTINE, FLORIDA*

Jonah had been asked by Wayne to join him when he went in to see his wife, Catherine. The doctors had warned them that she'd been talking nonsense, but otherwise seemed to be doing good.

When the guys walked in, she'd smiled groggily at them and said, "Hey, Babe, have I got, a story, for you...who's your friend?" She stared at Jonah in complete confusion.

"Hey Cat," Wayne said, walking over and kissing his wife on the forehead. "This is my new friend, Jonah. How are you feeling?"

"Cat?" she replied in deep thought. "My name IS Catherine...not Brandy..."

Wayne glanced at Jonah and smiled. "Brandy?"

"Bethany called me Brandy because I couldn't remember my name," Catherine replied with a distant look.

Wayne slid her hair behind her ear and combed it with his fingers. "Wow, Babe, it sounds like some dream you had."

"No!" Catherine responded, trying to sit up, but Wayne held her down. "No, it wasn't a dream...not at all...it was so real!"

"Calm down, Cat," Wayne whispered in her ear and continued rubbing her hair. "Don't work yourself up."

"Just listen!" she said in a calm voice, closing her eyes and catching her breath. "I was in a place; it was what she called the Valley of the Shadow of Death...with this young woman named Bethany...she'd been in a car crash. Somehow, we were both there. It's apparently where you go to wait for Death...and oh, Death is an actual person...well, not a person, but a living being. That's actually funny if you think about it...Death is living."



✝

Wayne and Jonah shared a look.

"I know this sounds crazy, but it's true! Honey, I prayed to give my life to Jesus! I'm a believer now!" Catherine announced. Both men stood up straight and Wayne started to cry. "What? What is it, Wayne?"

"He gave his life to Jesus as well," Jonah replied when he saw that Wayne was too choked up. "That's where I come in." Wayne could only nod and squeeze his wife's shoulder. They both hugged and sobbed together. Jonah stepped out of the room and pulled out his phone. He knew Brianna would be asleep, so he didn't want to bother her, but she'd given him Mark's number if he ever needed to talk to a guy about Christian stuff. He knew that Mark was back in America and shot him a quick text. "Hey Mark, it's Jonah, Brianna's friend. I hope your flight was good. I have a crazy question to ask you!"

Within seconds the reply came. "Hey Jonah! Just landed in Jacksonville and about to head home!  What's up?"

"Have you ever heard of the Valley of the Shadow of Death?"

"Wait...WHAT!?"

Jonah's phone immediately rang...it was Mark. "Hey, Dude!" Jonah said.

"Why do you ask!?" Mark sounded shocked. "What's happened?"

"Long story short, I'm here in St. Augustine in the hospital with a couple that God sent me to minister to...and the woman was basically in a coma with brain cancer. She suddenly woke up, completely healed and starts telling us about meeting some girl named Bethany in a place called the Valley of the Shadow of Death! Is she crazy?"



✝

"Jonah," Mark said. "I literally spoke to my sister, Bethany, about an hour ago and she told me she was there! It's a real place, Bro! I've been there myself!"

Jonah couldn't stop the tears...or the chills. "Holy…WOW!!! Are you kidding me!?"


## PENNINGTON SPRINGS, TENNESSEE

A child was screaming...no, wait. It was her. Why did she sound like a baby? Oh, her mother was holding her...rocking her in her arms. Her mom looked so young...so beautiful, so...upset. Why were there tears in her eyes? That's when she noticed the lights. The flashing blue lights dancing off the wall behind her mother.

"It's okay, Bree...Mommy has you now...everything's gonna be alright." Her mother wiped a tear that slid down her cheek. She pulled Brianna up close to her chest and held her tight.

"Excuse me, Ma'am, you said the boy headed back into the forest?" A man's voice from behind Brianna asked. Her mother nodded.

"Have you not found him!?" She asked in a panic. "That's where he lives! In that god-awful…"

"Ma'am, we've been in there, and Mr. Willoughby has informed us that no child lives at that... residence."

"Well, he's lying!" her mother said. "I've been taking care of him for weeks...that's where he comes from and that's where he goes!"

"But have you ever actually seen where he goes? Have you ever seen him with an adult? You told us earlier that he just showed up one day and said that his mother needed to find someone to keep him…"



✝

"Yes, she wrote a note that she was away a lot on business and that he was a very smart boy, he could basically take care of himself at his young age, but she didn't want to get in trouble with the authorities for leaving him alone."

"So, you've never met her?" the man asked. "According to Mr. Willoughby, there's no woman that lives there either."

"No, he would come out of the forest every morning and on Fridays he would have cash to pay me."

"Has he ever done anything like this before? Anything to harm your child?"

"Thinking back now...I think so. Brianna would scream a lot when they were alone. He's very smart, Officer. I mean, for his age. He MUST be gifted."

"Well, we have several officers scouring the area. I'm sure the boy will turn up. I'm sorry, I know you told the other officer, but what was his name again?"

"Micky...Micky Nesmith...he was so proud of that name. He would say it to himself over and over."

✝

Brianna jumped awake with a loud gasp and found herself covered in sweat. She had to remind herself where she was. Pennington Springs, Tennessee, at an Inn. The dream...the name...Nesmith! No way!

Something moved out of the corner of her eye and before she could react, she was pinned to the bed by two very strong hands. She struggled to free herself but whoever it was had a powerful grip on her wrists. Her eyes adjusted slowly and the large man holding her down was wearing a ski mask and breathing very hard. His breath was atrocious, and she tried to turn her face away from it. He lifted her arms over her head and held them with one hand against the

147

✝

headboard...then pulled a syringe from his jacket pocket with the other hand and quickly jabbed it into her arm. Her body immediately began to relax and there was nothing she could do about it. He let go of her and stepped back, raising up. He panted as he reached up and removed his mask.

"Hello, Brianna Bowers..." Michael Nesmith, the town's Medical Examiner said, smiling down at her. "I've waited a long time for this." She closed her eyes in surrender.


*GATEWAY, FLORIDA*

Mark awoke with a jolt and sat upright looking around the room. He was home. His beautiful wife was asleep beside him, breathing softly.

"Pray," the still, small voice whispered in his ear.

"Yes sir," he said softly into the night, sliding out from under the covers and padding out of the room, grabbing his robe from the door. He headed to the kitchen and started up his Keurig. If he'd learned anything in his life, it was that when God woke him up to pray, it was usually an all-night battle.

"Pray...now," the voice seemed urgent.

Mark abandoned the kitchen and headed to his study. A pain shot through his stomach like he'd never experienced. He bowed over and his knees hit the ground.

"Brianna Bowers...pray for Brianna!"

Mark lay prostrate on his office floor and cried out to God on behalf of Brianna...completely and totally lost in the presence of his Lord. He couldn't discern most of what he prayed, but he knew there was a fight going on in the spirit realm and God was using his prayers for the strengthening of his army.



✝

Jonah had been offered the opportunity to stay at Wayne and Catherine's house for the night.  Wayne was spending the night in the hospital with his wife, so Jonah chose to just get a hotel room nearby. He'd fallen asleep almost as soon as his head hit the pillow.

He'd been allowed to stay at the hospital for quite some time after visiting hours had ended. Wayne joked that the nurses might have a crush on Jonah and that was why they hadn't kicked them out. The three of them rejoiced in the couple's stories of salvation and praised God at Catherine's total healing...something the doctors were still amazed by...leading to further tests.

Wayne and Catherine also told Jonah their story. How they'd met in the small town of Friendsville, Tennessee...population 903. Catherine had often visited as a child, because she had family there. They'd been best friends ever since the summer of first grade when Wayne stood up to a bully who was picking on Catherine. "She was a very large and intimidating bully…" he joked.

They had a good laugh. Jonah really enjoyed their company. He'd planned to stop by in the morning and pray with them, say his goodbyes and head to Gateway. He'd get to meet all of Brianna's friends who he had just found out were now, finally, back in the country.

Jonah woke up and glanced over at the red numbers on the clock beside his bed. It was just after four. He'd been asleep for over four hours. He slid out from the covers and walked to the bathroom.

When he came back out and headed for the bed, a voice from the corner said, "Good morning, Jonah...how are you?"

It surprised Jonah how an audible voice in the middle of the night in a strange hotel room brought him peace and not sheer terror. He smiled at the silhouette of the older gentleman sitting near the window with his fedora still on. "Good morning, Holy Spirit...I'm



✝

excellent, thank you." He reached over and turned on the lamp that sat on the nightstand.

"Come," the Holy Spirit motioned for Jonah to sit in the chair next to him. "We need to talk."

"Yes sir," Jonah replied and walked over, not feeling in the least bit embarrassed that he was only wearing his boxers.

"Jonah, do you trust me?" the Holy Spirit asked, removing his old gray hat.

"Of course I do, sir," Jonah replied.

"I mean...really truly trust me...no matter what happens?"

Something about the way He said it, the seriousness in His voice, the look in His eyes made Jonah feel...nervous...terrified even. "Yes...I trust you with my very life."

"Every part of it?"

"I would die for you," Jonah replied, knowing this to be a fact with every fiber of his being.

"But, Jonah Westbrook...would you live for me...if I took everything from you?"

"I have nothing...nothing that isn't already yours...is there something else I have that I…"

"Brianna Bowers?"

Jonah only stared at Him...what did that mean? It was a question, not a statement.

"What if I took her?"

"I...I...what do you…"

"Do you remember reading about when the storm hit the disciples when they were on the lake? How they were afraid even while Jesus was in the boat with them?"

**150**

✝

Jonah nodded. "I remember...they woke Him up in a panic, and He rebuked them for their lack of faith."

"Well, remember that story, Jonah...for an even greater storm is coming." He stood up and placed His hand on Jonah's shoulder. "You did well on your last mission...now listen closely."

## GATEWAY, FLORIDA

Mark had no idea how long he'd been praying, but he did notice that the sun was starting to come through the window of his office. He raised his head up and opened his eyes and that's when he realized that Maria, his beautiful wife, was lying beside him, deep in prayer. He couldn't help but smile as he sat up on the floor feeling the stiffness in his back. "Thank you for my amazing, supportive wife, Holy Spirit," he whispered. As he grabbed the desk to pull himself up, he heard her stir.

"Hey there, my handsome warrior of a husband," she said, as she raised her head. He helped her to her feet and they hugged. "Brianna?" she asked with her head cocked to the side.

"Yep," Mark replied. "But it feels different this time."

"Should we call her?" Maria asked, as she attempted to stretch out her back.

"Yes," Mark answered. "But first...coffee." They both headed to the kitchen. The boys were at Mark's parents...allowing Mark and Maria for a nice, quiet evening together after being apart.

"Why don't I put the coffee on while you call Brianna?" Maria said.

"Yes, Dear," he replied and headed back to the bedroom to retrieve his phone. He picked it up and called Brianna. It rang several times and went to voicemail. "Hey, Brianna! It's Mark! Just checking up on you! Making sure everything is okay. Give us a call at your earliest convenience." He headed back to the kitchen and reported to his wife that Brianna had not answered her phone. Just then, their doorbell rang, causing both of them to tense up. "I'll get it," Mark said, but Maria followed him to the front door.

He opened the door and was taken aback to see Scotty, Gabi, Yvette, and some other guy standing on his front porch. All of them looking very serious. "Whoa…"

"Hey guys!" Maria said. "What's going on!?"

"We were told to come here immediately!" Scotty replied.

"By whom?" Mark asked.

Scotty glanced over his shoulder at the tall, good-looking guy standing at the back. "Jonah?"

Jonah smiled at Mark and Maria… "Um," he cleared his throat. "The Holy Spirit."

Mark only nodded and stepped aside as the motley crew walked into his house. He shook Jonah's hand and told him it was nice to finally meet him. They all gathered in the living room and Maria offered them coffee.

"Has anyone spoken with her yet?" Mark asked, assuming they all knew this was about Brianna.

"She isn't answering her phone, but I was hoping you would call Jas…" Gabi was saying when Mark's phone rang.

He looked down at it. "It's Brianna!" he declared with a big smile and answered it. "Brianna!? Is…oh, hey Jason! Hold on! I've got the whole gang here, let me put you on speaker. We've all sort of been called to pray for Brianna this morning…is everything alright?"

"No guys, it's not…" Jason replied. "I showed up this morning to pick up Brianna to take her to the airport and her door was open…" Jason sounded like he'd been crying. "It appears that



✝

Brianna is missing. All her things are here, but she's gone. Guys, we supposedly got the guy that was after her! What's going on!?"



✝

# CHAPTER 17



Captain Butler was sitting at his desk in the Gateway Police Department, working on paperwork from a routine traffic stop yesterday. It had led to an altercation with a woman who'd had a little too much to drink. His mind kept going back to Ramsey. He lowered his head and fought the urge to let the tears flow.

He and Ramsey had worked together for a long time before Ramsey had transferred to Jacksonville. They'd been friends for as long as he could remember...7th grade, actually. He smiled back to when he'd first met him. He'd been standing at the bus stop with some friends when this kid walks up wearing shorts and a t-shirt, with cowboy boots and knee high socks. His friends had started snickering but he had compassion on the newcomer who'd just moved into the neighborhood.

He became Ramsey's protector that day, knowing that every bully in Gateway Middle would have a field day with him otherwise. He found out that they shared a love for music and within weeks they were inseparable. Even though he'd been known as a troublemaker in the neighborhood previously, Ramsey's parents had taken him in and treated him like he was family. They were the reason he'd straightened up, gone to college, and eventually became a police officer.

Now...he couldn't believe that Lieutenant Ramsey was dead. He and his wife had been heading to St. Augustine to see his sister in the hospital. A semi-truck lost control and flew right into their lane, killing them both instantly. He'd been in shock when he'd taken the call...and then to have to break the news to Matt. That was one of the worst things he'd ever had to do. The poor kid had just moved back home to be with them...



✝

"CAPTAIN!" one of his officers yelled from the front office, bringing him back to reality. "911 calls are pouring in! Active shooter at Gateway High!!!"

Jumping up from his seat, he grabbed his vest from behind him and slipped it on. "Call everybody in!!! Get JSO on the call, give me everything you know!!!"


## *PENNINGTON SPRINGS, TENNESSEE*

Chief Jerry was coordinating a search party to canvas the entire town. About forty-five people were there to volunteer in the search and rescue of Brianna Bowers. Unfortunately, they had absolutely no leads. Someone had apparently jimmied her door open from the hallway, entered the room, and taken her from her bed. There was no sign of a struggle, which told him that she'd most likely been drugged.

"Who could've done this, Chief?" Pastor Jason asked. "We got Harley! Did he have an accomplice? Was Harley not the guy!?"

"I don't know, Pastor!" Chief Jerry replied. "I thought this nightmare was behind us."

"Was there anything on her phone that could be a clue?" Pastor Jason asked.

She sent her mom a text after getting back to her room from having dinner with us. Something about a kid she used to babysit."

"Her mom!" Jason said. "I should let her know." Using Brianna's phone, he obtained her number and dialed it on his own phone.

"Hello?" a woman answered.

"Mrs. Bowers?" Jason asked.

"Yes, this is she…" she replied.



✝

"This is Jason Green, do you…"

"As I live and breathe!" she screamed into the phone. "Pastor Jason Green! It's so good to hear your voice! I always loved your energy! So crazy and fun to be around!"

"Oh, well thank you!" Jason would have to remember this compliment later, but for now he had to focus. "Mrs. Bowers, have you heard from Brianna recently?"

"No…" she hesitated. "Jason, what's going on? She's supposed to be at the airport by now. I've been waiting for a text from her."

"Well, she's missing…we can't find her."

"WHAT!?" Mrs. Bowers replied. "What do you mean, you can't find her!?"

"We literally have half the town out searching for her, Mrs. Bowers…but we believe that someone broke into her room last night."

"Jason, she told me the guy that was after her was killed yesterday! What's going on!?"

"I don't know, this is just as much a mystery to us…she sent you a text last night…" Maybe it WAS a clue.

"Yes, asking me if I remembered ever keeping a kid that may have been disturbed…which I thought was a strange question."

"Why?"

"Because, when she was a baby, I watched this little boy that…and I never told her about it…he tried to hurt her. He tried to kill her one night. I walked in and he had a pillow over her face…pressing it down so hard…and he looked, almost possessed. Anyway, he got away…ran into the woods…and the police never found him."

"Wow, that IS strange…do you remember his name?"



✝

"Of course I do, Jason. I babysat him for weeks. His name was Micky...Micky Nesmith."

Jason almost dropped the phone. "Did you say Nesmith? How old was he???"

"Yes, he was about seven or eight years older than Brianna, why?"

Jason caught Chief Jerry's eye. "Has anybody seen Michael this morning!?"


## *GATEWAY, FLORIDA*

Gateway High School was completely locked down by the time Captain Butler arrived on the scene. Police from his department, the county, Jacksonville, and the state were surrounding the property. Nobody was allowed in or out. News vans were across the street. One person was confirmed dead and others had been injured. "Talk to me," he said as he approached the command tent that was set up next to the front gate of the school. Several people were gathered around computers anxiously watching live video footage of what was going on inside.

"There appears to be just one shooter...possibly two," said a woman from the state police, looking up from her computer. She held out her hand. "Deb...Deb Rath." Wally shook her hand and looked over her shoulder at the screen. There was a young, male with a hood pulled up and a skull mask over his face. He appeared to be tall and thin, but not much else about him stood out. "He seems to be talking to someone on his phone."

"Captain, check this out!" one of his deputies approached him holding a laptop. "We found this purchase on the dark web...well, the Feds sent it over."



✝

"Jeremy Stiles," Wally read on the screen. "Of Gateway, Florida...AK-47...which is what the suspect is holding." He turned and pointed back at Deb's screen.

"He's also purchased several handguns including a recent purchase of a Glock 9mm, and we've just confirmed that he is a student at this school." the deputy added.

"What do we know about Mr. Stiles?" Captain Butler asked.

"Looking at his social media page, he seems to be a normal kid...Star Wars fan...Lord of the Rings...no red flags." The officer scrolled through several pages on her computer. "We've contacted his parents and they are on their way here now."

"Don't bring them here!" Captain Butler said. "Just get them on the phone...I want to talk to them! I also want to know who he hangs out with...who are his friends!?"

†

Matt Ramsey was a mess. He was presently lying in his bed on his back...fully clothed in what he was wearing yesterday. After finding out that Bethany was doing fine with no complications, he'd been told that not one...but both of his parents were dead. Then...he'd had to go to the morgue to identify their bodies. Officer Butler had volunteered but Matt had insisted in doing it himself. Images that he would never be able to forget. His phone had been buzzing all morning...his doorbell ringing...but he couldn't move. His parents were dead...they were NEVER coming home...EVER. No more birthdays, no more family Christmases, no more hugs from his mom, no more…anything.

"What are you doing, God!?" Matt closed his eyes. So much death in his life. His best friend, his cousin and her fiancé, his many friends…Christina! "I'm done."

His phone buzzed again with a call. Instinctively he reached for it, without looking at the screen and answered it. "Whoever this

158

✝

is...it's a really bad time to be calling me! For God's sake..." He heard sniffing and someone was crying.

"I'm sorry, Matt...I didn't know who else to call," whoever it was, was whispering...and crying.

`Matt looked at his screen. "Daniel?"

"He's shooting people, Matt...Jeremy already killed Chris...and he's shot I don't know how many others...they're going to think I'm part of this."

Matt sat up. "Dude, what are you talking about!?"

"I'm sure this junk is on the news, Bro!" Daniel said. "Gateway High School is locked down...Jeremy Stiles is shooting people...and he's calling and texting and talking to me like I'm his accomplice!"

"Daniel, where are you!?" Matt stood up and looked for his keys.

"I'm hiding in a supply closet in the teacher's lounge...man, I got a gun on me!" Daniel was clearly freaking out. "Can your dad help me!?"

"No..." He didn't feel it was the right time to explain his dad's death. "I'm going to do the best I can to help you, though." He ran downstairs and grabbed his dad's cellphone.

†

Captain Butler was coordinating with SWAT from Jacksonville on the best places to enter the school. They would be going in fast and quiet. The gunman looked as though he was getting antsy...waving his gun around in the library with about sixty or more students. Captain Butler had learned that around forty students had managed to escape before the shooter and his associate closed off all the exits. As he was showing them on a map where to wait for his command, he

**159**

✝

looked down at his ringing phone to see he was getting a call from...
"WHAT THE..."

"Everything alright, Cap!?" one of his deputies asked.

"Hello!?" he reluctantly answered the call from his old friend who'd just died yesterday....

"Captain Butler! It's Matt! I've got something big that might interest you!"

"Now's not a good time, Matt!" Wally replied, feeling bad for him but being a little overwhelmed. "There's a shooting at..."

"Gateway High School, I know!" Matt said. "I've got someone on the phone who you might want to talk to!" He set the phones to conference. "Daniel, this is Captain Butler on the phone with us, tell him everything you know!"


## SOMEWHERE IN THE MOUNTAINS OF TENNESSEE

"Praise is your weapon..." the voice whispered in her ear and stirred her from her slumber.

Brianna opened her eyes and attempted to see into the total darkness that surrounded her. Reaching out, her hands hit a solid surface...wood...she tried to sit up and hit her head on something.

"What? Where am I?" Her head was spinning as she tried to remember what had happened...she'd been in Pennington Springs...she'd been staying at Carolyn's Inn...Chief Jerry had killed Harley...MICHAEL!!! She hit her head again, attempting to get up.

Where was she!? She needed to call the chief...or Jason. She felt around...there was a thin mattress beneath her...was this a box? She pressed on the wood above her and it gave a tiny bit but would not open. "Oh Jesus...I'm in a casket...Michael Nesmith is the town's



✝

pathologist and has access to them and he has buried me" She began to panic.

"Praise is your weapon…" the voice said again. "Through the praise of children and infants, you have established a stronghold against your enemies, to silence the foe and the avenger."

She recognized it from the Psalms. Right now claustrophobia was her enemy. She needed to get out of this casket! She pressed on the lid again and it only slightly moved. She didn't feel like she was buried...there was a slight rocking...was she in a car? Where was he taking her? "HELLOOOO! SOMEBODY HELP ME!!!" she screamed, but knew there would be no one to save her.

"And whenever the harmful spirit from God was upon Saul, David took the lyre and played it with his hand. So Saul was refreshed and was well, and the harmful spirit departed from him."

Why was Michael doing this? What had she ever done to him? Had he really tried to kill her as a child? "What is going on, Jesus?"

"Praise is your weapon…"

Brianna closed her eyes. She took a deep breath, wondering how much longer she would have air….then...she smiled. "My situation is grim, Father...it's scary. It's completely hopeless...but YOU! You are my provider. You are my breath. You are my life. I am YOUR servant...and if this is where you need me right now, then this is where I will praise you. Paul and Silas praised you in prison and you shook the very foundation of that place! You rescued them! My situation is not MY problem, Father...it's YOURS! This casket is my church, and I will praise you...I will worship you...I will glorify your name...I place ALL my hope in YOU! Whether I die or whether I live, let your praise be on my lips!"

Brianna heard a horn blow and a man's voice mumbling something. Michael. Michael Nesmith, her captor. A lost soul on his



✝

way to hell. He needed Jesus. Brianna would pray for him. She would tell him about Jesus, given the chance. Michael was not her enemy...though he was definitely being used by her enemy.

"Father, I pray that you would begin to soften the heart of Mr. Nesmith. Holy Spirit, I pray that you prepare him to hear from you, through me hopefully! But through one of your children. Bring him to Jesus."

She slid to the side as if he'd made a sharp turn. Opening her eyes, she began to sing…

"When peace like a river attended my way. When sorrows like sea billows roll. Whatever my lot, thou hast taught me to say...it is well, it is well, with my soul."

# CHAPTER 18



"To my knowledge, Michael left early this morning to transport Christina's body to the airport so that she could be sent back to New York," Chief Jerry replied. "At least that's what he informed me via email yesterday afternoon."

"Brianna, for some reason, asked her mom about a child she used to babysit," Jason said. "Someone she couldn't remember, I don't know, she said she'd been having strange dreams...someone that may have been creepy or violent towards her when she was a kid. Turns out, according to her mom, there was a boy that she kept when Brianna was a baby that had tried to kill Brianna."

"Oh my…" Chief Jerry grabbed his cell phone as he listened.

"He got away and her mom never saw or heard anything about him again," Jason continued. "Chief, his name was Micky Nesmith...Michael literally knew our every move when she was here."

"Michael?" the chief was taken aback. "You think he is behind this?"

Jason nodded. "I remember mentioning to him once when she was on the news that I had grown up with her. Maybe he used that information, thinking I could get her here. He used poor Harley as a scapegoat...played him like a fiddle."

"If that's true," Chief Jerry replied. "He played us all like a fiddle." He dialed Michael's cellphone and it went straight to voicemail. "Michael...it's the chief, I have a quick question concerning Mrs. Gavins, give me a call at your earliest convenience, please." He clicked off the call. "Pastor, if you're right, then maybe he didn't take Christina's body at all…"

"But Brianna!" Jason finished his sentence.



†

"We need to get into the morgue!" Chief Jerry said, heading out the door.

## *GATEWAY, FLORIDA*

The incessant knocking at his door and ringing of his doorbell was driving Matt crazy. He'd just hung up with Daniel and Captain Butler, letting them sort things out without him needing to be the middleman. Who was banging on his door!? Who could possibly be this insensitive...his parents had just died for crying out loud, couldn't a guy have a chance to grieve?

He stomped down the stairs and through the living room ready to lambast whoever the jerk was that was interrupting his quiet morning. He swung the front door open and his heart skipped a beat...Andy and Eddie, his two best friends in the world, stepped forward and wrapped their arms around him. Matt gave way to the tears he'd managed to hold off until that moment.

They stood there like that for several minutes before his friends helped Matt inside and led him to the sofa where he could sit down. Andy went into the kitchen and put on a pot of coffee while Eddie sat with his arm around Matt, holding him close. No words were spoken...so much was said.

Fifteen minutes later, they were sitting in the living room quietly drinking their coffee. "So, have you guys heard what's going on at the school?" Matt asked, breaking the silence. He cleared his throat realizing how hoarse he sounded. He figured they hadn't, or else Andy would be up there checking on his brother.

"Nah, Bro," Andy replied. "We've been all about you this morning. Camped outside your front door for the past three hours."

"What's going on?" Eddie asked.



✝

"A shooting," Matt replied. "At least one dead." He looked hard at Andy. "Stay seated, Bro...but Daniel's involved."

Andy shot up from his seat, almost spilling his coffee. "Do what!?"

"Sit down and I'll explain!" Matt patted the cushion beside him to encourage his friend to sit.

Andy plopped down hard. "Involved how!? And how do you know!?"

"He called me this morning from a storage closet...it's why I've been ignoring the doorbell!" Matt replied. "I put him in contact with Captain Butler, who's in charge of the situation. Turns out that Daniel has been getting bullied by these four punks for years and he'd had enough..."

"That's no excuse!!!" Andy shouted.

"Dude, listen..." Matt said, placing his hand on Andy's arm. "A friend of Daniel's...well, more of an acquaintance, a kid named Jeremy, who'd also been getting bullied by the same punks, put Daniel onto a site on the dark web that sells items illegally, like guns and other dangerous things. Anyway, Daniel went on and bought a gun to scare the bullies. He used Jeremy's account.

Well, that meant that Jeremy knew when the gun came in. He used that information to blackmail Daniel into helping him set up the...event. All Daniel did was lock a few doors before he realized what was happening and that Jeremy was actually shooting people. So now, Daniel is hiding in this storage closet, with a 9mm in his bag, while the school is surrounded by trigger happy cops."

"I'm not getting any less anxious here, Bro!" Andy replied, standing up and walking across the room.

"Captain Butler is presently on the phone with Daniel...he's using him to help get the SWAT team in place to take out this Jeremy



✝

kid. I'm sure Daniel will probably get into some trouble for having the gun on school property and locking the place down, but at the end of the day, he'll be a hero...I prayed with him...he's terrified, Andy. We need to use this opportunity as a teaching moment for him!"

Andy nodded slowly. "After I beat the living daylights out of him…"

"That's the spirit!" Matt said, standing up and walking over to his friend. "Right now, it might be best if you go inform your mother of what's going on before the media does."

"Yeah, good idea...then SHE can beat the living daylights out of him." Andy said, grabbing his keys and heading for the door. "I'll keep you guys informed!"

"So," Matt said, looking at Eddie. "Anything new in YOUR life?" He was hoping to put his mind on something positive.

"Did you hear about Brianna?" Eddie asked, leaning back on the couch.

"No, what's she gotten into now?" Matt asked, with a slight grin. "And I thought I kept busy."

"Yvette texted us earlier that she's missing," Eddie replied. "You know, yesterday they caught...or killed the guy that was after her?"

"Yeah, the guy that killed Christina...I still can't wrap my brain around THAT!" Matt said, getting up to make another cup of coffee. "Christina was SOOO awesome! I feel so bad for Tyler...God please give him a peace that passes ALL understanding."

"Well, when Jason went to pick up Brianna this morning, to take her to the airport, she was missing. Dude, they can't find her anywhere."

"Maybe she just went for a walk and lost track of time...it IS the mountains, you know?" Matt said, trying to add a dash of hope.



✝

"Without her cell phone?" Eddie asked. "And Yvette said she hadn't even packed yet."

"Yeah, that IS odd," Matt said.

"Mark, Scotty, and Jonah are getting on the next flight up…" Eddie started to say.

"Jonah? Who's Jonah?"

"That guy Brianna was on the run with…"

"He's here!? I thought he lived out west somewhere?"

"Yeah, I have no idea, I'm just passing on the information that Yvette is telling me." Eddie stood up. "Is there anymore coffee?"

"Yes," Matt replied, picking up his phone and checking his messages. He saw where Bethany had texted him a few times, and caught himself smiling. "Help yourself." He read her texts.

"Good morning, Matthew. I'm so sorry to hear about your parents. I wish I could be there with you to go through this nightmare." "Thinking about you and remembering you in my prayers." "The doctors are saying that I could possibly be released later today. I hope I can see you."

"That actually sounds amazing, Bethany!" he replied. "Thank you for your prayers."

"So, Dude," Eddie said, coming back in from the kitchen. "What's going on? The others were saying this feels like before, when we were kids. Do you think this is a demonic attack?"

"Absolutely, Bro," Matt replied. "Cover yourself, your family, and your friends in prayer! Rusty and his hounds of hell are on the prowl!"

✝

"Okay, Daniel," Captain Butler said into the phone. "Are you ready?"

167

✝

"Yes sir," Daniel said, standing up and stretching his legs in the tight space of the storage closet he'd been hiding in. "Do you promise that I'm not going to get into serious trouble?"

"I promise to do what I can to help you, Son. You've made some seriously poor decisions in the past several hours, but so far you haven't done anything to hang yourself." Wally checked to make sure his SWAT team was in place. Daniel would be opening a back door for them to come in. "Now, start making your way toward the door…"

Daniel slowly opened the closet door and peeked out. The teacher's lounge was empty. He made his way quickly to the door that led into the main hallway with the Main Office just across the hall. Captain Butler had told him that Jeremy was holding most of the students at gunpoint in the library, which was to the right...so he would go to the left.

He peeked out and saw where a few students and teachers were hunkered down in the Main Office, peeking out over the counter. He made his way down the hall as fast as he could go. When he rounded the first corner, he came to a screeching halt and nearly threw up. There in the middle of the hallway lay Chris Norton...looking straight up to the sky. Skin as white as a piece of paper. Jeremy had called his name from down the hall and watched as Chris and his boys had mockingly approached him.

As soon as they'd gotten close enough to him, he'd lifted his AK-47 out from under his coat and fired a single shot into Chris' forehead. He'd been dead before he hit the floor. The others had run but Jeremy had fired right into the crowd they'd run into. All down the hallway Daniel could see trails of blood. He prayed that nobody else had been killed, though he hoped Fred, Jarod, and Malcolm had been the ones to get hit and not somebody innocent. It was their fault that any of this was happening.



✝

He stepped past Chris' body and slowly made his way down the second hallway toward the door where he was to let the SWAT team in. Just as he was about to reach it, something moved to his right. Somebody lunged toward him and tackled him to the ground. Their bodies slammed into the wall and Daniel scrambled out of their grasp. He looked down into the face of Malcolm...who was looking up at him with so much hatred.

"You killed Chris!"

"I didn't kill anybody, you idiot!" Daniel yelled back. "I'm trying to help!"

"I heard you were the one to lock the doors!" Malcolm said, standing up and squaring off with Daniel. "You're just as guilty as Jeremy!"

"Don't you start pointing any guilty fingers, Malcolm...if you guys didn't spend your days wandering around looking for whose lives you can ruin every day, Chris would still be alive! Piece of garbage had it coming!" The door was only about ten feet away. He just needed to get it open and let the cavalry save the day.

"Well, well, well!" Came a voice from behind Daniel, and he spun around. "Good job, Daniel!" Jeremy said, aiming his AK-47 directly at Malcolm. "Where's the other two?"

"Come on, Jeremy!" Malcolm said, lifting his hands. "Jarod is hit...he needs help, man!"

"Help!?" Jeremy yelled. "Where was help when you twits were tormenting me every day for the past three years!? Where was help when you would pick on smaller unsuspecting people just so you could feel bigger!?"

He pointed the gun right at Malcolm's head. "You want mercy!? WELL, I BEGGED FOR MERCY EVERY DAY AND NONE WAS SHOWN TO ME!!!" He pointed toward the room behind Malcolm. "Go inside!"



✝

He followed Malcolm into the classroom where about twelve students were crouched behind a wall of tables and desks. He saw Fred in the corner, kneeling over Jarod, with a look of complete terror on his face. Jeremy started laughing. "If I'm going to prison, you idiots are going to hell…" He placed his gun against the back of Malcolm's head and….

†

The SWAT team had been told that one of the students was on his way to open the rear door for them. The plan was to make their way to the library, sweeping each room along the way. One minute ago, they'd received word that the monitors had lost sight of the shooter.

The team leader told them that if the door didn't open in twenty seconds to blow it open. Explosives were in place. Five seconds into the count, they heard someone yelling, and then...a gunshot...the explosive blew the door open and the team stormed in.

"Team Leader, this is Captain Butler, talk to me!" He could hear shouts and screams over the radio. Someone was being told to get on the ground.

"The shooter is down, Captain! Repeat the shooter is down...second shooter in custody."

"Second shooter?" Captain Butler asked. "Repeat Team Leader, what second shooter?"

Wally's cell phone rang and he looked down to see that it was his Team Leader, Sargent Luke Colson, calling him. "Talk to me, Sarge!"

"Your guy...Daniel...he killed the shooter...single shot to the back of the head. He saved the lives of several people, Captain...kid did what had to be done!" He looked at Daniel… "Shouldn't have had a gun in school, though!" He smacked Daniel on the back of the head and then pulled the terrified teen into a hug.

**170**

†

Chief Jerry and his team managed to get into the morgue through a small window in the back. He and Pastor Jason walked into the back and opened the cooler. Jason pulled back the sheet on the one body that was left out and not in a drawer.

"Oh God," Jason said, seeing the bashed in skull. "It's Christina…"

"Are you kidding me!?" Chief Jerry said. "Michael can't be our culprit! He just can't be! He's so…unassuming."

"They always say it's the person you least suspect…" Jason added.

"CHIEF!!!" Officer Clark called from across the room. "You need to see this!"

Chief Jerry and Pastor Jason looked over to find that the officer had pulled and left open three drawers.

"Whatcha got, Clark?" Chief Jerry asked.

"These are the missing persons from the woods…the ones we thought had been taken! I recognize their pictures…that's little Emily Madison…age eight…" he said, checking the notes in his phone. "These are Rose and Angela Pegalo…sisters…ages twenty-nine and thirty-one."

"Pastor, what is going on!?" Chief Jerry asked. "How in the world did Michael orchestrate this whole thing right under our noses!? How did he wrangle Harley into it? Was Harley just a pawn? A crazy, easy to manipulate pawn!?"

Pastor Jason just stood there shaking his head. "I was wondering why he was in church on Sunday, Chief! He's always made it clear that he had no interest in religion. I guess he just wanted to see his old friend, Brianna… he sure did work hard to get her here.



✝

Now...there ain't no tellin' where he's got her...or if she's even still alive."



✝

# CHAPTER 19



Dustin had opted to get a hotel room rather than stay with someone. He knew they'd all been on the road for months and wanted to get back to some kind of normalcy. He still had money from his small moment of fame and figured it wouldn't take him long to find something to rent. He wasn't sure if Gateway was where he was supposed to put down roots but for now it was where God had him. This Gateway hotel was not a vote of confidence for his future there, though. It was barely a step up from camping, but he was thankful for what he had.

He'd been told about what was going on with Brianna, but felt a strong pull to let the others deal with that. He was still searching for more of God. He really hadn't had a lot of time to dive into the Word and was itching to get at it. Gabi had loaned him an old study Bible of hers and he laid it out in front of him on the small table in his room.

"Father, I pray that you would guide me to where you want me in Your Word. Speak to me in these pages I pray…" Gabi had said it was a good idea to pray before you read, but if God didn't specifically tell you where to read, then try starting in the book of John. Having received no divine intervention, he decided to do just that and began with John chapter one.

"In the beginning was the Word," he read out loud. "Hey, she was right...this is talking about the beginning! And the Word was with God, and the Word was God. He was in the beginning with God. Wait...who was in the beginning with God?" He started over. "The Word WAS God...and was WITH God...sooo, the Word is a person?" Dustin asked out loud. He decided to keep reading in hopes that somehow this would all be explained.



✝

Luckily, it didn't take him very long to understand who this mysterious Word was, though. "Okay, here we go...verse fourteen...And the Word became flesh and dwelt among us, and we have seen his glory, glory as of the only Son from the Father, full of grace and truth."

"WAIT!?" Dustin smiled. "JESUS IS THE WORD!? SERIOUSLY!? Oh wow, this is exciting!"

Just then, there was a knock at his door.

"Who could that be?" he got up and opened the door, completely shocked by who stood there… "Jessie!?"

†

Gabi, Maria, and Yvette pulled back into Maria's driveway. They had just dropped Mark, Scotty, and Jonah off at Jacksonville International Airport. They'd decided that it was best if just the guys went to help with the search for Brianna. The ladies felt a stirring in their spirit that God had something else in store for them...though they had no idea what that was. Until then, they would pray.

"I need more coffee!" Maria said as they piled out of the minivan.

"And lots of it," Yvette added, noticing that Gabi had walked over to the curb and was staring at something down the street. "You okay, Gabs?"

Gabi nodded and walked slowly down the sidewalk.

"Gabi!?" Maria called after her. "What's up?" She and Yvette watched as Gabi approached a small car that was parked on the side of the road about two houses down. "I feel like we're supposed to…"

"Pray!" Yvette finished her sentence. Both women bowed their head right there in Maria's driveway and began to call on God.



✝

Gabi approached the driver's side of the small, older car. She could hear a female inside crying...angry crying. She lightly tapped on the window and what appeared to be a teenage girl jumped and looked up at her.

"I'm okay...please go away!" the girl said through her tears.

"I can't do that, Sweetie," Gabi replied, smiling at her in a way that let the girl know that she wasn't going anywhere. "Either unlock your door and let me in the passenger side or roll your window down...otherwise I'm going to have to shout through the glass!"

The girl rolled her eyes and unlocked the door. Gabi walked around and climbed in.

"I'm Gabi," she said, turning to face the girl giving her a big smile. "You may have messed up your makeup a bit."

The girl begrudgingly smiled and looked at herself in the mirror. "You think?"

"What's your name?" Gabi asked.

"Emma..." she put her head down on her steering wheel and sobbed.

Gabi placed her hand on the girl's back. "Well, Emma...whatever is wrong...you're not in this alone."

Emma's head shot up and she looked at Gabi in shock. "Who sent you? I mean...how did you know to say that!?"

"To say what?" Gabi asked. "That you're not alone?"

She nodded frantically. "I was sitting here screaming at God for abandoning me in the worst time of my life! I literally JUST said that I felt like I was going through this completely alone right before you tapped on the window."

Gabi smiled at her. "That sounds like God...are you a believer?"



✝

She looked back down and placed her forehead against the steering wheel again. "I used to be. I was raised in church. I know God...or of Him." She reached over and grabbed a well-used tissue and dabbed at her nose. Gabi reached into her purse and handed the girl a clean tissue. "So, is this your house?"

Emma shook her head. "My boyfriend's...or I guess I should say, my ex-boyfriend."

"So, you guys just broke up?" Gabi asked, hoping that was all this was about but knowing it wasn't.

Emma nodded and looked over at Gabi. "He dumped me when I told him I was pregnant. It didn't fit into his plans...he's about to go to the University of Mississippi to play football...but he said he'd pay for my abortion though...and we could maybe stay together if I did it." Gabi squeezed her shoulder. "I don't know what to do, Gabi! I love him so much!"

"What are your parents saying?" Gabi asked.

"OH...I haven't opened THAT can of worms yet!" Emma replied, looking absolutely terrified at the idea. "Maybe I SHOULD get the abortion...they'd never have to know." She started crying again, and Gabi pulled her into a hug. It was then that Gabi looked in the mirror and could see Maria and Yvette standing in the driveway praying. She smiled. "Hey," she squeezed Emma's shoulder. "Come with me."

"Huh?" Emma replied, looking up at her.

"Trust me," Gabi said, opening her car door. "I have a friend that lives two houses away. Come on, just for a few minutes."

Emma opened her door. "Okay, but I can't be long." She walked around to the sidewalk with Gabi and headed toward the two women standing at the end of the driveway. "Oh my gosh, hey Mrs. McGee! You're home! It's so good to see you!"

**176**

✝

Maria held out her hand to Emma and the girl wrapped her arms around her in a big hug. "Hey, Emma. How are you, Sweetie!?" She gave Gabi a concerned look.

"Let's go inside for a second, so we can talk," Gabi said. "Come on, Emma." They led her into the house and Maria made coffee for everyone as they sat around the kitchen island. "So, guess what, Emma!" Gabi smiled at her and broke the ice. "I and Mrs. McGee are both pregnant!"

Emma looked at both of them with eyes as big as saucers. "No way...are you serious?"

"Yep, and this is my first one," Gabi replied. "Isn't that exciting?"

Maria, catching on fast, added, "yeah, we're having another one...and…"

Tearing up a bit, Emma reached over and gave Gabi a big hug. "It IS exciting." She began bawling into Gabi's shoulder. The other two women came around and stood behind them, stroking her back.

"You're not alone, girl," Gabi said. "We can walk through this side by side. We can even be with you when you tell your parents." Emma, unable to speak as she cried, just nodded her head and squeezed Gabi even tighter.


## *SOMEWHERE IN THE MOUNTAINS OF TENNESSEE*

"I'll praise in the valley, praise on the mountain (yeah). I'll praise when I'm sure, praise when I'm doubting (yes, sir)! I'll praise when outnumbered, praise when surrounded! 'Cause praise is the water, my enemies drown in! As long as I'm breathing, I've got a reason to...praise the Lord oh my soul (c'mon)! Praise the Lord oh my soul (hey)! I'll praise when I feel it, and I'll praise when I don't!



✝

I'll praise 'cause I know, you're still in control! Because my praise is a weapon, it's more than a sound (more than a sound)! Oh, my praise is the shout,  that brings Jericho down! As long as I'm breathing…" Brianna sang the Elevation Worship song as loud as she could, hoping that Michael could hear her.

The road had gotten much bumpier in the last few minutes as if they were on a dirt road. Every so often they would hit a pothole so big that her head would slam into the lid. It just made her sing even louder.

"SHUT UP!!!" Michael finally screamed. "I SWEAR TO GOD I WILL SLICE YOUR THROAT IF YOU DON'T SHUT UP!!!"

She smiled, knowing that he could hear her. Knowing that she wasn't broken. It also made her smile to think of Gabi…every time someone said, "shut up", she could hear her best friend saying how that was an ugly word.

"Father! I pray that Your Spirit would be with Michael Nesmith! Touch my captor, Father! Touch his mind, his heart, his spirit, and his soul!" she cried out, just loud enough for him to hear her. "Help him to find You, God, to…" Her head slammed into the wall behind her. He'd apparently slammed on brakes.

She could hear him cursing and then heard his door slam. The car shook and then…was he messing with the latch? The casket lid flew up and Brianna immediately sat up and took a deep breath…only to be greeted by the barrel of a large pistol being pressed against her cheek.

"If I hear so much as another moan out of you before we get there, I will kill you," Michael said in as calm a voice as he could muster. "Do you understand me?"



✝

His skin was pale and pasty...he'd been sweating. He looked terrified. Brianna felt sad for him. "Michael...please let me pray for you."

He reached back and slammed the pistol into her face as hard as he could. "I SAID SHUT UP!!!" She dropped back into the casket with blood pouring from her nose and mouth. Her eyes were closed, and he wondered if he'd killed her. He reached down and touched her neck feeling a pulse. "Just shut up, Brianna. It will all be over soon enough."

He closed the lid and hooked the latch. He climbed out of the back of the van and closed the door. Sliding the pistol back into the waist of his pants, he walked back to the front of the van. "I'm sorry, Micky...I promise she'll be quiet now." He got in and started the vehicle.

"Good...her words were burning me..." Micky replied. "I hated her words..."

The van continued down the long dirt road to the cabin in the woods. The one he'd come to long ago...the one where he'd made peace with Micky...and the others. He would finally be able to keep his promise...the one about Brianna Bowers, anyway. Then, he would go after the other one...the friend. They'll be so happy, the voices in his head...maybe they'll finally leave him alone.


*SOMEWHERE OVER THE STATE OF GEORGIA*

Jonah sat across the aisle from Mark and Scotty. He had hoped to have the seats to himself, but a young twenty-something man had plopped down next to him at the last moment. He'd slid a small laptop bag under the seat and buckled up. After they'd taken off Jonah had placed his Bible in his lap and was reading out of the book of Acts. He heard the young man snicker to himself and lay his



✝

head back. Jonah decided to ignore it and whispered a silent prayer that God would lead the situation.

"What are you reading, Jonah?" Mark, who sat in the aisle seat, asked.

Jonah smiled to himself at God's sense of humor. "Acts chapter 7...the story of Stephen."

"One of my favorites," Mark replied.

"Yes, it's my third time reading it, and I just love Stephen's attitude...for such a young man."

"He was the first martyr for Christ," Mark said. "And did you notice how he described Jesus?"

"What do you mean?" Jonah asked. "He says he saw Him." He looked back down at his Bible.

"He saw Him standing at the Father's right hand," Mark said. "It's the only time in the Bible that Jesus is recorded as standing...instead of sitting at God's right hand. That's why the leaders were so mad...they considered it blasphemy."

"That's interesting…" Jonah replied, making a note in his Bible.

"Not really…" the young man beside him replied, sliding his ear buds in.

Jonah and Mark shared a look and they both shrugged.

Mark looked over at Scotty, who was gazing out the window. "How are you feeling?"

"Fine," Scotty said.

"I still think we should've waited for you to see a doctor before going on this trek."



✝

"I don't really think Brianna would agree," Scotty replied. "Can you believe he's back, Mark...Rusty? The threats he made."

"I'm not surprised," Mark replied. "But the good news is that he lost. He made all those threats and then you and Bethany are fine."

"That actually worries me," Scotty said, still looking out the window. "It just means he'll up his game."

"Well, with Matt's parents...situation, I guess you could say he already has," Mark said. "You're not afraid of him, are you? You know we win in the end, right?"

"Yeah, I know," Scotty said, glancing over at his best friend. "It's the getting to that end that I'm afraid of. What with the threat on my unborn baby and all."

"But seriously, you don't actually believe any of that to be true, do you?" the young man beside Jonah asked, removing his ear buds.

"What? Yeah, every word," Jonah replied, being caught off guard. "Are you a skeptic?"

The man laughed. "Atheist. It's all a bunch of..."

"Yeah, I would've said the exact same thing about a week ago," Jonah said, interrupting him. "But Jesus changed my life."

"How? Did you get chill bumps at a church service?" the young man asked, sarcastically. "Did they tell you a sad story so you'd give them your money?"

"Nope," Jonah replied. "I was hanging from chains after having my face beat in by a group of child traffickers and about to be set on fire...when I witnessed an absolute miracle."

The guy looked over and noticed Jonah's bruised face and looked away. "Oh...child traffickers? How did you..."



✝

Jonah smiled and thanked God for the opportunity. "First of all, my name is Jonah...here's what happened..."



✝

# CHAPTER 20



"How did you know where I was!?" Dustin was clearly freaked out over seeing Jessie again.

She laughed and attempted to step into the room. He quickly blocked her entrance and gave her a look of concern.

"Dustin!" she said, stepping back. "Oh my gosh, I saw you getting out of your car in the parking lot! I had to run a quick errand and came back.

"And my room number?"

"The guy at the front desk," she said with a smile. "He apparently has a thing for blondes...what can I say?"

"Last question," he said, looking down at her. "What do you want?"

"Just thought you might want some company?" she replied, attempting to get past him again. He held his ground. "And why is a guy of your stature staying at a dump like this?"

"First of all, I don't want or need any company right now...and secondly, I do need to be in Gateway...unfortunately, this dump is the only option."

"You could come stay with me!" She smiled and showed him a picture on her phone. A quaint little cottage that looked to be quite secluded. "Airbnb."

"Now, why didn't I think of something like that?" he replied and looked her over. "What happened to you on the airplane? You literally vanished."



✝

"Yeah, sorry about that," she replied. "My boss was sitting up front and needed my help with something.  So, what do you say? You wanna come stay with me? It's about a ten-minute drive."

"No, Jessie," Dustin replied. "I'm a Christian now, and that wouldn't be appropriate."

"Come on, Dustin, it's a two bedroom...I'll behave."

"No thanks," he replied. "I'll be fine here until I find something more permanent. It'll give me reason to look for something." He gave her a 'that's my final say' smile.

"Well, at least let me take you to lunch," she said. "It's the least I can do after abandoning you!"

He let out a huge sigh and resigned himself. "Okay," he said, pulling the door closed behind him. "Lead the way."

✝

"Can you keep a secret?" Matt asked Eddie as they sat on the sofa drinking coffee and talking about anything they could to take Matt's mind off his parents.

"Of course," Eddie replied. "Even from Andy?"

"From everybody...for now." Matt answered. "There's...a female...someone I may...you know."

"Dude, you've only been back in town for a minute!" Eddie replied, sitting up straight. "You sly dog! Anybody I know!?"

"Actually, it is," Matt said with a smile that he couldn't fight. "Remember, not a word,"

Eddie put his hand over his heart. "Not a peep, my brother!"

"It's Bethany," Matt said, ecstatic about being able to tell someone.

184

✝

"Bethany who?" Eddie asked, and then his eyes got as big as saucers. "Wait! Bethany McGee!?"

Matt nodded, grinning at his old friend. "Yes!"

"Dude!" Eddie was highly impressed. "I recently saw a picture of her and was totally blown away! She's HOT! Wait, is she aware of this relationship goal of yours or…"

"Of course she is, you dork!" Matt said, shoving his friend lightly. "What do you think, I'm stalking her? We've been texting...she works at the church, you know. Anyway, what do you think?"

"I think she's out of your league and you totally deserve someone that's out of your league...wait...does Mark know?"

"Why do you think I've sworn you to secrecy?" Matt said, finally losing his smile.

✝

"This is so awesome!" Emma said as she sat on Maria's couch drinking her coffee. "Just when I thought that all hope was lost…" She teared up again. "God sent me three angels."

Yvette put her arm around her and gave her a light squeeze. "You just rest in Him. Let His love for you flow over you like oil."

"Yep, because once that baby comes…" Maria said with a chuckle. "There ain't no more rest!" They all laughed. "I'm being serious...but honestly, I wouldn't change it for a moment. These kids are my world. I mean, Jesus is my world, but these kids are His blessings into my world."

"Emma, what's your family situation like?" Gabi asked. "Your parents are still together, right?"



✝

Emma nodded. "Yes, ma'am, they've been married for eighteen years. They go to Gateway Baptist...my dad is a deacon. My mom runs the nursery...she has for over five years."

"The nursery, huh?" Yvette chimed in. "Maybe the idea of a grandbaby won't be so bad."

"No, my parents are big on image. Keeping up appearances, even if it isn't necessarily true. A baby out of wedlock would devastate them."

"A lot of Christians are like that," Gabi replied. "It's sad, really. People should be more concerned with impressing Jesus than others...He's way more forgiving."

"What do they do for a living?" Maria asked. "Are they at work right now?"

"My dad works from home. He's in insurance and my mom cleans houses...she has her own business. Yeah, they should both be home, today is her early day." She checked the time on her phone. "Wait, why do you ask?" Emma looked panicked.

"We need to rip this band-aid off, Emma," Gabi replied. "Trust me, no matter how bad it goes, you'll be glad it's over."

"Unless I'm dead!" Emma replied, sitting up and setting her empty coffee cup on the table.

"Don't be dramatic," Maria said with a smile. "Come on, let's pray."


*KNOXVILLE, TENNESSEE*

Mark headed to the car rental kiosk while Scotty and Jonah walked with Jonah's new friend, Aiden, who was heading to baggage claim. Aiden had been intrigued with Jonah's story and was



✝

especially fascinated that Mark and Scotty were a part of the whole dragon incident from Florida.

"Well, you guys have definitely given me a new perspective on things," Aiden said, as they approached the conveyor belt. "Not to mention, that flight has never gone by so quick." He smiled and stretched out his hand to Jonah.

Jonah took his hand and squeezed it firmly. "Can we pray with you, Aiden?" He asked in a gentle tone, trying to be led by the Holy Spirit.

"Um, no…" Aiden looked around nervously. "But…give me your number, and if I maybe have any questions later, I'll text you."

Jonah assumed he was just trying to get rid of them but gave him his number anyway. "It was very nice meeting you, Aiden."

"It was nice meeting you, Jonah… and…"

"Scotty," he replied and shook Aiden's hand. "We're going to be praying for you, Aiden. God didn't put you in our path by mistake. Please give this some serious thought."

"Well," Aiden replied with a smile. "It's not like my eternity depends on it." They all laughed, and he thanked them. Jonah and Scotty went to find Mark.

Mark finished taking care of getting the rental and walked over to a seating area to text Scotty. Just as he was about to sit down, someone bumped into him. "Stay alert!" the man said, and kept walking. Mark looked back at him and started to say something when he realized that the man looking back at him was none other than...

"Topher!" Mark called, but he got swept away into a small crowd and vanished from Mark's sight. "Topher!"

"Mark!" Scotty called from behind him and Mark turned around. "What's going on?"



✝

"It was Topher! He bumped into me...and said..." Mark started to say.

"Said what!?" Scotty asked.

"Stay alert," Mark replied and looked back in the direction that Topher had gone.

"Who's Topher again?" Jonah asked. "I feel like Brianna may have mentioned him."

"He's a messenger angel," Scotty replied. "He was a big part of our 'adventures' as kids."

"That's right," Jonah said nodding. "Wait, a messenger angel just told you to stay alert!? That can't be good."

"No, it can't," Mark replied. "Come on, let's pray." The three men sat down right there in the middle of the airport and joined hands, calling on God to protect them from whatever lie ahead.


## GATEWAY, FLORIDA

Dustin sat across from Jessie at the small barbecue restaurant. "So, how long are you in Gateway for, Jessie?"

"Maybe just a few days," she replied. "It depends on how long this job takes."

"What exactly do you do?" he asked, pouring some mustard sauce onto his plate so that he could dip his fries into it.

"I'm basically a headhunter for my company," she replied. "I find people that interest my boss and try and recruit them."

"That's fascinating," Dustin replied. "Do you enjoy it?"

"Yes, I absolutely love what I do." Jessie set her fork down and smiled at Dustin. "I've never met anyone like you, Dustin."



✝

"Oh, I'm nobody special," he replied. "Music is really the only talent I have."

"And you're so good at it. You have the voice of an angel...and I ought to know...my boss is big into music. But that's not what I'm talking about. Most men...well, all men really, would've jumped at my offer to come stay with me."

"Don't get me wrong, Jessie," Dustin said, taking a bite of a chicken thigh and wiping his chin with his napkin. "You're a beautiful woman and your offer is quite tempting, but I'm not like that anymore."

"Like what?" she asked innocently. "You don't like women?"

"Like I told you before, I'm a Christian now."

"Oh, you're still on that?" she replied with a smirk. "That's usually just a quick phase that people go through until they decide what they really want to do with themselves."

"Well, I haven't perfected it yet, but I'm doing my best," Dustin said. "And I really believe that this IS what I want to do with myself."

"No offense, but...that's such a waste of your talents."

"Giving my talents to God could never be a waste, Jessie."

"Well, when you could be making a thousand times more money doing something else, it is!" Jessie replied with maybe a little too much passion.

Dustin stopped eating and looked at her for a few seconds. "Wait a minute...are you here to recruit ME!?"

Jessie smiled and took a drink of her sparkling water. "It took you long enough to figure THAT out, sweetheart."



✝

"Well, regardless of who you work for or how much money you're prepared to offer me...the answer is no."

"So, what, Dustin?" Jessie asked. "Are you just going to keep on working with that...dragon slaying circus show? That's so far beneath you, and honestly, makes you look like an absolute joke."

"Well, Jessie...it's also, none of your business what I do with my life," Dustin replied. "And we're done here." He stood and picked up his plate. "Thank you for lunch and...whatever this was." He walked over to the trash can and dumped his plate in. When he turned around, she was standing behind him.

"Allow me to make one more pitch to you, Dustin," she said, her face only inches from his. Her perfume was quite intoxicating. "Come meet my boss...maybe he can work something out with you where you can stay with this whole...church thing." They stared at each other for several seconds. "Please...after that, if you still don't want to do it, I'll take you back to your little hotel room and you'll never see me again."

"Promise?"

"I promise," she replied with a wicked grin. "Now, come on...it's not far from here." They headed outside, walking across the parking lot towards her little red convertible.

†

Maria, Gabi, Yvette, and Emma piled into Maria's minivan for the small trek to Emma's house. Emma had pulled her car into Maria's driveway after they'd all decided that staying together was the best plan. The others could encourage her and give her the support she needed. They would bring her back later to get her car.

"So, what kind of plans DID you have for after high school, Emma?" Gabi asked her.

190

✝

"I wanted to be a nurse," she replied. "I guess that's never going to happen now."

"Never say never," Maria said. "It won't be easy, but women do it all the time."

"I suppose," Emma said. "We'll just have to wait and see...once this little one makes her appearance."

"Her?" Gabi asked.

"I really hope it's a girl," Emma said, rubbing her flat stomach. "But a boy wouldn't be so bad either. Do you know what you're having yet, Gabi?"

"Nope, but like you, I'm hoping for a girl. I haven't run it by Scotty yet, but I really like the name Cassini."

"Oh, I like that too!" Emma replied. "I haven't even given names a thought yet."

"The name Yvette is a really good one," Yvette said, giving Emma a light shove and a wink. "I think you're going to have so much fun planning for this little..." As they passed by a small strip mall something caught Yvette's eye. It was Dustin Knight walking across the parking lot with... "PULL OVER, MARIA!!! THAT'S JESSICA LYONS!!!"



✝

# CHAPTER 21



Chief Jerry had put out an APB on Michael Nesmith over an hour ago. He'd used an old photograph taken at a town meeting about four months ago. Darlene had found it stuffed in a drawer in the Chief's desk. He was supposed to have gone through the pictures weeks ago for a local story on community happenings.

Luckily it was available because it seemed that after a thorough search through Michael's apartment that he had absolutely no photographs of himself...or anyone else for that matter...unless, of course, you counted the wall of photographs in his basement, consisting of none other than Brianna Bowers... and some boy that Jerry had never seen. He would have to do a search as to who that might be. There was also no clue as to where Michael might be taking Brianna. His phone buzzed with a call from Pastor Jason. "Hey, Pastor, what's up?"

"Just calling to see if anything useful turned up at Michael's place," Jason replied.

"Nothing so far...he did, however, have a healthy obsession for Brianna."

"Pictures?"

"And newspaper clippings and pictures of screenshots. He's been at this for a while, Pastor. There are pictures of her as a teenager, pictures of her when she was in college, clippings from international newspapers. Tons of stuff. If Brianna had a fan club, Michael was the president."

"Hang on, Chief, I'm getting another call," Pastor Jason said. "Let me know if you find anything useful." He hung up with the chief and clicked on the other call. "Is this that guy who still thinks he's Mark McGee's best friend!?"



✝

"Pastor Green!" Scotty Morgan said with a smile as he remembered how he and Jason had first met...by arguing over who was Mark's best friend. "I still am, but that's not why I'm calling! We are just now pulling into the beautiful town of Pennington Springs...where might we find you?"

"Oh, seriously!?" Jason replied, taken aback. "Not sure when I expected you guys, but it wasn't this fast! I'm in the downtown area. There's a park across the street from Town Hall. Pennington Park."

"We'll find it," Scotty replied. "There's a lot of traffic here!"

"Tourist area...plus people are turning out to help look for Brianna. That's what I'm coordinating right now."

"I see the park," Scotty said. "See you as soon as we find a parking spot!"

Fifteen minutes later the three men spotted Jason working under a canopy, sitting at a table with several maps laid out. He was speaking into a walkie-talkie. "Okay Team X, you'll need to make your way north about five hundred feet. Remember to move slowly. You should see Team B at some point." He handed the device to a young woman sitting next to him and walked over to embrace the guys. "Mark!" He squeezed him tightly and grunted. "It is so good to see you!"

"You as well, my friend," Mark replied. "I just wish it was under better circumstances."

"Yeah, look at what I have to pull off to get you here!" Jason said jokingly. "How are you doing, Scotty?"

"Jason," Scotty said, accepting his bear hug. "This is Jonah Westbrook...Brianna's...boyfriend?"

"Trial basis," the tall good-looking Jonah said with a smile. "Haven't officially gotten the job yet."



✝

"Well, Jonah," Jason said. "I think you've come closer than anyone ever has. It's a pleasure to meet you!" He shook Jonah's hand. "Hopefully we can reunite you two a soon as possible."

"Hopefully…" Jonah looked around at the operation. "So, how many people do you have involved?"

"Last count was two-hundred," Jason replied. "But they keep coming. We have state police, FBI, and local cops in all the surrounding areas on the lookout as well. Her face and the face of who we believe has her is all over the news."

"So, who do you believe has her?" Jonah asked.

"His name is Michael Nesmith, he's our town's pathologist...and get this...he's from Gateway."

"What!?" Mark looked shocked.

"No way!!!" Scotty added, leaning in close. "He's not a demon, is he?"

"I don't think so," Jason replied. "But possibly possessed?" He said it as a question because he honestly had no idea. "Chief Jerry said they found pictures of Brianna in his apartment that dated back to her teen years. Apparently, her mom used to babysit him. He tried to kill her when she was an infant."

"Still doesn't give me assurance he isn't a demon," Scotty said.

"I've given that some thought myself, Scotty," Jason said. "He was manipulating the town crazy to kill people and lure her here. He orchestrated this guy, Harley, to kill several people so that he would take the blame. He even had him break into the room he thought was Brianna's and kill Christina. Then, we kill Harley, and he takes matters into his own hands and breaks into Brianna's room himself. Only, he doesn't kill her...he takes her." Jason steps back and



✝

looks at the three men. "I don't think a demon would've done that...just a thought though, I could be wrong."

"Literally everything you just said, sounds like a demon...manipulating someone else?" Scotty replied.

"I don't know, Scotty...Michael just doesn't seem…confident enough," Jason said.

"So, what can we do?" Mark asked. "We didn't fly all the way to Tennessee to stand around."

"Well, I'm going to be honest with you, Mark," Jason replied. "I was hoping, given who you guys are...that you could take this battle to the spirit realm." He reached into his pocket and produced a set of keys. "My church is right there," he pointed across the street.

Mark took the keys. "Now THAT sounds like a battle plan."


## GATEWAY, FLORIDA

By the time Maria had gotten into the parking lot of Gateway Barbecue, Jessica had pulled out into traffic. Maria pulled through and attempted to keep up.

"Hurry!" Yvette said in a panic. "She's getting away!"

"I'm trying, Yvette, she's in a sports car for crying out loud!"

"Who in the world is Jessica Lyons!?" Emma, clearly distraught, asked.

"I'm so sorry, Sweetie!" Yvette replied. "I didn't mean to scare you, but that girl killed me!"

"I'm sorry?" Emma was even more confused now. "She killed you!?"

Yvette wasn't sure whether to tell Emma that Jessica Lyons was indeed a demon from hell...literally! She had shot Yvette in the



✝

chest, and she'd been declared dead...only to be raised back to life by Jesus in the morgue...of all places.

"She shot Yvette in the chest when they were teenagers," Gabi said, turning around in the front seat. "Yvette was declared dead on the scene...but, as you can see...God healed her. We'll tell you the whole story another time."

Jessica made a right turn at the light, but Maria caught the red light behind several other cars. "UGGGHH!"

"We HAVE to catch them; she has Dustin with her!" Yvette said. "There's no telling what kind of garbage she's feeding him!"

"Father God!" Gabi began to pray. "We ask for your favor in helping us to catch up with Jessica and Dustin right now in Jesus' name!"

"Amen!" Maria said, as the light turned green, and she made the right turn.

"Sorry for asking, but who's Dustin?" Emma asked.

"Have you heard of Dustin Knight!?" Yvette asked.

"Um, yes, please!" Emma beamed. "He's only the hottest singer in the world! Wait! He's in that car!? How do you know HIM!?"

"Long story, but he's a part of our ministry now!" Yvette replied.

"NO WAY!!!" Emma yelled. "You guys are going to have a lot of stories to tell me later!"

"Gabi, look!" Maria said triumphantly. "There's a huge traffic jam!" The red sports car was about ten cars up, just sitting in traffic.

Yvette slid her door open and jumped out.

"Yvette!" Gabi yelled. "No! Remember who she is!!!"



✝

"SHE better remember who I am!" Yvette replied and stomped toward the sports car.

"God, please protect her and keep your angels surrounding her!" Gabi replied.

†

Dustin had gotten into the car with Jessica against his better judgment. He had a sinking feeling in his gut that something wasn't right, but his fear of offending people and his slight attraction to her had led him to this point. Now, as they sat in this traffic jam, he was extremely tempted to jump out of the car and make a run for it.

"I wonder what's going on?" Jessie said. "I can't believe there's a traffic jam in a small town like Gateway...it looks like there's something going on at the school up there."

"Yeah, there's a huge police presence up there," Dustin replied. "Hey, why don't we postpone this…"

"What in the world!?" Jessie swore under her breath. She was looking in her rear-view mirror.

Dustin whipped his head around and saw a dark-haired woman walking down the center of the road, straight for them. "Yvette? Do you know her?"

"She's not the one I'm worried about!" Jessie said, looking around for an escape route. "It's those three big guys with her!"

Dustin looked again and Yvette was one car back and all by herself. "What are you talking about!?" He looked back over, and Jessie was gone. The seat was empty. He scanned the area and...nothing. "How does she keep doing that!?"

Just then, Yvette walked up and slapped the side of the car. She didn't even seem shocked that nobody was in the driver's seat. "YOU BETTER HIDE!!!" Yvette screamed at the sky.

197

†

"Did you see her jump out!?" Dustin asked. "Because I didn't!"

"No, but she's glad she did!" Yvette replied and parked herself in the driver's seat. "We need to discuss something."

†

While sitting on the couch catching up with Eddie and trying to keep his mind off his parents, Matt received a text from Bethany.

"So, my mother has made up a lame excuse for not being able to pick me up from the hospital and then she conveniently suggested I ask you. I know you have other way more important things on your mind, Matthew, but I thought I'd at least mention it because she's going to ask."

"LOL, I would be happy to. What time?" Matt smiled as he hit send.

"Must be Bethany," Eddie replied. "Can't think of anybody else on the planet that would make you smile at a time like this."

"You would be correct, sir," Matt replied. "She may need me to pick her up from the hospital."

"Well, praise God, she's getting out so soon!" Eddie replied.

Another text came through. "RU SURE!?"

"Positive," Matt replied.

"They are about to release me, so whenever you're ready."

"Oh, I need to go," Matt said to Eddie. "Do you want me to drop you off somewhere?"

"Yes, if you don't mind dropping me off at my mom's," Eddie replied. "Andy and his mom are probably dealing with Daniel. I'll just go home."

198

†

An hour later, Matt was walking into Bethany's room. She was sitting in a wheelchair reading her Bible when she looked up and smiled at him. "Hello, Matthew," she said softly. "How are you?"

"Presently, I'm somewhere between the twilight zone and hell," he replied. "If I'm being honest."

She held up her arms to hug him and he graciously accepted her embrace. As soon as he knelt to hug her, he lost it completely. He bawled like never before. Bethany wrapped her arms around him tightly and prayed for him. They stayed like that for over fifteen minutes. Matt was drained and sat down on the floor in front of her.

"Sorry about that," he said, slightly embarrassed.

"Don't be sorry," Bethany replied. "Your parents just died, Matthew! I would be a basket case."

After a few moments of silence between them, Matt looked up and took Bethany's hand. "Don't take this the wrong way, but one of the last things my mom said to me..." He wiped his eyes. "We were talking about you...and...I said something about focusing on God and taking things slow...and she said...she wanted grandbabies." He started crying again. She would never see his kids. She wouldn't be there when they brought them home or...

"I've always imagined that those in heaven can see us, you know," Bethany said, as if reading his thoughts. "I'm not sure if it's scriptural, but I just know they can. She'll be there through every step of your life...our life...if that's what God wants."

Matt nodded and smiled at her. "Thank you."

"AWWW!!!" came a voice from the doorway, causing them both to jump. "That's got to be the sweetest most disgusting thing I've ever heard!" He laughed out loud and... "How's your parents, Matthew!?"



✝

With one motion, Matt was on his feet stepping toward Rusty. "I COME AGAINST YOU IN THE NAME OF…" Rusty was gone in a flash. Matt ran out into the hallway to make sure he wasn't out there. When he came back into the room, Bethany was bent over praying. "Stupid demon," he muttered under his breath.

"We're at war, Matthew," Bethany said softly without looking up. "You're at war!" She looked up into his eyes. "You're a marked man!"

"What do you mean?" Matt asked.

"I mean, I almost feel like this whole attack that's going on...against our entire gang...is literally a war that Satan is waging on YOU!"

"On ME!?" Matt asked, extremely confused. "Like a generational curse? Like the war waged on you and Mark?"

"Something like that...only...that may have had something to do with you as well...do you remember how you were hit harder than anyone else with deaths before!?" Bethany asked.

"Are you saying there was a connection to me in those attacks? Not just the McGee clan?"

"Possibly," Bethany said. "Or it could've been a two birds one stone situation...but I don't think so."

"She's not wrong, Matt?" someone said from the door behind him. Matt heard Bethany gasp as he swung around.

"Topher!" Matt said, embracing his old angelic friend. "You have no idea how good it is to see you!"

"It's good to see you as well, my friend!" Topher said, giving Matt a good squeeze. "But I'm afraid I'm not here to catch up." He released him and glanced at Bethany. "We need to talk, Matt."



✝

# CHAPTER 22

*SOMEWHERE IN THE MOUNTAINS OF TENNESSEE*

It's been a while since he's been here, but Michael found the well-hidden cabin. He thought he might've taken the wrong dirt road. It was grown over and it seemed that nobody had been back here in a long time. He made his way along the winding clay road doing his best to miss as many potholes as he could, though they were everywhere.

He figured if that didn't wake Brianna up, she may already be dead...which would be unfortunate for him. Micky had told him that it would be best if they took her out here alive, so they could give her a proper death...one that people would talk about for years to come. He didn't understand why Micky hated her so much, but he'd never been one to question Micky either. It was always best to just do as Micky said.

After staring at the old cabin for several seconds, he decided to go inside. It looked way gloomier than he remembered. There was a lot of overgrowth on the walls and front porch. He would need to find some sheers to see if he could make it more attractive. One of the porch rails was hanging down as well...he would need a hammer and some nails.

He parked the van on the backside of the cabin, close to the lake and nearer to the trees. He decided it would be best to go ahead and take Brianna inside as well. Opening the back of the van, he pulled out the casket trolley and proceeded to set it up.

"Hurry up, Michael!" Micky said urgently. "You're going too slow! We should have been here hours ago!"

"I'm sorry, Micky!" Michael replied. "I'm doing the best that I can."



✝

"Well, we both know that's rarely good enough!" Micky jabbed. "If it was, Brianna would've been dead already!"

"Isn't it a good thing that she's still alive?" Michael asked, quite confused. "Since Master wants her for himself."

"A happy mistake on your part...and nothing else...now get the casket into the basement, you fool!"

Fifteen minutes later, Michael had the casket in place. It was set up on a table in the main room of the basement. It was the room he remembered as the game room. The foosball table had been pushed out of the way as well as a folded-up ping pong table. He saw the old dart board he'd played with still hanging on the wall. He used to imagine throwing the darts at Brianna...when she was a small child. He also imagined throwing them at…"

"Good, you've finally done something right!" Micky said. "Now, check and see if she's still alive. If she is, then give her the shot."

The next shot had been Micky's idea. The first shot knocked her out completely...this one would leave her awake and aware of what was going on, while being totally paralyzed and unable to do anything but blink her eyes. He unlocked the casket and slowly opened it, half expecting her to lunge at him. She was, however, still unconscious.

He checked her neck for a pulse and found it to be weak. Reaching into his bag, he pulled out a syringe. The first shot would be a jolt to her system, in hopes of waking her up. The second shot would render her invalid for several hours. He smiled at the thought. Finally, after all these years...he was going to be able to destroy his worst enemy...well, one of them. He still needed to find the other one.

Brianna awoke with a jolt, attempting to blink away the fog in her head...which just so happened to be pounding. It felt as if her



✝

nose was broken, and her mouth was...something stung her on the arm.

"There you go, my dear," a familiar voice whispered from above her, as her eyes began to focus. It was Michael...Michael Nesmith. He had kidnapped her...she was in a casket...it was all coming back.

She attempted to sit up and he held her down with his strong arm. Why did she feel so weak? It was as if all her strength was leaving her body.

"Take it easy, Brianna," he said with a gentle voice. "I've given you something to help you relax."

"I need to sit, pplleeee," was all she could manage before losing her ability to speak. She couldn't even move her tongue. What was happening? What exactly had he given her?

"That's it, just lie there and ponder all of the horrible things that are about to happen to you," he said with a smile, sliding her hair out of her face. "You have no idea how much joy this brings me. Why, I haven't been this happy in...well, ever."

He slid his fingers along her cheek, smiling at her like a mother would smile at her child. "Oh, Brianna...after all these years..." A tear slid down his cheek. "I'm getting ahead of myself," he said, clearing his throat. "There's so much work to do." He reached for the lid and began lowering it.

"NOOOO!!!" she screamed in her head. "NOOOO, PLEASE LEAVE THE LID OPEN!!! I CAN'T ESCAPE!!!" She tried to say it out loud, but only drool formed in her mouth. Miraculously, he stopped and lifted the lid back up. "Thank you, Jesus," she thought, closing her eyes...which just so happened to be the only things that she had control of.

Michael lifted the lid back up and walked across the room. "I almost forgot about the gift I prepared for you. He picked the large



✝

jar up off the shelf and shook it, watching the contents inside scurry about. He'd been gathering them for her ever since he'd left church that day.

He walked back over to the casket and set it down. "I know you're probably getting lonely being cramped up in that little casket all by yourself, Brianna." He smiled at her, noting the fear in her eyes as he lifted the jar full of hundreds of cockroaches. "So, I thought maybe you would enjoy some company." He opened the lid and set the jar beside her in the casket. Smiling down at her, Micky winked a wicked wink as he closed the lid.

As Brianna lay paralyzed in the dark casket, she could hear the roaches crawling out of the jar. She was absolutely terrified of the thought of them crawling all over her...and at the fact that she couldn't close her mouth.


## GATEWAY, FLORIDA

"Have you taken care of everything here at the hospital, Bethany?" Topher asked.

"Yes, I was just waiting for Matthew to come get me, I'm already checked out."

"Great, let's go then," Topher said and immediately the three of them were at the park across the street, sitting on a bench.

"Oh wow!" Matt said, looking around. "That was awesome!"

"Yes, it was!" Bethany added with a giggle.

"Okay, listen up," Topher said, standing up and facing the two of them. "Matt, I'm going to need you to remember back to when you were a kid. Do you remember when you would go stay with your Aunt Catherine, sometimes over the summer?"



✝

"Of course, I used to love staying with her and Uncle Wayne...sometimes all the kids from the neighborhood would go with us to..."

"Good, you remember that as well," Topher said. "That's where our story begins."

Matt glanced over at Bethany, and she smiled at him and laced her fingers through his.

Topher saw this and smiled at them. "By the way, Matt...your parent's homecoming was phenomenal! They've never been happier...in fact, they're presently sitting at the feet of Jesus, worshiping Him!"

Matt teared up and quickly wiped his eyes. "Thank you...for saying that."

"They're constantly praying for you...and can't wait until you get there!" Topher was so excited to give this news.

"Well, hopefully that won't be too soon!" Bethany said, squeezing Matt's hand. "I kind of need him to hang around here for a while."

"I make no promises either way," Topher said with a wink. "Okay, listen up...your Aunt Catherine was going through a difficult time in those years. You see, her and your Uncle Wayne couldn't have children and when they went to their church for prayer...well, let's just say things didn't go as they should have."

"What do you mean?" Matt asked.

"I mean," Topher replied. "After much prayer and counseling, they were accused of having a secret sin in their lives that they hadn't dealt with and told that was the reason they couldn't bear children. The entire church eventually knew about it, and they were not allowed to hold any positions in the church. Your aunt had been involved with the nursery because of her love for babies and children.



†

This decision absolutely devastated her...and she vowed to never step foot in another church for the rest of her life."

"So that's why she's always been basically an atheist?" Matt asked, more to himself than anything. "I never really thought about the reason. My parents weren't into church for a long time until...well, you know how that came about." He smiled at Topher, remembering the whole castle incident thing.

"That was the reason your dad refused to go to church, as well," Topher added. "Of course, truth be told, he was looking for any reason he could find to not have to go to church."

"Okay, now that you mention it, I remember him saying that Aunt Catherine had been hurt by church people pretty bad. Unforgivably was how he'd worded it, I believe."

"Well, it was so bad that Catherine started to build a hatred for God...for allowing any of it to happen. She became extremely bitter...which you may or may not know this, but bitterness is a doorway to demonic influence. Drugs and sexual immorality also open doors to demonic influences. So, this bitterness led her to cursing God...daily she would scream at God for making her barren. For turning her entire church against her. For basically anything that went wrong in her life."

"Wow, bitterness is that powerful?" Bethany asked.

"Absolutely, what do you think led to Lucifer's rebellion?" Topher asked. "His jealousy of God turned to bitterness and...well, here we are."

"That's crazy," Matt replied.

"Anyway," Topher continued. "One day, while having one of her rants...you happened to be at her house. She was keeping you and several other children that day...and when she cursed God...the demonic influence of her bitterness impacted one of the children



✝

present...for, you see...he was already possessed by thousands of demons."

"Wait...WHAT!?" Matt asked in shock. A child my aunt was keeping was possessed by demons!?"

"Yes," Topher replied. "And when the demonic influence connected with him...there were only two other children in the room at that time…"

"Was Matthew one of them?" Bethany asked.

"Yes...and the other one…was Brianna Bowers."

†

"Wait, you're actually sitting here telling me that Jessie was a demon!?" Dustin sat up in his seat and squared off with Yvette. "Listen...this is a bit…"

"Dustin," Yvette replied. "You KNOW demons exist already!" They were still sitting in traffic with Yvette in the driver's seat of Jessie's sports car.

"Yeah, but she was so...so...real!" Dustin just couldn't wrap his brain around the fact that the hot blonde that had been stalking him and literally driving him around...was a demon.

"Do you remember the story of me getting shot and dying?" Yvette asked. "How I said it was actually a demon that had done it?"

"Yes, it took me a few minutes to digest that, but of course I remember it."

"Well, she's the one who did it!" Yvette lowered the front of her t-shirt to show Dustin the scars. "She goes by the name of Jessica Lyons!" Just then, there was a light rap on the side of the car and Yvette jumped. It was a police officer.

**207**

†

"Ma'am, we're asking everyone to turn around. This road is going to be closed for quite a while. There's been a shooting at the high school."

"Oh no!" Yvette replied. "Is everyone alright?"

"To my knowledge there was a single fatality...and the shooter has been subdued."

"Okay, thank you officer," Yvette replied. "I need to go back into town anyway." She checked her mirrors and turned the car around quick enough. She slowed down as she passed Maria's van. "I'll just take Dustin back to his hotel! Gateway Hotel?" she asked Dustin, and he nodded. "Pick me up there?" They agreed and she zoomed off.

"So, where was she actually taking me?" Dustin asked Yvette. "I was supposed to meet her boss who was going to try and convince me to go back into music...though she did say I could keep working with you guys."

"I'll just bet she did...the little minx." Yvette was furious. "Dustin, listen...her boss...is Satan...also known as Lucifer. Do you know what Lucifer did before he became the devil?"

"I know he's a fallen angel, but not much else."

"He was literally the worship leader of heaven. He oversaw music before music was even invented here on Earth!"

"Okay…" Dustin wasn't sure where this was going.

"He has since taken what was meant for goodness...and twisted it...he uses music to influence millions every day. How many times has a song moved you? Influenced you? Changed your mood? Taken you back to a specific time or place?"

"All the time!" Dustin replied. "Music is powerful."



✝

"Exactly," Yvette said. "People lose their minds over music artists all the time...simply because of what their music does to them. How it makes them feel. Sometimes they worship these people to the point of making them idols or gods."

"Okay," Dustin said. "So, what are you saying, Yvette?"

"What I'm saying," Yvette replied, as she pulled into the hotel parking lot. "Is this...what do you THINK she was going to do with you when she introduced you to her boss? Satan or whatever demon she answers to would have made a deal with you, Dustin...it may even have seemed innocent. Like allowing you to stay on with Dragon Slayers. Think of the influence that would've brought into our ministry! Into your life! Into all of our lives! You would've literally been striking a deal with the devil!"

She pulled into a parking space and saw where Maria had pulled up behind her.

"Wow," Dustin replied. "And to think I'd just pulled out my Bible to read it when she knocked on the door.

"Of course," Yvette replied. "That's how the devil works. Listen...if you see her again, tell her to leave you alone in the name of Jesus! Demons hate that name. Don't bargain with her, don't listen to her, don't even allow words to come out of her serpent mouth! Just rebuke her in Jesus' name!"

Dustin smiled at her. "You're really passionate about this." He put his hand on hers and squeezed it. "Thanks Yvette...thank you for caring."

Yvette's heart rate increased at his touch a little more than she'd care to think. "Of course, Dustin...now go read that Bible….and call me if you need anything."



✝

# CHAPTER 23



Maria, Gabi, Yvette, and Emma pulled into Emma's driveway after their little sidetrack with Dustin. Gabi looked back at Emma who looked like she was about to be sick. "Are you sure both of your parents are home?" Emma nodded, reluctantly. "It'll be okay, girl!"

"Let's pray," Maria said, and they all closed their eyes. "Father, we thank you for our new friend, Emma...of course, I already knew her...and we pray Your blessings over her and her precious baby. God, I pray that You would wrap Your arms of peace around this sweet young woman and show her Your unconditional love. Give her courage for all the things to come. I also pray that You would open the hearts and minds of her parents to see their child's need for their support. We thank You in advance...in Jesus' sweet name, we pray...AMEN."

"Are you ready for this?" Yvette asked Emma, putting her hand on Emma's arm. "We've got your back!"

"I know," Emma said with a weak smile. "And thank you." Emma slid her door open and stepped out. The rest of them followed suit. "How do you want to do this; I probably shouldn't just walk in with you guys..."

"Do you have like a front room we could sit in until you get your parents?" Gabi asked.

Emma nodded and led the way. She let them in the house and pointed toward the formal living room at the front of the house, and she walked toward the back looking as if she was going to run out the back door. "Mom!? Dad!?" she called out as she headed toward the kitchen.



†

"Hey, baby!" her mother replied from somewhere in the kitchen as Emma entered. "I guess it's a good thing you didn't go to school today! Have you heard what happened?"

Gabi and the others could only hear mumbling in the kitchen and then Emma's mother... "What!? There are people in our house!?" More mumbling and then... "You can go inform your father...what is this about Emma? We don't have time..." They heard Emma shush her mother and then footsteps going upstairs. All went quiet in the house for about three minutes as the women each seemed to be silently praying for the terrified Emma.

Emma finally stepped into the room where the three women were seated on the small sofa. "Hey, guys, this is my parents...Rick and Pauline Harrison." The poor girl was trembling. "Mom, Dad, this is Gabi, Maria, and Yvette. Maria lives near Toby."

Her parents smiled as the three women stood and shook their hands. "It's a pleasure to meet you, Mr. and Mrs. Harrison," Maria said, taking the lead. "You have an amazing daughter."

"Why, thank you, Maria," Mrs. Harrison replied. "May I get you ladies something to drink?"

"No ma'am, we only intend to be in your hair for a few seconds," Maria replied, and that seemed to put them at ease. "If you would be so kind as to take a seat, there's something that your amazing daughter would like to tell you."

"We're just here for support," Yvette added.

"Well, that's not encouraging at all," Mr. Harrison replied, taking a seat in the loveseat next to his wife. "What is this about, Emma?"

Emma remained standing at the entrance to the room, and for a second Gabi thought she was either going to throw up, pass out, or make a run for it. "Well, Mom...Dad...I um." She paused and looked at the ladies for help.



✝

"You're pregnant..." her mother said as a matter-of-factly. They all looked at her in amazement.

"What!?" her father asked, turning toward Emma, his face turning red. "Is this true, Emma!?"

Emma looked directly at the floor and nodded in shame. Neither parent spoke. The room was quiet. "I'm sorry, Daddy," Emma managed. "I know you're disappointed...I...

"Where is Toby!?" her father asked. "Why didn't he man up and tell us himself!?"

Emma wiped a tear rolling down her face. "Toby...broke up with me when I told him."

"What!? The COWARD!!!" Mr. Harrison stood up and walked over to his daughter. He lifted her face to look him in the eyes. "Emma Harrison," he said softly, and everyone braced for what was coming. "You're the most valuable thing I've ever possessed...you are like a jewel...a priceless jewel. I love you more than words could ever say." He paused to wipe his own eyes.

"So, you made a mistake." He looked over at his wife. "A mistake that makes us grandparents is a mistake I'm somewhat okay with." He reached his hand up and wiped his daughter's tears. "My sweet EmmaGirl." And with that, he wrapped his arms around her, and they both wept. Mrs. Harrison joined them, wrapping her arms around Emma from the back. The three of them cried and Emma's parents showered her with love.

Maria, Gabi, and Yvette stood up and quietly left the house...each of them needing a tissue for their own eyes. "That was amazing," Maria said, after they got into the van.

"Thank You, Jesus!" Yvette exclaimed.

"Now, I think we may need to pray for this Toby kid..." Gabi said. "His future ain't lookin' too bright!" The others nodded.

**212**

✝

"Not when her daddy gets a hold of him…" Maria added.

†

"So...this is crazy, Topher…" Matt's mind was going a thousand miles an hour. "What does it mean? Does it have something to do with what's going on with Brianna!?"

"It has everything to do with what's going on with Brianna!" Topher replied. "The person who has taken her is Michael Nesmith. He's the boy that was there that day...he has been unable to hurt the two of you for all these years because of God's protection on your lives...but now...God needs the two of you…" He poked Matt in the chest. "You and Brianna...to help bring him to Jesus."

"You want me to witness to the guy who's been stalking Brianna for her entire life, has killed innocent people, including Christina, and has kidnapped Brianna...and lead him in the sinner's prayer...seriously!?"

"Which of those sins are greater than yours, Matthew Ramsey?" Topher asked. "Which of your sins are more easily forgiven by the Savior!?" Topher stepped closer to Matt. "Or better yet, which drop of Jesus' blood that He shed on that cross is unable to cover the sins of Michael Nesmith!?"

"I'm sorry, Topher…" Matt said, looking down. "This isn't about me."

Topher lifted Matt's head and smiled. "Michael Nesmith was born into child trafficking. He was raped and abused thousands of times before his first birthday. He did not choose that...he was born into it. He was beaten, starved, and cursed for most of his early childhood. He has NEVER known love...except for what was shown to him by a few people who watched him as a child in Gateway. It's why he hates that memory...or should I say, it's why his demons hate that memory. YOU must show him love, Matthew. You and Brianna

213

✝

have got to be the love of Jesus to him…or he is going to burn in hell forever."

Matt nodded and looked over at Bethany. She gave him a weak smile to encourage him. "What's next?"

"You're going to have to figure out where Michael has Brianna," Topher replied.

"And how am I supposed to do that?" Matt asked in a panic. "He could have her anywhere. Wait...I'm sure YOU know!"

"I do...but unfortunately I do not have the authority to give you that information."

"Sooo…." Matt just put his arms out in frustration.

"So, you'll need to speak with Jonah...he has the information...he just doesn't know it yet," Topher replied.

"Who is Jonah!?" Matt asked.

"Brianna's boyfriend!?" Bethany asked.

"Oh!" Matt exclaimed, remembering that Andy had mentioned him earlier. "That's right!"

"Yes," Topher replied. "Now, let's go…" He held his hands out for them to accept.

"Wait!" Matt said. "Go where!?"

"Pennington Springs, Tennessee, of course!" Topher replied, grabbing their hands. Two seconds later, they were standing in the middle of a park in a small town. There were people milling about and a large tent set up to their left. "Find Jonah!" Topher said, and he was gone.



✝

"Pastor!?" Chief Jerry called Jason from across the tent. "Where was Team C when you last spoke to them!? I'm seeing an area here that may merit looking...it's about seven miles North near Louisville, Tennessee."

"Let's see," Pastor Jason replied, checking his laptop. "They're in Louisville right now. Derek is talking with the local police there."

"Okay...send him a text and have him…" Jerry started to say until something caught his eye. "What in the world!?" He made his way out from under the canopy and stared at a couple that was heading their way.

"What is it Chief!?" Pastor Jason asked and followed him out. "Well, I'll be a preacher's cousin!!! If it isn't Matt Ramsey and Bethany McGee!!!" Jason exclaimed as he walked out to meet them and embraced a grinning Matt.

"Pastor Jason Green!" Matt said, accepting the hug from his old friend. "It's so good to see you!"

"Wow, Jason!" Bethany said. "Where'd your hair go!?" She gave him a big hug.

"Look at YOU, Bethany!" Pastor Jason replied. "You're stunning! All grown up!"

Matt's eye caught the fact that there was an older police officer standing behind Jason staring at him as if he wanted to say something. "Yes sir!?" Matt said, holding out his hand. "I'm Matt Ramsey, this is Bethany McGee!" He put his arm around Bethany and pulled her closer. She smiled and glanced at him. "We go way back with Pastor Jason, here."

"Chief Jerry," the chief replied. "Any relation to Mark?" he asked Bethany.



✝

"Sister," she replied.

"And you…" Chief Jerry pointed at Matt. "I've recently seen you!" Noting his confused look, the chief glanced at Jason. "I suppose I should've brought the pictures with me. I told you there was a ton of pictures of Brianna at Michael's house...well, there was just as many of this guy right here…" He pointed at Matt. "I just didn't know who he was."

"Matt!?" Pastor Jason replied. "Why would Michael have pictures of Matt!?"

"I mean, he WAS from Gateway!" Chief Jerry replied.

"Wait!" Pastor Jason said. "When did you two get here? And how!?"

Matt laughed. "Funny you should ask…" he smiled at Bethany. "We just now got here...and Topher brought us!"

"Topher who!?" Pastor Jason asked as he tried to remember every Topher he'd ever known...then. "OHHHH!!! NO WAY!!!"

Matt and Bethany both nodded.

"We need to talk with Jonah," Bethany said. "Apparently, he doesn't realize it, but he knows where this guy has taken Brianna.

"He's with Mark and Scotty in the church," Pastor Jason replied. "I sent them there to do battle."

"Well, if he knows," Chief Jerry said. "Let's go pick his brain."

†

Mark sat in the front row of the small church and talked to his best friend. His eyes were shut, and his head was bowed. He called on the Holy Spirit for help. He knew that with all the technology in the world, all the cameras, all the tracking devices and ways to find people...the Holy Spirit already knew where Brianna was. He didn't

216

need those things. In fact, compared to Him, those things were incompetent. "We need Your help, Holy Spirit. Just help us to move in the right direction. Guide us."

Scotty was walking slowly around the sanctuary of the church. He was praying God's favor over those who were searching for Brianna. He was praying for God's protection over Brianna. He even threw in a prayer for God's protection over Gabi and their unborn baby.

Jonah sat on the stage of the church with his back against the wall. He'd received a surprise text from his new friend, Aiden, from the plane. Aiden had thanked him again and told him that he'd found a Bible and was considering reading it. Jonah replied to him and told him to start in the book of John...like Brianna had told Him.

There was a big cross hanging just over Jonah's head. He didn't have a lot of experience at this praying and 'going to battle' stuff, but he knew how to talk to God. He kept glancing up, expecting the old man to walk into the sanctuary and tell them where Brianna had been taken.

"We need YOUR help Holy Spirit! Give us our mission...our call of duty!" It was at that moment that the door opened. Jonah straightened up and watched as Pastor Jason came in with the police chief and two other people. A young couple. Pastor Jason caught Jonah's eye and motioned for him to come back. Jonah stood up and made his way to the back of the church. He noticed that Mark and Scotty had seen what was going on and were coming to join them as well.

"Jonah," Pastor Jason said quietly, motioning to the young couple. "This is Matt Ramsey and Bethany McGee...she's Mark's sister."

"Nice to meet you," Jonah said, shaking their hands. "I'm Jonah Westbrook. I was with Brianna during the whole child trafficking thing."

**217**

✝

"Yeah, she told me ALL about you," Bethany replied. "It's a pleasure to meet you."

Mark ran and embraced his baby sister thanking God that she was alive and okay. Scotty walked up and hugged the two newcomers, asking them how they'd gotten there and how Matt was holding up and then Mark asked Matt jokingly why he was with his little sister.

"To answer your first question," Matt replied. "Topher brought us."

"WHAT!?" Mark and Scotty replied together.

"So, listen up guys!" Pastor Jason said to the entire group. "Matt and Bethany have something they need to discuss with, well, Jonah." Everybody looked at Jonah, who looked just as confused as they did. "Matt," Jason said, giving him the floor.

"All we know is, Topher...he's an angel...literally," Matt said, noticing Jonah's growing confusion.  "Told us that you already know where Brianna is at...even though you don't realize it."

"What's this Topher angel talking about?" Jonah asked. "I literally know less about what's going on than any of you."

"That's not saying a lot," Scotty added. "None of us know anything."

"Hold on," Mark said, looking at Jonah. "What do you know that the rest of us doesn't?" Jonah shrugged. "Let's start from the beginning...didn't you say that the Holy Spirit told you to go to St. Augustine?"

"Yeah, but that doesn't have anything to do with this," Jonah replied.

"Maybe, maybe not," Mark said. "He could've called any number of local believers to do what you did. Why did he have YOU fly all the way across the country to pray with someone?"



✝

"That's actually a good point," Jonah replied. "So...why?"

"Who was the person you prayed with?" Pastor Jason asked, catching onto where Mark was going with this.

"His name was Wayne...Wayne Lutringer," Jonah replied. "His wife was having brain surgery."

"WAYNE LUTRINGER!!!???" Matt replied, in total shock. "That's my uncle!!! My Dad's sister was the one in surgery!"

"Lutringer!?" Bethany added. "Matthew! That's the woman I prayed with in the valley of the shadow of death!! Catherine Lutringer!!!"

"Alright! Alright! The ball is rolling now!!!" Chief Jerry said.



✝

# CHAPTER 24



*GATEWAY, FLORIDA*

"So, I have a question for you, Gabi," Maria said, as she sat down at the dining room table with Gabi and Yvette. They had opted for ordering Chinese food and were just now sitting down with their freshly delivered meals. Emma's parents had swung by to pick up her car. They had thanked the women for being there for their daughter.

"Okay, whatcha got?" Gabi asked with mild curiosity as she helped herself to a delicious pork dumpling.

"Did you get any vibes earlier from Yvette that she may very well be harboring some feelings for Mr. Dustin Knight?"

"Oh my...WOW!" Yvette cut in, almost spitting a mouthful of fried rice across the table.

"Oh!" Gabi replied. "I've been getting that vibe since Cairo!" She looked at Yvette and gave her a wicked smile. "And don't you even think about denying it!"

"He's half my age!" Yvette shouted.

"Half!?" Maria replied. "So, he's what, fifteen!?" She and Gabi laughed.

"You know what I mean!" Yvette said, trying to look innocent while taking a big bite of her egg roll. "He's too young for me...plus, I don't need all the baggage he would most likely possess."

"Even while denying it, she's proving that she's given it some thought," Gabi said with a chuckle.

"And I don't recall Yvette ever appearing to be this red before," Maria added. "Did you get some sun today, Yvette? You know, when you were in that convertible...rescuing Dustin..." Her and Gabi both laughed out loud, while Yvette continued to eat.

"Will you pass me a packet of soy sauce, Maria?" Yvette asked, in a desperate attempt to move the conversation away from her love life...or lack thereof.

"I don't think she likes us anymore, Gabi," Maria said, handing Yvette the packet.

"That's okay," Gabi replied. "We LOVE her!"

Yvette shook her head, unable to hide her grin...as her two goofy friends just stared at her. "But don't you think he's hot!?"

"Oh, he's gorgeous!" Maria replied. "And from what I've heard, the man sings like an angel!"

"I've never heard an angel sing," Gabi replied. "But they'd have to do an amazing job to beat Dustin Knight! Is it any wonder that hell sent their best-looking demon to woo him?"

"So, what are your plans?" Maria asked Yvette. "You two would make beautiful babies, by the way."

"Oh, wow!" Yvette replied and stuffed her mouth with a dumpling.

"Beautiful babies indeed," came the familiar voice of their old friend, who was sitting on the sofa in the living room with his back to the women. He set his hat on the coffee table and turned his head to glance back at them. "But we, however, have more pressing matters to deal with this afternoon."

Each of the women stood up from their seat and walked over to where He was. They each knelt on the floor silently and bowed before Him, tears flowing down their cheeks. Gabi began to sob, crying out in worship.

"In the past..." the Holy Spirit said. "You have fought and won many battles. Tonight...a great battle will be fought over one soul. A soul that was claimed for the enemy years ago...the soul of Michael Nesmith. I need you ladies to prepare for this battle," he said,



✝

with a smile. "You need to pray...worship...fight...but you must be prepared for what I have planned. What do you think? If a man has a hundred sheep, and one of them has gone astray, does he not leave the ninety-nine on the mountain and go in search of the one that went astray? Michael Nesmith is loved by God...tonight he will find out exactly how much."

†

Dustin had been shaken to the core to find out that Jessie, or Jessica, had been a demon. I mean, he knew that something was off about her but wouldn't have come up with that in a million years. Apparently, he had a lot to learn about this whole being a Christian thing.

When Yvette had dropped him back off at the hotel, he'd immediately gone back to his room and fallen on his face...on the bed, not the floor...the floor was disgusting. He'd prayed for over an hour, calling out to God to help him to have the wisdom and knowledge he'd need to make this work. He'd even prayed for his new friends, that they'd have the patience to help him play catch up. He'd even thanked God for Yvette...she was a good friend. She'd seemed legitimately concerned for him earlier. Of course, that was probably just the kind of person she was...and she would've done that for anyone. Still, Dustin had drifted off to sleep with a big smile on his face, just thinking about her.

Now, he stood in front of the bathroom sink, clearing the fog from his brain by rubbing soap and water over his face. "Okay, Lord," he started. "I'm not sure where to go from here or what to do, but I trust that you do."

Just outside his room, standing in the parking lot of the small hotel, were two black, leather-skinned demons. They too were plotting their next move. "We cannot fail her," the first one said.

"He is praying, you fool!" the second one chimed in. "We must move with caution. The angels of God are near."

222

†

"I am not afraid of the angels or of God!" the first demon declared defiantly. "In the end, they will all meet my blade!"

"I have accurately called you a fool," said the second. "Just be ready to act...for at the right moment...we will strike. Lucifer himself will be proud of us on this day."


## *PENNINGTON SPRINGS, TENNESSEE*

Everyone was gathered around Jonah, trying to help him figure out what he knew that he didn't know he knew.

"Did the Holy Spirit say anything else to you?" Scotty asked.

Jonah shook his head. "Nothing that would've told me where Brianna was, no."

"Matt," Bethany whispered in his ear. "Can we talk privately for a moment?" She pulled him by his arm and led him out of the church and down the front steps. They headed slowly down Main Street.

"Is everything alright?" Matt asked, truly concerned by the worried look on her face.

"I suppose I should've asked Topher about this, but it didn't cross my mind as anything but a lie until the revelation that Catherine, my Catherine, was your aunt...and your family is steeped in this whole thing pretty deep."

"Asked Topher about what?" Matt asked. "What did you think was a lie?"

"Something the dragon said when I was in the valley," Bethany replied. "About you."

"Oh, this is going to be good," Matt replied. "What did that slimy lizard say?"



✝

"Well, first he said that he didn't care about me going to heaven when he killed me, it was more about how badly it would impact YOU!" She poked him in the chest, and they stopped walking and faced each other. "He said he wanted to destroy the man who would give me his heart."

Matt felt embarrassed at first. Was this not something she believed? Was this not something that she wanted? Had he been reading her wrong? "Okay…"

"That's not the part that bothered me, silly…" She gave him a light shove. "You BETTER give me your heart!" She blushed a little and it made him smile. "No, he then went on to say that this whole thing...from the castle until now...has been about YOU...not the McGees. I mean, it's what put me on that line of thought just before Topher showed up."

"What?" Matt said, attempting to process what she'd said.

"I mean, think about it, Matthew," Bethany replied. "Rusty killed Billy to get to you...your cousin...her fiancé...Christina was close to you...and now your parents."

"And his attempt on YOU even…" Matt stepped away and walked over to lean against a post. "Maybe, I mean it lines up with what Topher said about this curse thing with Michael."

"Exactly," Bethany replied. "I guess I just want you to be careful. Rusty seemed pretty adamant about ruining your life."

"Well, either way," Matt said, walking over and putting his arm around Bethany. "I don't really care about anything that liar says. He thought he was about to kill you...and look how that worked out for him." They both smiled and he led her back to the church. "Now, let's go ruin some more of his plans."

As they entered the church, they heard Mark praying over Jonah. "Father, I pray that You give my friend wisdom and



✝

understanding...that You bring things to light that are hidden...touch his mind and memory. We thank You in advance…”

“WAIT!” Matt yelled out, and everyone jumped. “Oh, sorry! Jonah, you were with my aunt and uncle! Did they happen to say anything about a cabin in Tennessee!?”

“YES!” Jonah jumped up from his seat in the pew and swung around. “It was in...Friendly...Friendship…”

“Friendsville?” Chief Jerry asked.

“YES!!!” Jonah replied, pointing at the chief. “They had a cabin in Friendsville, Tennessee!”

“That’s only twenty minutes from here!” Pastor Jason replied. “Matt, call your uncle and get an address!”

“I’m on it!” Matt said, fist bumping Jonah and heading outside so he could call Uncle Wayne.


## GATEWAY, FLORIDA

“Yes, the other officer that was here earlier said that I may be able to see my son, Daniel Cruz, in a little while,” Mrs. Cruz said to the young officer behind the counter at the Gateway Police Department. Following the school shooting, the place was abuzz with reporters and more police officers than usual. There were police from local, state, and federal levels milling about. The small lobby was presently packed to overflowing, and most of the reporters had been asked to step outside.

“Yes, ma’am, Captain Butler just sent me a message that he was almost done questioning the suspect...err, your son.”

“Suspect!?” she snapped a little too harshly. “My son is a hero!”



✝

"Yes, ma'am! But he did have a loaded weapon on school property, so that's a third-degree felony in Florida by itself."

"But he shot the actual shooter, young man!" she retorted. "There's no telling how many innocent people would've been hurt or killed if he hadn't acted!"

"I understand that, ma'am," the officer said, attempting to remain as patient as he could. "He could possibly still be charged...that decision has not yet been reached."

"So, what does that mean?" she asked. "A third-degree felony...what could happen?"

"A third-degree felony brings a possible $5,000 fine and 5 years in prison, ma'am."

"WHAT!?" Mrs. Cruz replied, in a panic. "My baby can't go to prison!"

"Officer, what's going on here!?" Captain Butler asked, walking out of a room behind the counter. "Are you alright, Mrs. Cruz!?"

"He said my Daniel is going to prison!" she replied.

"I said…" the young officer started to say.

"Officer Samuels, why would you say something like that!?" Captain Butler asked. "Why don't we just get rid of the justice system, and let you hand out penalties!?"

"But sir," he said, attempting to explain himself.

"Just go make sure those reporters outside are staying away from the front door!" Captain Butler demanded. "I'm sorry, Mrs. Cruz, why don't you come back? I've got Daniel in interrogation room two."



✝

"Would it be alright if Andy and Eddie came back as well?" she asked, turning to point at the two men sitting patiently in the lobby.

"Hey guys!" Captain Butler said, walking toward them. Andy and Eddie stood up to shake his hand. "I didn't realize you were back in town!"

"Yes, sir, just got in yesterday!" Andy replied.

"That's awesome, great to see you! I wish it was under better circumstances! Come on back, you don't have any weapons on you, do you? I have to ask."

"No, sir, Officer Butler," Eddie replied. "It's not like the old days." They both shared a laugh.

He led the three of them back to the room and told them they could visit Daniel for about ten minutes.

"Captain Butler," Andy asked as his mother stormed into the room to hug Daniel. "What are we looking at?"

"Long story short, Daniel did a stupid thing today, Andy," Captain Butler replied. "Fortunately, he did a good thing as well. I'm just not sure the good is going to outweigh the bad. That's going to be up to a judge to decide. I'll do everything I can to help him."

"Well, thank God you're here!" Andy replied, shaking his hand. He turned and went into the room where his little brother sat, scared out of his mind.

✝

Dustin had prayed and studied his Bible for several hours and was finally realizing that he was quite hungry. He remembered seeing a taco truck up the road earlier and wondered if it was still there. It was only a block up the road, so he decided to walk over and see. If it wasn't there, maybe another option would present itself. He slid his shoes on, checked himself in the mirror and headed out the door.

227

✝

As the three women prayed in Maria's living room, they sought after God's will. They prayed for God's favor over Mark, Scotty, and everyone else that was looking for Brianna, for Brianna's safety, for Andy's little brother, Daniel, for Dustin...Emma...and for the Holy Spirit to guide their steps.

"Yvette," a sweet voice whispered in her ear, causing her to open her eyes.

"Yes, Lord?" she replied.

"Dustin Knight," the voice said, making her heartbeat faster. "Go to him...he needs your help."

Yvette stood up and walked across the room, grabbing her purse.

"Everything alright, Yvette?" Maria asked, looking up from her place of prayer on the living room floor.

"I'm supposed to go help Dustin with something," she replied. "The Holy…"

"Do you need to use my van?" Maria asked, and noticed the fact that Yvette was without her car register on her face...and the red sports car had mysteriously vanished after she'd parked it.

"Oh yeah...is that okay?"

"Keys are on the table by the door," Maria said, and went back to praying.

"Thanks!" Yvette replied and headed out the door.

†

Dustin hadn't realized exactly how far away from the hotel the taco truck was. He could see it in the distance, but he had to cross several empty lots cluttered with trash, rubble, and what in the world was that smell…

"Hey, Buddy!" a voice from across one of the lots called out.

228

✝

Dustin looked over and saw a short, stocky, white man that looked like he'd just risen right out of a pile of trash, walking toward him. He was wearing a pair of dark pants, a button-up shirt with the sleeves rolled up, black boots, and gloves with the fingers cut out. There was a cigarette hanging out of his mouth and as he got closer, Dustin noticed he had a tattoo across his forehead.

"Can I help you?" Dustin asked, not sure how exactly to handle this situation as a Christian.

"Can I get some change from you?" The guy continued to walk toward Dustin.

Dustin instinctively patted his pockets, though he knew he never carried cash. "Yeah, sorry...no cash, but listen, I'm heading to the taco truck over there, can I get you something?"

The guy walked right up to him and leaned in close to Dustin and showed him the large knife in his hand. "Just give me your wallet and cellphone, pal...NOW!"

Dustin took a step back and held up his hands. "Listen, man..." The guy lunged at him and the pain in his stomach was searing as the knife was pushed in. The entire world seemed to be spinning faster than ever before as Dustin struggled to remain upright. He felt the guy rummaging through his back pockets and then heard him running away. The next thing Dustin realized was that he was lying in the grass, surrounded by garbage...and his shirt was extremely wet.



✝

# CHAPTER 25



*FRIENDSVILLE, TENNESSEE*

Chief Jerry had been on the phone with various law enforcement agencies. He was getting everyone on alert that they may have found the suspect's hiding place. He was riding shotgun in his cruiser as one of his deputies drove to the address that Matt had provided. There was another patrol car and Pastor Jason driving the church van hauling Mark, Scotty, Jonah, Matt, and Bethany. They had insisted on following him, with the stipulation that they wait at the end of the driveway for the officers to make sure the coast was clear...or not. He received a call from a number that he knew would be a federal agent. "Chief Jerry Winkler of the Pennington Springs Police Department!"

"Chief Winkler!" the man said. "This is Agent Donnie Wright of the FBI, how are you doing, sir!?"

"Donnie Wright?" Chief Jerry replied. "Why do I know that name?"

"Well, I'm world famous, of course," Agent Wright replied with a chuckle. "But seriously, you probably heard of me through the whole Brianna Bowers incident with the child trafficking."

"Of course!" Chief Jerry replied. "She spoke highly of you, by the way!"

"Well, she's an amazing young woman," Agent Wright said. "I can't wait to see her again! Sooo, on that note...where are we?"

"On our way to check on a very promising lead at the moment. I have four officers and a van load of Brianna's friends in my entourage."

"Where is this location?" Agent Wright asked. "I am presently on route to Pennington Springs from the Knoxville airport."



✝

"Friendsville, Tennessee...we believe that Michael Nesmith went there as a child."

"Friendsville," Agent Wright said to himself, as he pulled up a map. "Perfect, I'm about twenty minutes away. Shoot me the address and I'll meet you there."

"Absolutely!" Chief Jerry replied and clicked off the call. He sent the agent the location just as their procession entered the town of Friendsville. He quickly called the local sheriff and let him know they were there. He was told that the sheriff and several officers were already at the end of the driveway waiting for them. Based on the map Jerry had seen, the driveway was quite hidden and long. Hopefully Michael wouldn't know they were there until it was too late.


*GATEWAY, FLORIDA*

Yvette silently prayed for the Holy Spirit to guide her steps and to protect Dustin from any further attacks from the enemy. There were three red lights between where she was and the hotel, and it seemed like those lights were working overtime today. "Come on!" she yelled.

"Wait…" a voice whispered in her ear.

"I'm sorry, Holy Spirit...forgive my impatience," she replied, and the light turned green. She punched it and still managed to catch the last light. "It's fine!" she said through gritted teeth.

"Pray for those around you," the voice said.

Yvette looked around and it just so happened that there were no other cars around her at that moment. She thought it was strange for God to say that when… "What is that?" She saw what appeared to be someone lying in an empty lot to her left.

"Is that a person? A homeless person maybe? Are they alive?" The light turned green, and she started to drive, glancing over



✝

at the person lying there awkwardly. It appeared they were wearing a light blue shirt...kind of the same color shirt that..."DUSTIN!!!" she screamed and did an immediate U-turn back to the lot. "Dear Jesus! Let him be okay!"

She pulled into the empty lot and jumped out of the van, cellphone in hand. She ran over and saw that it was Dustin...and he was covered in blood. With shaky hands she attempted to dial 911. She put a finger to his neck and felt that his pulse was extremely weak. "DUSTIN! BE OKAY!"

"911, what's your emergency?" Yvette heard a voice say from the phone lying on Dustin's chest. She quickly scooped it up.

"Yes, I'm in Gateway, Florida on US1...um near...there's a Burger King across the street! I'm in an abandoned lot!"

"Ma'am, I need to know your emergency," the calm female voice said.

"My friend, Dustin...he's bleeding...his pulse is weak! He's unconscious!"

"Do you know what happened to him? Has he been shot? Stabbed?"

"No, I'm not sure!" Yvette lifted up his shirt and saw the blood coming out of a good-sized hole in the side of his stomach. "It looks like maybe he was stabbed! Please hurry! He's losing a lot of blood!" It was at that moment that she heard the sirens and remembered that the fire station was literally a block away. "Thank you, Jesus! I hear them coming!"

"Ma'am, stay calm, they'll be right there. Can I get your name?"

"Yvette...Yvette Turner," she replied, watching the fire truck and rescue squad make their way toward her. She waved them over. "They're here! Thank you so much!"



✝

Yvette clicked off the call.

†

Gabi and Maria had gone right back to praying after Yvette had left and about three minutes later, Gabi felt a stirring in her spirit. She looked over at Maria, who looked over at her at the same time. "Dustin?"

"Yeah," Maria replied. They grabbed each other's hand and began to lift Dustin up to the throne room of God.

Gabi felt a breeze blowing on her face and opened her eyes. She and Maria were standing in an empty lot in the middle of Gateway...they were both over ten feet tall and in full battle gear. She looked around and they were surrounded by black leather-skinned demons. They were closing in and ready for a fight.

"You don't want THIS!" Maria screamed, raising her sword and swinging it at the closest demons.

Gabi joined her friend in the fight as she noticed Yvette kneeling next to a body, talking on the phone. It must be Dustin. "Let him be okay, Jesus!" she prayed as she swatted demons with her sword like they were large flies.

"IN THE NAME OF JESUS!!!" Maria screamed, really seeming to be in her element. "I COME AGAINST YOU!!!" The demons just kept coming, attempting to get past the two of them to attack Dustin.

Just then, a bright light pierced through the demonic darkness and shone from behind them. Gabi squinted her eyes and what she saw made her break out into laughter. "OH YEAH!!! PRAISE YOU JESUS!!!" Her excitement caused her to take out three demons in one swing as she watched the warrior angel Daniel along with about fifty others join the fight.

**233**

†

Within five seconds, every demon in sight was thoroughly vanquished. She turned around and saw that there were now several rescue workers kneeling over Dustin. Yvette was standing nearby, head bowed, eyes closed...leading the fight.

## FRIENDSVILLE, TENNESSEE

"The driveway is long and treacherous," Sheriff Boyett told the chief. "It's maybe two and a half miles with mud, potholes, and steep hills. I went up there years ago...just wanted to see if anyone lived there. It looked like what used to be a nice cabin. I think it's been abandoned for quite some time. These tracks are fairly fresh, though. Looks like it COULD be the vehicle you described."

"Like I told you over the phone, I'm not sure if Michael has actually killed anyone or just coordinated their murders, but I believe he is capable. We'll need to proceed with caution."

"Well, as far as I'm concerned, this is your rodeo, Chief!" Sheriff Boyett replied. "Me and my men are at your disposal."

"Thank you for that, Sheriff," Chief Jerry replied. Just then a large black SUV pulled up behind their line of cars.

"You expecting more company?" Sheriff Boyett asked.

"That's most likely Agent Donnie Wright," Chief Jerry replied. "He knows the victim."

"Well, well," the sheriff said. "We don't get many feds in these parts."

Four federal agents in shirt and tie, one of them wearing a suit coat, walked over toward where the sheriff and the chief had set up a makeshift workstation on the tailgate of the sheriff's pickup truck. "Gentlemen!" the agent wearing the jacket and standing almost a head taller than the rest said. "I'm Agent Donnie Wright." He held out his hand to shake the chief's.



✝

"Agent! I'm Chief Jerry of Pennington Springs and this is Sheriff Boyett of Friendsville." They all shook hands. "We were just discussing the lay of the land. It appears that the cabin where the suspect could possibly be held up is approximately a mile and a half up...some fairly rough terrain."

"Well," Agent Wright replied. "We have drone capability, if you'd like to have a peek at what's going on up there before you send a team in. My guys can have it in the air in two minutes."

Chief Jerry and Sheriff Boyett glanced at each other, and they both shrugged. "As long as it doesn't give us away."

"He'll never know it's there," Agent Wright assured them, and turned toward one of his men giving him the thumbs up. "Chief...Sheriff...if you'd like to accompany me back to the comfort of our SUV, we can watch the footage of what the drone is seeing without the glare from the sun.

He led them back to his truck and they climbed in the backseat while he got in the passenger seat and turned on his laptop. They watched as one of the other agents pulled out a drone the size of a small cat and set it on the hood. He took a remote control out of the same box and fired everything up. Within seconds it was airborne, and they were watching the screen, seeing what the drone was filming.

The agent directed it about fifty feet above the ground and proceeded to follow along with the direction of the driveway. After a few minutes, he took it higher and just over a slight ridge they spotted a mid-sized log cabin sitting along the edge of the forest, next to a large lake. It looked quite abandoned with all the overgrowth of trees, bushes, and vines. "There it is...and there's a van just under those trees."

"Yep, that's Michael's van!" Chief Jerry replied. "We've found him!"



✝

Across the street from where the chief was talking with the local sheriff, Pastor Jason had parked the church van. Chief Jerry had asked them to stay in the vehicle until he told them otherwise. They saw the big black SUV pull up and what appeared to be several federal agents get out.

"FBI," Pastor Jason said.

"Oh wow!" Jonah replied from the back of the van. "That's Agent Wright from the child trafficking situation! He knows Brianna! That dude don't play!"

"WHOA!" Scotty said and sat up straight in his seat. "I just got a text from Gabi! Apparently, Dustin was stabbed and left for dead in an empty lot in Gateway!"

"WHAT!?" the others chimed in.

"Yvette found him after being guided by the Holy Spirit. Apparently, Gabi and Maria slugged it out with some demons in the spirit realm! Rescue is taking Dustin to the hospital as we speak!"

"Let's pray!" Bethany said, and she began to lead them in prayer for Dustin.


## GATEWAY, FLORIDA

Dustin had been taken to an emergency center in Gateway, where he was treated for his stab wound to the abdomen. Yvette sat in the lobby texting Gabi and Maria. She couldn't believe that they had been there fighting with her for Dustin's life. They each continued to pray. Gabi also told her that Scotty and the others were praying for him.

"Thank You, God!" she said out loud, initiating some stares. "Thank You for Your protection and provision!"



✝

"Amen, Sister!" an older black woman sitting across from her replied with a big, sweet smile. "My grandbaby, Jerald, is back there having his eyes checked after a lawn mower accident! Protect him and keep him, Lord!"

Yvette smiled back at her. "May I pray with you?"

"Of course you can, sweetie!" the lady replied. "My name is Geraldine!"

"I'm Yvette," she replied and slid into the seat next to Geraldine. "My friend was stabbed in the stomach and robbed, and I have no idea why he was even there in the first place."

"Well, the good Lord knows it all, Baby!" Geraldine replied, taking Yvette by the hand. "Let's talk to Him about it!"

Yvette felt such a peace wash over her as Geraldine called on the name of the Lord with abandon. Neither woman cared that there were about eight other people in that waiting room listening. As far as they were concerned, these people NEEDED to hear what they had to say to Jesus.


## FRIENDSVILLE, TENNESSEE

"SWAT team out of Knoxville will arrive in fifteen minutes," Chief Jerry said to Agent Wright. He put his cellphone away and focused on the map they had laid out on the hood of one of the squad cars.

"We're going to need to act fast, Chief...we'll need to get them in place as soon as they get here. It's going to be dark in less than an hour."

"I agree," Chief Jerry replied.

"These people in the van..." Agent Wright said. "Do they need to be here?"

"They're friends of Brianna and have been helping with the search...if it wasn't for them, we wouldn't be standing here right now." The chief waved to Jason and motioned for him to join them. All of them exited the vehicle and crossed the street.

"Chief!" Pastor Jason said. "What's going on?"

"Jonah!?" Agent Wright exclaimed. "Jonah Westbrook!?" He met him as he crossed the street and shook his hand. "Never thought I'd see you again!"

"Agent Wright!" Jonah replied. "Once again meeting under bad circumstances."

"Well, unfortunately, considering my job...everyone I meet is under bad circumstances," Agent Wright replied.

"I must say," Jonah said. "I was relieved when I saw they'd brought in the big guns."

"Well, I wasn't exactly sent," Agent Wright said. "I'm solely here because of my connection to Brianna. I just want to help."

"Well...thank you for that, sir!" Jonah said, again shaking the man's hand. "And please...if I can help with anything."

"Sorry Jonah," Pastor Jason said. "The chief just said they need us to go back into town and wait this out from there."

"Okay," Jonah replied, understanding that they'd just be in the way. "Please let us know when you have ANY information on Brianna!" He looked directly at the chief when he spoke, then turned and followed the others back to the van.

"Um...guys!?" Bethany asked, turning in place and looking in every direction. "Where's Matthew!?"



✝

# CHAPTER 26



Michael was hurrying about, preparing for tonight's event. All of Micky's friends would be joining them. Michael didn't like them per say...but he knew better than to go against anything they said or did. They were very powerful friends.

"Oh...it's perfect, Michael," Micky said. "I absolutely love what you've done with the place."

Michael beamed at the rare compliment from his only friend in the world. "I'm glad you approve, Micky."

"The candles placed all over the house...give it such a perfect atmosphere, don't you think?" Micky said in a cheerful voice.

"Yes, that's exactly what I was going for...atmosphere. I want your friends to be happy."

Micky laughed at that statement. "Oh, Michael...I don't know if my friends are capable of being happy...but they sure are going to be as close to it as they possibly can be when they see what we have in that big box over there."

"Good," Michael responded with a smile. "Do you think they'll leave us alone for a change...after tonight, I mean?"

"Alone?" Micky asked. "Why would we want them to leave us alone? Don't you understand, silly man...they're going to be with us forever!"

Michael moved quickly into the kitchen and busied himself with the grand meal he'd prepared. He had no desire to be with Micky's friends for one more minute, let alone forever. Perhaps if he ignored that statement, then it was never said.



✝

Mrs. Gilmore, Mark's mom, had taken Maria up to the ER to get her van and dropped Gabi off at her house. She had been keeping the grandbabies all day and was tired when she'd dropped Gabi off.

"Thanks, Mrs. Gilmore," Gabi replied. "I may go back up and sit with Yvette for a while."

"That's a sweet idea, Gabi," Mrs. Gilmore replied. "Let me know if there's anything I can do."

"Will do," Gabi said as she got out of her car. "You go home and get some rest." Gabi headed into her house, checked herself in the mirror, grabbed her keys and headed back to the ER. Yvette had told them that Dustin was stable but still unconscious. She'd been told she could go back to his room and sit with him in about twenty minutes. Gabi pulled into the parking lot and parked her car. Just as she was about to get out, her old friend appeared beside her. "Well, hello there, Holy Spirit!" she said with a big smile. "To what do I owe this honor!?"

"I wanted to stop you before you got out," He replied.

"Okay," she replied, leaning back in her seat and looking at Him. He was staring at something across the parking lot. Gabi looked over and recognized the blonde that was standing next to the little red sports car. "Aha," Gabi said. "Thank You for protecting me."

"Why don't you just sit here for a little while and pray, Gabriella?" He reached over and placed His hand on hers. "Some things are about to happen...and I'm going to need you to be ready."

"Trust in the Lord with all your heart, and lean not on your own understanding..." Gabi began.

"...in all your ways submit to Him," the Holy Spirit continued. "And He will make your paths straight."

Gabi remained there praying for well over an hour. When she opened her eyes, the Holy Spirit was gone...though still there, technically. The good news was...Jessica Lyons was also gone. She climbed out of her car and went inside the building. "Good evening," she said to the young woman working the front desk. "I'm here to see Dustin Knight."

"Yes, ma'am," the woman replied. "Room 107...visiting hours end in fifteen minutes."

"Okay, thank you." Gabi walked through a door that led to a long hallway. She immediately felt the presence of evil. Stopping in her tracks, she quietly began to pray. She prayed God's protection over Dustin, Yvette, herself, and every single person in the building.

As she began to walk toward Room 107, she whispered the name of Jesus over and over. "...at the name of Jesus every knee should bow, in heaven and on earth and under the earth, and every tongue acknowledge that Jesus Christ is Lord, to the glory of God the Father."

Yvette looked up as Gabi entered, having heard her quoting from Philippians chapter two. "You feel it too?" she asked her friend.

"Thick as thieves in this place," Gabi replied. "I have a strong feeling that the enemy isn't quite ready to let Dustin go."

"I've anointed his room," Yvette said. "They said I couldn't stay the night...I'm afraid to leave him."

"Well, thankfully you're not the one protecting him," Gabi said, walking over and placing a hand on her friend's back. "And the One who is, isn't going to leave him."

"I know...but still," Yvette said, looking down at the sleeping Dustin. "There's no way I'm going to sleep tonight."

**241**

✝

"Why don't you come to my place tonight?" Gabi suggested. "We can put on a pot of coffee and pray for...well, basically everyone we know."

"Any word on Brianna?" Yvette asked, having not checked her phone in a while.

"Last I heard, they found where she's being kept. Scotty said they'd been told to leave, so he wasn't sure what was going on. And oh...Matt and Bethany turned up in Tennessee with them...thanks to our old friend, Topher."

"WHAT!?" Yvette exclaimed, looking at her friend.

"Yeah, apparently this all has something to do with Matt's family...some curse from when he and Brianna were kids...and Michael Nesmith, the guy who took Brianna is a part of it as well...and get this...now Matt is missing."

"Matt and Brianna are involved in the same curse?" Yvette was thoroughly confused. "From when!? I didn't realize they were friends as kids...until later."

"Apparently Matt's aunt...who caused the curse, babysat Brianna...at least once...and she also babysat Michael...or Micky...I don't know his real name."

"Wow, it's like a soap opera that was written in hell..." Yvette replied, looking up as the nurse walked in.

"Visiting hours are over in five minutes."

"Okay, thank you," Gabi replied to the nurse and turned her attention toward Dustin. "Now, let's pray over the future Mr. Yvette Turner."

Yvette turned a dark shade of red and gave Gabi a gentle shove. "You're so crazy."



✝

One of the officers had told Jason, Mark, Scotty, Jonah, and Bethany to go to Small Town Barbecue, telling them it was pretty much the only restaurant in Friendsville that was still open. "Great food, though...get the Friendsville Hot Chicken!" They'd found it easy enough and pulled into the parking lot.

"I can't believe that Matthew just took off!" Bethany said. "I hope he knows what he's doing and not just trying to be the hero."

"That doesn't sound like Matt at all, Bethany...and I think you know that" Scotty replied.

"I know, I'm just upset that he didn't let me in on his little escapade."

"Chief Jerry wasn't too happy about it either," Jason added.

"He was protecting you, Bethany," Mark replied. "You would've insisted on going with him. Besides, seeing how an angel brought you to Tennessee, Matt may not have even known he was leaving us until he did."

"I didn't think about that," Bethany said. "Mark, I'm worried about him. He's as wrapped up in this mess as the McGee family was years ago."

"And we survived...and so will Matt." Mark wrapped his arm around his little sister. "Now, until we know what we're supposed to be doing, let's get us some of that Friendsville Hot Chicken."

"Yeah," Scotty added. "I'm starving."

✝

"Okay, everybody listen up!" Chief Jerry said, as about twenty-five officers and agents of various branches and divisions gathered around him. "This is a photo of the man we are looking for!"

**243**

✝

He held up a picture of Michael Nesmith and let them pass it around. "To our knowledge, he is working alone...but stay aware that may not be the case! We aren't sure if he is armed, so again...be aware! Either way, the man is extremely dangerous!"

He sifted through his phone until he found the Facebook photo that Pastor Jason had sent him and held it up. "This is Matt Ramsey! He is a friend of the victim and has entered the property without our authority. It's because of him that we need to go in hot and fast!

Basically, before he gives away our element of surprise. If you run across him, detain him, but not with force. I believe that you've all seen photos of and know what Brianna Bowers looks like...if not, we have photos up here on the hood!" He turned and gave the floor over to the SWAT sergeant in charge. As he gave orders to his men and told everyone where they would be expected to be, Jerry once again dialed Matt's number that Mark had given him. No answer...he'd most likely turned his phone off.

The chief had been livid when he found out that Matt had gone against his orders and entered the property. He'd allowed them all to come against his better judgment to begin with. Depending on how this all played out, Matt could be looking at charges for interfering in a police investigation.

"Chief Jerry!" Agent Wright called to him. "I believe we're ready! You're with me and my men!"

"Perfect!" Chief Jerry replied. "Let's do this!"

†

As Brianna lay there in the darkness of the casket, feeling the tiny legs of the cockroaches as they crawled all over her body and face, she attempted to sing praises to God. She sang a dozen or so songs over and over in her mind. She'd made a list of things she was thankful for and repeated it in her mind over a hundred times. She'd

244

✝

always known she was a blessed woman...but until now...she'd never realized HOW blessed.

Her list had gone on and on, covering things from her childhood up until she met Jonah. She'd grown up in Gateway with great friends, then her parents had moved to California, where her older sister still lived...oh Ariel...how Brianna longed to hear her laugh...to meet her children...Brianna was an aunt!

She made a note to go see them when this was over. She thanked God for her parents. She loved her daddy so much! He'd always been her hero...her rock...her image of the perfect father. It had always been easy to see God as her father because of the example of her own.

Her mother...now there was a good woman. Always putting others above herself...a trait Brianna had always been proud to acquire from her mother. So beautiful as well...she missed her parents now more than ever. "I need you, Daddy…" she thought, and a tear rolled down her cheek.

Gabi...where would she begin to thank God for her best friend in the world? Sweet Gabi...and pregnant...how much Brianna wished she were married already and could raise a baby alongside Gabi's. That had always been their plan as kids. Jonah...was he the one? He was good looking for sure, but that wasn't everything...he was also kind...and a great listener...and good looking. She smiled.

"Thank you, Jesus for ALL the blessings in my life! For everything!" She couldn't thank him out loud, but knew He could hear her heart. She felt a bug crawl across her face, and it brought her back to reality. "Oh yeah, Jesus...please get me out of this little jam I've found myself in. I know I don't stand a chance without You."

✝

Matt walked along the forest line keeping with the driveway. He moved slowly and deliberately, not wanting anyone to know he

245

✝

was coming. It was starting to get dark, and he had to use the flashlight on his phone. He wasn't exactly sure what his plan was...but when he'd heard that voice telling him to go, he'd gone.

When he was sitting in the van with the others, waiting to see if they were in the right place, the Holy Spirit had whispered in his ear that He was about to use Matt in a mighty way...and to be ready. He'd known instantly that he couldn't say anything to the others, especially Bethany. He didn't want any of them to be put in harm's way.

Then, moments later, the chief asked them to get out and join him across the street. He looked over while the FBI agent was talking to Jonah, and saw a small opening in the trees. The Holy Spirit had nudged him to go. "Now, Matthew…"

He topped a small hill and looked over to his left. In the distance, he could barely make out a light. It appeared to be coming from a house window. He held his phone's flashlight lower to the ground so as to not be seen. He scurried across the gravel driveway as fast as he could go and saw that there was an overgrown trail to the back of the house.

He decided to take it and instantly regretted it as he walked through what was possibly the thickest and largest spiderweb that he'd ever encountered. He attempted to do his spiderweb shuffle as quietly and calmly as possible, but it had managed to stick to every part of his body, especially in his hair. He could only imagine the size of this mammoth spider...probably one of those bird eaters he'd seen pictures of online.

After several seconds of some impressive dance moves, he calmed down...especially grateful that nobody else had witnessed that. He picked up a long stick and waved it around in front of him to knock down any further arachnid nests of death. "Oh, I hate spiders!"

The thin trail winded around, and for a moment Matt thought he'd made a mistake, because it seemed to be moving away from that



✝

light in the window and more toward the lake. Then he heard a babbling brook to his right and saw where a small walking bridge had been constructed that led right into the back yard of the cabin...where he hoped to find Brianna.

He walked across the backyard and saw where there were tons of foliage growing over the house and it was totally unkempt. The back porch looked to be falling apart and had junk piled up all over it. He could barely even make out the back door.

"Well, it looks like I'll need to try the front. Father, I pray that You would continue to give me favor...and no more spiders." He checked both sides to see which side would give him easier access to the front yard and provide him more cover from prying eyes. It seemed that the left side was more accessible, but also more open.

Squatting down as low as his large frame would allow him, he moved slowly to the front corner of the house. He looked over to his right and could barely make out the front porch. "Okay, Lord...here goes..." He never saw what hit him from behind, but the pain that shot through his skull was intense. The last thing that Matt Ramsey remembered was...hoping there were no spiders on the ground...as he slammed into it.



✝

# CHAPTER 27

*FRIENDSVILLE, TENNESSEE*

As the guys sat eating a big barbecue dinner in downtown Friendsville, literally just waiting to hear something from the chief, Jonah's phone rang. He didn't recognize the number, but he did recognize the area code. "This is Jonah!"

"Jonah! Glenn Bowers, Brianna's dad! How are you, son?"

"I'm okay, sir...a little stressed, I'm not going to lie," Jonah replied.

"What have you heard, Jonah? Nobody is answering our calls out there," Mr. Bowers said.

"Well, sir, I don't know how much you know, but they've found where they think she's been taken to..." he paused.

"So, he took her to Friendsville? The last we heard, that's where the entourage was heading to investigate."

"Yes, sir...Friendsville, Tennessee," Jonah replied. "That's where we are now. I actually tried to get the FBI agent, the one from the Wyoming...Agent Wright."

"He's there!?" Mr. Bowers asked, interrupting Jonah.

"Yes, sir, he arrived only about an hour ago...I tried to get him to let me go in with them, but it was a big no...he's not exactly in charge of THIS operation."

"Chief Winkler SHOULD be in charge!" Mr. Bowers replied. "This is his..."

"Yes, sir, he is!" Jonah added. "He was the big no...he's trying to make sure he does everything by the book."

"So, nobody has seen or heard anything regarding my baby girl?" Mr. Bowers asked, lowering his tone.

"No, sir, not that I've heard...all I can say right now, is just pray!" Jonah replied, hating that he didn't know more...that he couldn't do more.

"Yeah, her mother and I are holding a big prayer meeting as we speak...half the church is at our house."

"That's awesome, sir!" Jonah said. "This situation needs all the prayers it can get."

"Keep me in the loop, son...we're praying for you as well."

Hearing the heart behind Mr. Bowers' words made Jonah realize how he was more than just a contact to him...to his family. It immediately bonded him to them...they were family. He reached up and wiped a tear and glanced at Mark, who was looking at him.

"Thank you, sir...you'll know things as I know things." He clicked off his phone and slid it in his pocket, then stood up and excused himself from the table. He walked outside and headed across the street to a small park that overlooked a river. He stared out at the beautiful scenery with the lights from the homes on the other side shining in the night and only saw emptiness...darkness...chaos. "What's happening, God?"

"What is your foundation?" a voice whispered in his ear.

Jonah, being an architectural engineer, understood the importance of a good, solid foundation. It was the strength of the entire structure. "I've always been my own foundation...but I can't be anymore. I need YOU to be my foundation, Father. Otherwise, I won't be able to withstand this or ANY storm that comes my way."

"Hold firm to Him, Jonah," Mark said from behind him, causing Jonah to jump. He placed his hand on Jonah's back and stood next to him. "I wouldn't be here right now, if I hadn't made that exact decision years ago."



✝

"He has to be my foundation," Jonah replied. "There's no bottom without Him...it's completely dropped out. I just...I hate to say it, but I have a sick feeling in my stomach about what's about to happen."

"Trust Him," Mark said. "No matter what."

"What if I lose her?" Jonah hung his head, ashamed of himself for doubting. "I mean, we haven't even had a chance to be us yet...and I...I think I love her." He started to cry. Mark just squeezed his shoulder and continued to stand beside his new friend in Christ, silently praying that God would take care of the entire situation.

## GATEWAY, FLORIDA

Dustin opened his eyes in total confusion. Where in the world was he? He turned his head and looked around. Monitors beeping, cables, tubes, a needle in his arm with something dripping into his veins...why was he in a hospital? What had happened?

He remembered leaving the motel...heading for the taco truck...wait, a knife...somebody had a knife! Immediately a sharp pain in the side of his abdomen brought him back. He looked down and saw the bandages wrapped around him. Had he been stabbed?

"You're awake!" an older, dark-haired nurse exclaimed, as she walked over to the side of his bed. "How do you feel?"

"Confused...what happened?" Dustin asked.

"You were stabbed," the nurse replied. "In the abdomen...left for dead...it's a good thing that angel of yours found you!"

"HUH!?" Dustin was really confused now. "Angel!?" With all the demons and angels being talked about by his new friends, was it possible that one had actually come to his rescue?



✝

"Oh, I don't remember her name, but we practically had to kick her out of here." She walked over and checked his vitals on the machine. "Said she saw you lying in the empty lot, covered in blood...called 911 and came in with you. If she hadn't found you at exactly the time she had...I can almost guarantee you that you would not be alive right now."

"And you don't remember her name?" Dustin said, feeling a little bit frustrated.

She pressed the call button on his bed and a voice came through. "Yes?"

"Hey, Shirley, check the sign in sheet, what was that woman's name that brought Mr. Knight in?"

"Hold on...it was...Yvette...Yvette Turner...sweet girl...let him know she saved his life!"

"Thanks, Shirley!" the nurse replied and gave him a big smile. "There you go...your angel has a name."

Dustin couldn't help but smile, remembering how fired up Yvette had been when she was running Jessica off. "Yes, she does."

†

Gabi and Yvette were sitting in Gabi's living room, working on their second cup of coffee and listening to worship music while they silently prayed and enjoyed being in the presence of God. Gabi had her Bible app open on her phone and was randomly jumping from scripture to scripture as the Holy Spirit revealed things to her.

Yvette was silently praying for God to protect Dustin from the attacks of the enemy. "Father, I pray that You would keep Dustin safe...I know that just because I'm not there, doesn't mean that You aren't. I pray that Your angels would surround that emergency center and..." A flash of blood splattering on the wall went through her mind. She stiffened and sat up straight, almost spilling her coffee.

251

✝

"You okay, over there?" Gabi asked from across the room, noticing Yvette's change in demeanor.

Yvette did not respond, but sat there with her eyes closed. Another flash of someone slamming into medical equipment...they were covered in blood. Yvette gasped. It was a nurse...she was struggling to get up...there was fear in her eyes. She saw Dustin covered in blood, running down the hall, looking over his shoulder.

"Yvette!?" Gabi was on her feet next to her friend in a moment. "What's going on, girl!?" She put her hand on Yvette's shoulder, and she jumped, spilling the coffee on her pajama shirt.

She looked up at Gabi with a terrified look on her face. "We have to go to the emergency center!" She yelled, jumping up off the sofa. "They're dying!"

"What!?" Gabi asked, grabbing her arm. "WHO!?"

"EVERYBODY!!!"

†

"Okay, Sweetie," the nurse said to Dustin as she headed to the door. "I'm going to make my rounds. This isn't a real hospital, so there's only me and Shirley working tonight. I have seven other patients to check on, but don't hesitate to press that button if you need anything. Otherwise, just try and rest. Your remote for the television is on the stand beside you there. Don't have it up too loud if you turn it on, though."

"Thank you Ms…? I didn't catch your name," Dustin said.

"Just call me Nurse Patty," she replied with a big smile. "I'll check on you again in a little while."

That's when they both heard a crash and a loud commotion coming from down the hall. Nurse Patty stuck her head out the door cautiously and peered in the direction of the crash. Just then there was a loud scream and Nurse Patty took off running toward the front

252

✝

lobby. Dustin heard her scream as he attempted to sit up, fighting the pain of his freshly dressed wound.

The next thing he heard was Nurse Patty running while screaming no at the same time. She appeared inside his room and slammed the door, sliding a chair up under the door handle. "She killed Shirley!" Nurse Patty screamed as she pulled out her cellphone and dialed 911. "Yes, there's been a murder at the emergency center in Gateway! She's still in the building, please send someone NOW!"

She screamed again and jumped back as the doorknob turned. "YES, PLEASE HURRY!!! SHE KILLED MY COWORKER WITH WHAT I'M GUESSING IS A KNIFE!!!" The door thumped as if someone had hit it on the other side, and Nurse Patty screamed again.

"What's going on!" Dustin yelled to whoever was behind the door and the door shook again. Dustin heard the wood splitting. "That's a woman!?"

"Nurse Patty nodded and slid a heavy table over and pushed it against the chair as hard as she could. "Shirley's throat was slit...there was so much blood!" Patty said in a panic. "WHERE ARE THE POLICE!?"

"DUSTIN!!!" a low growling, eerie voice called from the other side of the door. "GAME OVER, DUSTIN! YOU HAD YOUR CHANCE!!!" Again, the door shook with excessive force and the middle of it began to crack.

"Wait..." Dustin said to Nurse Patty. "Is it an extremely attractive blonde!?"

She nodded, having backed up against the far wall. "Is she here for you!? Who is she!?"

Dustin stumbled over to the door as it was hit again. "Jessica!!!" He was trying to remember everything he'd learned so



✝

far through Yvette and reading his Bible. "I come against you in the name of Jesus Christ!!!"

The thumping against the door stopped.

"You have no authority here!" Dustin yelled. "Do you hear me?" There was silence...

"Dustin!?" a female voice called to him through the door. "Dustin, it's Yvette! Are you okay!?"

"Yvette!?" Dustin attempted to slide the table out of the way, looking to Nurse Patty for help, but she was sitting on the floor, leaning against the wall behind his bed. "Hold on!" He moved the chair, and the door swung open. Yvette ran in and wrapped her arms around him.

"Thank you, Jesus!" she said as she hugged him tightly. Dustin flinched and she remembered his wound. "I'm sorry! Are you okay!?" He nodded and she helped him onto the bed just as Gabi and a police officer entered the room.

"Is everyone okay in here?" the officer asked. Dustin pointed behind the bed to Nurse Patty.

"She's a little shaken up," he told the officer, who walked around and checked on her.

He helped Nurse Patty up and led her down the hall in the opposite direction of the front lobby, where Shirley's body lay.

"Jessica?" Gabi asked.

Dustin shrugged. "I never saw her, but Patty said it was an attractive little blonde that was about to beat through that solid door. Her voice sounded quite...evil."

"Yeah, Jessica," Yvette said. "Are you okay?" Dustin nodded.



✝

"Thank God you came," he said. "I wasn't exactly sure of how to get rid of a demon."

"Sounded to me like you had it under control," Yvette replied. "She was gone when I rounded the corner."

"Hold on…" Dustin said, looking at both of them. "Why didn't that cop question us as to who it was or where she'd gone? Did you already tell him?"

"This is Gateway…I think they just know…" Gabi said with a smile. "But that was Captain Butler, he's quite aware of who it was. Her car was still in the parking lot."


*FRIENDSVILLE, TENNESSEE*

"No sign of Ramsey," one of the officers said into Chief Jerry's earpiece. "Team three is in place. Also, there appears to be no lights on in the cabin."

"Team four in place, all quiet."

"Team two in route, moving to the front of the cabin…two minutes out, no Ramsey."

"Roger," Chief Jerry replied. "Team one in place at the rear…no Ramsey here, keep your eyes open for him and don't be trigger happy." He looked over at Agent Wright, who was instructing the SWAT members that had come with their team what might be his best vantage point. Each team had taken one of the sides of the house, so that it would be thoroughly surrounded. Each team also had a member of the SWAT team that would try and get a bead on the target…Michael Nesmith.

"Team two in position," came the call. "No Ramsey…also, there's a light coming from what appears to be the basement…seems to be candlelight."



✝

"Can your sniper make anything out through the window?" Chief Jerry asked. He turned to Agent Wright. "If this is all going down in the basement, we may just need to rush the place."

"I agree," Agent Wright replied. "Let's see what the sniper finds."

"Bush overgrowth, we're sending in an officer to cut a hole."

"Ever had an operation that required you to trim the hedges so that you could get a good shot?" Agent Wright asked with a grin.

"Yeah, that's a first for me," Chief Jerry replied. They waited as apparently one of the officers from team two snuck up to the front of the house and cut a hole in the bush that was blocking the sniper's view. After about three mind numbing minutes, Chief Jerry heard someone whispering to another.

"Team two...opening is clear...window is uncovered. SWAT has line of sight into the room, but target has not yet been acquired."

Chief Jerry's phone lit up with a call that was from team two's team leader. "Whatcha got?" Jerry asked in a whisper as Agent Wright watched him.

"Chief," the officer said. "Harris was the one I sent to cut the opening...he saw Ramsey inside, and Chief...he was literally nailed to a cross on the wall, and Harris had no idea if he was alive or not."



✝

# CHAPTER 28

*GATEWAY, FLORIDA*

"Dear Heavenly Father, we praise You tonight," Glenn Bowers, prayed. "Thank You for all the blessings in our lives, Father. We lift You up tonight...higher than our problems...higher than our valleys...higher than our mountains. You alone are worthy to be praised in our lives! Father, as we praise You, we also come before you humbly...seeking Your face. God, I pray Your blessings over my daughter, Brianna Bowers..."

†

Gabi and Yvette led Dustin out to their car. He had been cleared to leave with them as the other patients were transferred to a hospital in Jacksonville.

"I tell you what!" Dustin said as he buckled himself into the backseat as gently as he could without tearing his stitches. "The Christian life is anything but boring!"

Gabi and Yvette smiled at each other as they began to pull out of the parking lot. "No doubt about that," Gabi replied.

"Dustin," Yvette said, turning in her seat to look back at him. "The devil does not want to lose you...he'd rather kill you than have you doing God's work."

"Well, he can keep trying, because God is amazing, and I have no intention of stopping this train from moving down the track!"

"I'm glad to hear that," Yvette said, smiling back at him. "When we get to Gabi's house, I fully intend to pray over you, your future...we're going to anoint you with oil..."

"Yvette..." Gabi said, interrupting her... "Can you feel it?"

Yvette looked at her quizzically and then nodded. "Yes...Brianna and Matt."



✝

"What!?" Dustin asked. "What about…"

Gabi pulled her car over into a fast-food restaurant parking lot and put it into park. "Let's pray!"

## FRIENDSVILLE, TENNESSEE

Michael was kneeling in front of the casket, eyes closed. He was terrified at what was about to happen. Micky had been blessed with the favor of his god…who had unbelievably delivered Matt Ramsey right into their hands. He was the one they'd needed for tonight to go perfectly. Micky found him in the yard, knocked him out, and brought him down to the basement, where together they laid him out on a cross made from some two-by-fours that Michael brought in from the back porch.

Micky had been so excited to nail Matt's hands and feet to those boards. Michael had drugged him first, of course…but boy when he wakes up, will he be surprised…and in excruciating pain. They had leaned the cross against the wall behind the casket. However, the next step would be Teuflisch's arrival…Michael was really hoping that Micky would completely take over for that part. Teuflisch was horrible…he hated Michael…but loved Micky.

"Oh, great god of Teuflisch!" Micky cried out. "We welcome you into our presence! Please, great god, have mercy on us! Show yourself and grace us with your majesty!" Micky bowed his head low to the floor. The tears began to flow as he thought of being in the presence of one so powerful. "Please, god of Teuflisch! Show yourself and accept our sacrifices to you! I believe you will be pleased with our work, Oh god!"

"Indeed!" The deep voice behind Micky made him jump to his feet and spin around. When he saw the sight before him, the towering beast with horns that spiraled around and pointed to the sky,

258

✝

he fell on his face before the great Teuflisch and wailed out in praise to his god. "You have done well, Micky...well, indeed..."

"They are both here, my god!" Micky called out, without looking up. "Brianna Bowers AND Matt Ramsey."

"This is how you prepare a servant to serve you properly...Anansi..." Teuflisch said, making Micky realize that someone else was in the room.

Micky looked up and saw a young, red-headed boy standing next to Teuflisch. "Who have you brought, my lord!?"

"Rusty Staggerbush...Anansi...the Dragon from Gateway...I have allowed him to be a part of what success looks like. He will witness what I have planned for Brianna Bowers and Matt Ramsey! What he should've done to Mark McGee and his miserable family years ago!"

"Show me, oh great Teuflisch," Rusty said. "Peel the skin from their bones as they beg for your mercy."

"Peeling the skin from their bones...WILL be my mercy!" Teuflisch responded with a slight smirk.

†

High above the cabin in the mountains, above the trees, and even above the clouds, the armies of God had gathered by the tens of thousands. They were led by Daniel, the great warrior angel. He stood with his sword in his right hand and his left fist raised, informing his army to hold still...for the moment. They anxiously awaited his word to strike. The demons of hell would be struck down on this night...for this battle had been expected for many years. Teuflisch and Anansi would be bound in chains and cast into hell, where they would no longer be allowed to wreak havoc on the families they had tormented for decades and centuries. Their curses forever broken.

259

✝

*GATEWAY, FLORIDA*

"And Father," Pastor Brian Jones began praying after Glenn had finished. "We pray for Your hand to be with Brianna Bowers tonight. I understand that they have found where she is being held, Father...of course, you've known all along. I pray that You would give the law enforcement teams Your favor and Your wisdom tonight, God. Bless them...keep them safe...be with Matt Ramsey as well, Lord...after facing such terrible loss recently, God...give him Your favor and protection."

†

Gabi had led the prayer at first, lifting up Brianna and Matt. Then she'd begun worshiping God with a song and Yvette had joined right in. Dustin had sat in the backseat, praying along and listening to the women singing. That's when it happened.

A bright light burst all around the car as if there had been an explosion of brilliant light. Dustin tensed up, not sure what was going on. Then...he saw Gabi and Yvette rise up out of the car, over ten feet tall each, wearing what made him think of Roman battle gear. Each of them donning a massive sword and a gigantic shield.

"What in the world is going on with you two!?" Dustin yelled. "Are you angels!?"

Yvette smiled over at him and pointed her sword toward him. "If we are, then so are you!"

Dustin looked down and he was also standing there, over ten feet tall, holding a sword and shield. "WHOA!!! WHAT IS THIS!!!???"

"Dustin Knight!" Gabi said. "THIS IS WAR!!!" And instantly they were flying through the clouds as fast as a bullet.

**260**

†

Brianna started to notice that she was getting feelings back into some of her extremities. The bad news was that she could now feel the cockroaches crawling on her. It was like they were inside the legs of her pants. She tried, however, not to freak out. She just continued to pray that God would bring good out of what the devil had planned for evil. She had started hearing voices outside the casket about five minutes ago, as if Michael was talking to someone and wondered if it was just himself that he was debating again...although the voices did sound different. "Please, Holy Spirit," she prayed. "Please let him open this coffin...please, I need fresh air...I need…"

"Only a little longer, my child," the sweet, quiet voice whispered in her ear. "I have something big planned for you. There will be rest...and then, you will be about the Father's business."

With those words came a peace like Brianna had never felt. It was as if she were about to be on vacation in a relaxing place...with no worries. "The job is almost done," she thought. "God is about to rescue me...but first, Holy Spirit...let me be able to share Jesus with Michael."

"No, Brianna...you're going to be Jesus for Michael."

She smiled at that thought. Hopefully, she would be able to show him Jesus, help him to accept Jesus...and then lead him into an eternal relationship with Jesus. "After all that...I want to see my daddy. Help him finish restoring Bruce...that glorious car." She smiled at the thought of not only being used by the Holy Spirit to help Michael, but then she would get to rest…

*GATEWAY, FLORIDA*

"Dear Heavenly Father," Diana Bowers said, as the entire group gathered in a circle in their living room. "I lift up my baby girl, Brianna to You right now…" She began to cry. "Lord, I know that

You called her to serve You in some extremely dangerous ways, and I know that time and time again, you have kept her safe in Your hands." She pulled her hand away from her husband's hand and grabbed a tissue to dab her eyes. "It just feels different this time…" She began to sob and several of the women broke the circle and gathered around her to pray.

## *FRIENDSVILLE, TENNESSEE*

"My, lord…god of Teuflisch!" Micky said, groveling at the demon's feet. "I am unworthy to be in your presence!"

Teuflisch kicked him away and walked past him to the casket. "ENOUGH!" he said, snatching the lid to the casket open. "IT'S TIME WE HAVE A LITTLE FUN!!!"

Immediately, Brianna sat up and sucked in the fresh air, coughing at the same time…then she noticed Matt hanging nailed to the cross above her and screamed.

Teuflisch grabbed her by the throat and snatched her out of the coffin. He threw her body against the wall to the left of the casket, and she fell to the floor like a lifeless doll. Roaches were crawling out of the casket and off of Brianna. Teuflisch began to laugh. "Now that was a nice touch, Micky…you have done well."

"Thank you, Master…I…"

"SHUT UP!!! CAN'T YOU JUST SHUT UP FOR A SECOND…YOUR INCESSANT GROVELING IS…"

"TEUFLISCH!!!" Rusty called from across the room, pointing at Brianna, who was attempting to stand up behind the massive demon.

Teuflisch spun around and slapped her in the face, causing her to fly further away from the casket, toward the center of the room.



✝

Brianna reached up and put her hand over the side of her face he'd slapped and once again attempted to stand.

"STAY DOWN!!!" He ordered. "GET ON YOUR KNEES!!! BEFORE WE ARE DONE HERE, TONIGHT, YOU WILL WORSHIP ME!!!" His voice shook the very walls of the room.

Brianna stayed lying on her side and looked over to see Michael writhing on the floor about four feet from her. It looked as if there was a battle going on inside him. "Michael! Michael Nesmith!" she called.

"He is not here!" he replied, looking at her for just a second before turning his eyes toward Teuflisch. "He can no longer come out and play!"

"You will speak only to Micky!" Rusty said, with a smirk on his face. "For as long as you can still speak!"

"Okay," Brianna replied, without missing a beat. "Micky...I come against you in the name of Jesus Christ! I command you to leave right now in Christ's name!!!"

Michael began to convulse and shake, his body writhing on the floor.

"STOP!!!" Teuflisch commanded and in one swift motion, kicked Brianna in the chest and causing her to fly backwards several feet like a rag doll. "SPEAK THAT NAME AGAIN!!!" He challenged her, standing close enough to kick her again.

†

Thousands of feet above the cabin, the armies of angels were getting antsy. Silently they watched Daniel...waiting for him to give the word at any second.

"Not yet," he said, desperately wanting to be the one to separate Teuflisch's head from his shoulders. "Hold steady…" As he

263

✝

spoke, three bright lights shot across the sky and stopped right in front of the angelic army. "Gabi! Yvette...Dustin!"

"We await your orders, Daniel!" Gabi said, smiling at the angel with excitement in her eyes.

†

"Michael..." Brianna managed. "I know you don't want this!" She looked over at him as his convulsing began to slow.

"Michael is not here..." he said in barely a whisper.

"Michael...you can control this," Brianna said. "Just say His name...those who call upon the name of the..."

Teuflisch's giant foot caught Brianna on the side of the head, and she flew backwards again. She landed right next to Rusty, who shoved her against the wall with his own foot. "FIRST YOU CAN WATCH WHAT I WILL DO TO MATT RAMSEY!!!" Teuflisch said, turning away from her and stepping toward Matt's body that was nailed to the cross.

Michael looked up as Matt began to stir, he looked right at Michael and somehow, through the pain, managed to smile. "J-J-JES-JESUS!" Michael called out, thinking he'd just seen Him, and immediately stood to his feet. "JESUS!!! PLEASE HELP ME!!!" He screamed in pain as it appeared that the fight within him was coming to a head. "NOOO!!!"

†

"NOW!!!" Daniel called out as the trumpet sounded for battle. Hundreds of thousands of angels descended on the cabin in a split second and were met by just as many demons that had been waiting for the attack. In the spirit realm, you could hear the sounds of swords meeting swords. Gabi, Yvette, and Dustin were right in the middle of it, slashing demon after demon.

†

264

✝

Michael just stood in that spot as it appeared that the demons within him were fighting for his very soul. "NOOO!!! JESUS, I NEED YOU!!!"

A hand reached out of nowhere and took Brianna by the arm, lifting her up. She looked up into the face of her old friend standing there with his perfect gray suit and his fedora on his head, smiling at her. It was as if time had slown down. "Do you trust me, Brianna?" She nodded. "Then show him Jesus." He looked over at Michael just standing there convulsing when at that very second a red laser light appeared on his chest.

Without thought, Brianna knew exactly what to do...show him Jesus...Jesus had died to show the world his love...Brianna, using every bit of strength she had, threw herself in front of Michael...just as the bullet came through the window...and struck her right in the heart…

Falling back against the wall at the force of something slamming into him, Michael looked down...there in his arms lay Brianna Bowers...his enemy...the one he'd spent his entire life hunting...she'd taken a bullet for him...and she was looking up at him...smiling. For the life of him, he could've sworn at that moment that he was staring into the eyes of Jesus himself…



✝

# EPILOGUE



*GATEWAY, FLORIDA*

*One Week Later*

Hundreds of people had shown up for Brianna's funeral. There were people from all over the world. People she'd helped through her ministry of saving those trapped in child trafficking. There were friends she'd made along her journey. Nadia Skutnik, the friend she'd made overseas recently while on the run from some very powerful people, was there. She sat next to her little sister, Ana, who Brianna had rescued. They held each other's hand and cried at the thought of such a loss.

Brianna's closer friends were sitting up front...Gabi, her best friend, along with Scotty, Mark and Maria along with their children. There was also Yvette, Dustin, Andy, Eddie, and Daniel, who had been released by a judge, his trial pending. Pastor Jason, Chief Jerry and his wife Carolyn were there, as well. All of them sitting there wiping their eyes and watching the video montage of Brianna's life. Then there was Jonah Westbrook, sitting next to Brianna's parents and barely holding himself together. He knew he'd be okay in the end...but right now, he missed his Bree.

In the back, sitting along the wall in his wheelchair, was Jake, along with his sister JoAnn and her family. Next to them sat Bethany McGee, who was delicately holding hands with her new boyfriend, Matt Ramsey...who was also in a wheelchair and on the mend from having had large nails driven through his hands and feet. He had a new appreciation of what Jesus had gone through on the cross. Matt, at least, was unconscious for most of his ordeal.

Lastly, leaning against the wall, wearing sunglasses to hide his glassy eyes, was Agent Donnie Wright of the FBI. He would need to duck out for a flight back to Tennessee as soon as the funeral was over.



†

Pastor Brian Jones took the podium as the video ended. He stood there in silence for several seconds, looking down at his notes. Looking up, he saw Brianna's parents sitting over to the side looking as if they were made of glass and ready to shatter at any second. Brianna's sister, Ariel, was there with her family as well.

He choked up before he could even begin. "I've known...a lot of people, who have been involved in ministry in many different areas...at many different levels. I've NEVER in my life known anyone as dedicated to their ministry...to the work of God...as Brianna Bowers. There is so much I could say, so many testimonies I could share. I've been asked by most of the people in this room if they could say something about how Brianna has touched their life. I mean, there are literally people here today because Brianna Bowers saved their lives..." He took out his handkerchief and wiped his eyes.

"However, after much prayer...with the family, of course, we're going to have a single person come up and speak." Again, he wiped his tears. "I'm not even sure how to introduce this person..." Pastor Brian lowered his head and began to openly cry. Moments later a hand pressed onto his shoulder and squeezed it.

"Thank you, Pastor..." the man said as Pastor Brian gave him a hug and walked off the stage. Straightening his tie and wringing his hands nervously, Michael Nesmith cleared his throat. "Most of you have no idea who I am," he began. "My name is Michael...and in honor of Brianna's devotion to God and her sacrifice," he choked up. "She led me to Jesus...to the One who saved my soul. I want to tell you my story. I came to Gateway many years ago as a child. My mother, who, from what I've been told, was sex trafficked. She supposedly died giving birth to me. I was, for lack of a better term...the product of multiple rapes.

I was born into sex trafficking...sold by my...owners...as an infant. I have recently begun to understand the gravity of my situation during those days as I was basically possessed by many, many



✝

demons. The state of Arkansas was ready to commit me into a mental hospital after several attempts at saving me.

Then, according to my medical records that I have recently acquired, I, um...changed...and out of nowhere I became one of the smartest children of my age bracket. I was sent to schools where I succeeded at every level. My I.Q. was off the charts. What I didn't have during those days...was a family. I had no idea what love was. My doctors and teachers searched high and low to find someone that could adopt me...giving me both the education I needed and the love I craved.

Finally, at last, someone stepped forward that by all accounts, looked to be the proper family. They lived right here in Gateway, Florida...in a castle that used to stand on the far side of town." An audible gasp came from all over the church. "I honestly do not remember what they even looked like...my adopted parents. From what I now remember about that castle, they probably weren't even human...but that's for another debate.

Typically, I was sent out to be watched by others. Others that I could prey on. I was taught to hate...to wish the worst on others...to kill. In other words, I still never knew what love was...other than what I saw in other families...and when I saw it...I hated it. Brianna was the first person that I ever truly hated. I saw how much love that her mother gave her..."

He looked over at Diana Bowers and smiled. "I wanted so desperately to end her life...so that her mother would maybe love me instead." He walked down and stood next to the casket where Brianna lay. A tear slid down his cheek. "I spent my entire life hating this woman. Plotting her murder. Looking for the right opportunity. Then, I thought I'd never get the chance when I heard she was mostly living and working in Europe...and then I thought for sure that she would die when she took on Joshua Coff and his child sex trafficking ring...but she survived."

**268**

✝

He looked up at the crowd of mourners that were listening to him. "That's when I had to act fast...before she went back to Europe. I had been working as the town of Pennington Spring's Medical Examiner for quite a while. It was a nice place to hide away and blend in. I knew about the town crazy...Old Harley Thomas Linwood. He was an easy enough scapegoat...so I manipulated him...well, the demons in me manipulated the demons in him...and I began my plan to draw in Brianna Bowers. The rest, as they say...is history."

He walked over and faced Brianna with his back to the congregation. "It worked too...she came...I caught her...and had her...she was mine for the taking. Everything I'd ever wanted...except that I didn't. It was what...he wanted...the other me." He turned back around and faced the people. "I wanted out...and somehow Brianna Bowers knew it. She knew it...and she called my bluff. In one quick second...in one moment, she did what nobody in the world had done in my entire life. She showed me love." He used the sleeve of his jacket to wipe a stray tear. "She demonstrated love to me...because that's what Brianna Bowers did." He looked over at Chief Jerry and nodded.

At that moment, two federal officers came over and led Michael Nesmith out of the room. He would stand trial in the state of Tennessee for the deaths of sixteen people. Christina Bulford was one of them. He would most likely be given the death penalty...where he would get to see his friend, Brianna Bowers, once again...so he could properly thank her for helping to set him free.

**269**

✝

# THE HOMECOMING

For a single moment, she felt the pressure of the bullet as it pierced her chest. The pain only lasted for a split second, like having your finger pricked for blood. Then it was over. Everything went dark...for how long, Brianna had no idea. The next thing she knew, however, was that the light that pierced through that darkness was brilliant...perfect like nothing she'd ever seen.

There were colors beyond her imagination. The colors danced around her for quite some time, and she had no idea if she was standing, sitting, lying down, or floating. She just enjoyed the peace that seemed to dwell in the colors. Then, someone took her hand and pulled her...along.

She began to see a shape appear and realized who it was by the hat He wore, when all of a sudden, His appearance began to change. No longer was He an old man in a gray suit with a fedora...now He was radiance. He was light, and his robe filled the room where they were, like water flowing around Him...as he walked...or floated...she still wasn't sure.

As they moved along, the brilliant colors continued to dance around them... and then, they became... lifelike. They were... angels... made of brilliant colors that Brianna had never seen. There were hundreds of them celebrating her arrival, smiling at her, clapping, shouting words she didn't understand and yet she did.

"GIRL!!!" one of the angels came from behind her and squeezed her tightly.

"Topher!" Brianna screamed, recognizing her favorite messenger angel.

"Welcome home, GIRL!!!" he screamed and blended into the crowd of cheering angels.



✝

"Brianna!" a familiar voice called to her as the Holy Spirit continued to lead her on. She looked over and saw Christina Bulford, beaming at her. "We made it!!! And look who else came to see you!"

"Pastor Eric Osborne!" she hadn't seen him in so long. He'd passed away when she was a teenager, during the time when the dragon was killing off as many of their friends as he could.

"Hey, Brianna!" Pastor Eric yelled. "You lived an AMAZING life! We were all cheering you on!"

She beamed at his statement and then saw Billy Mumpower as he stood there smiling at her, waving. "BILLY!"

Then, standing alone and to the side...she saw her. Smiling. She seemed more excited to see Brianna than anyone had so far. With arms outstretched, little Maria Sanchez ran to greet the woman who was there when she died. The woman who had tried her best to save her but had helped to usher her into heaven instead. "Ms. Brianna!!! I love you soooo much!!!" Brianna hugged the little girl with all her might.

"Come, Brianna," the Holy Spirit said. "There's someone waiting to see you…" He pointed ahead...and then for the first time...Brianna saw the city...the streets of solid gold...the buildings made of crystal and beauty...she had no other word...but none of it compared...to who she saw walking toward her...with the nail scars on His hands and feet...and the smile on His face.

"JESUS!" she wailed and could no longer move. She found herself kneeling at His feet as He approached. "Thank You, thank You, thank You!" She kissed the feet that took those nails in order for her to be here. "THANK YOU, JESUS!!!" she cried, as He easily lifted her up to face Him. With a quick swipe of His hand, He wiped away her tears and smiled. "Welcome home, child…"



✝

# THE END



✝

This story is dedicated to those affected by human trafficking.

...and hope does not put us to shame, because God's love has been poured into our hearts through the Holy Spirit, who has been given to us.

Romans 5:5 NIV

**Praise is your weapon...**



✝

✝

www.ingramcontent.com/pod-product-compliance
Lightning Source LLC
Chambersburg PA
CBHW072028220726

48293CB00016B/568